'It's the right th___
it in my bones.'

'Have you taken leave ___
You're really suggestin___
stunned. 'I only asked you to give me moral
support.'

'That's what I'm offering.'

'But we're friends. We've never even…you know.'

He side-stepped her implication. 'I know we've
shared a lot over the years. More than most engaged
couples. I know we respect each other. Trust each
other.'

'But Dallas…it's not your problem. I'm strong
enough to go this road alone.'

'You may be, yes, but have you considered the child?
The baby needs a mother and father. Trust my
experience on this.'

She didn't answer for what seemed a long time.
'Dallas? What do you expect to gain from saving
me?' she asked at last.

His heart constricted. He hadn't anticipated this
question. 'Perhaps,' he finally replied with complete
candour, 'you're saving me.'

Dear Reader

Welcome to September's spectacular Special Edition™ line-up and six novels we know you're going to love!

Laurie Paige is the author of this month's **That's My Baby!** title, where stubborn widower Hunter McLean, finds his life changes when he becomes a *Father-To-Be*. And in Annette Broadrick's latest novel, gorgeous secret agent Nick Logan is torn between duty and desire when he falls for *The President's Daughter*!

Don't miss the second **Prescription: Marriage** title, *Prince Charming, M.D.*, where a 'sworn-off doctors' nurse is tempted by a dashing surgeon! Meanwhile, Dr Mike McCall proposes to a woman with a dark secret in Ginna Gray's excellent *Meant For Each Other*.

To complete the line-up, there's a strait-laced woman falling for a laid-back man in *Until You*. And a *Baby Starts the Wedding March* in the latest novel from Amy Frazier.

Finally, we're launching a brand-new series of twelve linked books this month called **MONTANA**. The first book, *Rogue Stallion* by Diana Palmer, should be in the shops now—look out for it!

Happy reading!

The Editors

Baby Starts the Wedding March

AMY FRAZIER

SILHOUETTE

SPECIAL EDITION

Silhouette, Silhouette Special Edition and Colophon are registered trademarks of Harlequin Books S.A., used under licence.

First published in Great Britain 1999
Silhouette Books, Eton House, 18-24 Paradise Road,
Richmond, Surrey TW9 1SR

© Amy Lanz 1998

ISBN 0 373 24188 7

23-9909

Printed and bound in Spain
by Litografia Rosés S.A., Barcelona

AMY FRAZIER

has loved to listen to, read and tell stories from the time she was a very young child. With the support of a loving family, she grew up believing she could accomplish anything she set her mind to. It was with this attitude that she tackled various careers as a teacher, librarian, freelance artist, professional storyteller, wife and mother. Above all else, the stories always beckoned. It is with a contented sigh that she settles into the romance field, where she can weave stories in which love conquers all.

Amy now lives with her husband, son and daughter in north-west Georgia. When not writing, she loves reading, music, painting, gardening, bird-watching and the Atlanta Braves.

Other novels by Amy Frazier

Silhouette Special Edition®

The Secret Baby
*New Bride in Town
*Waiting at the Altar
*A Good Groom Is Hard To Find

*Sweet Hope Weddings

To Jim and Peggy Lanz, who welcomed me into their irrepressible clan and who personify love in all its manifestations.

Prologue

Ten-year-old Julia Richardson put a pebble in the rusty chewing-tobacco can, then, in a predetermined signal, tucked the can amid the tall grasses next to the railroad-crossing warning lights. She sure hoped Dallas Parker discovered her "message" soon because her thoughts were sorely troubled.

She needed to talk to her best friend.

Having sent her SOS, she hoisted the heavy library book she'd been carrying from the gravel roadside and headed along the tracks toward the old oak tree. To her mind, there was nothing better than a long summer's day, a good book, a perch in her favorite oak's branches and the prospect of seeing Dallas. If only all those good thoughts weren't completely ruined by the memory of the horrid argument she and Mama had had over the breakfast table.

Every summer for as long as she could remember, Julia had run barefoot and free over the enormous Richardson property, Ten Oaks. An only child, the content of her days was hers alone to decide. She could pack the hours with activity or she could waste long stretches at a time with daydreaming. No one from the adult world interfered. Until now. This summer, if Mama had her way, would be different. This summer Mama and Big Daddy and Auntie Ouidie wanted her to attend Miss Peters's School of Etiquette and Grace over in Macon. Two days a week! Plus a dance on Saturday afternoons.

Angrily, Julia scuffed her bare toes in the thick red Georgia clay dust and fought the idea of her feet pinched by fancy patent leather shoes with lily white ankle socks, no less. Drat and double drat. Her family wanted her scrubbed and squeezed into Sunday-go-to-meeting dresses three more times than was necessary. Auntie Ouidie would surely take Julia's hair out of pigtails, brush it till her niece's eyes watered, then plop a big sissified bow over one ear. The mental image made Julia's young blood boil even now. How could you shoot marbles, or climb a tree, or catch crawdads in a creek in a fancy dress?

Earlier that morning, with tears in her eyes, she'd asked her mama *why*. Why were they all trying to torture her when she was perfectly happy making her own fun all summer long?

Her mama had gotten that girl-talk look on her face. She'd told Julia that it was time she learned to behave like the lady she would become. It was time to cultivate those young people who would eventually make up her adult social circle. It was time she learned to behave properly around boys.

Boys! As if Julia didn't know how to behave around them already. She'd been practicing ever since kindergarten with Dallas Parker. She'd found it was a simple process: she was herself around Dallas; all other boys she avoided.

During this morning's spoiled breakfast, she'd made the mistake of asking if Dallas Parker would be attending Miss Peters's school this summer. It would ease the pain some if he were with her. Mama had swallowed a horrified look before beginning her lecture. Whatever made Julia think that Dallas *Parker* would attend anything in the Richardson social circle? He might be their neighbor, but he was *not* the Richardsons' kind of person. It would take more than the firm hand of Miss Peters to make the wild and uncouth Dallas Parker into a little gentleman. Wherever did Julia come up with these questions? And while she was on the subject, Julia was not—repeat *not*—to cross the railroad tracks or associate with *Miss* Parker and her son Dallas.

Julia couldn't understand her family's rabid dislike of Dallas and his mama. Miss Parker worked harder than any adult in Cannons Crossing, and Dallas was going to be a rodeo star some day. When any of the Richardson adults referred to *those* Parkers, however, Mama frowned, Big Daddy's mustache quivered and Auntie Ouidie cackled with unladylike glee.

Despite her family's odd behavior, Dallas Parker was the best friend Julia ever had.

Best but secret.

Julia might be just a kid and ignorant of some adult behavior, but she wasn't dumb. She sensed that her family could and would squash her friendship with Dallas if they got wind of it.

And the last thing she wanted was to lose any time with her best friend.

During her covert meetings with Dallas at the old oak, she could tell him anything. Her hopes. Her dreams. Her problems. And in turn she listened to him and all that was on his young mind. But always they met without her family's knowledge. Always out of sight at the ancient, secluded oak.

When she saw Dallas in town, however, he acted too busy to notice her much. That bothered her. But considering the adult Richardsons' attitude, it was probably for the best. Maybe, even, he sensed that Ten Oaks hadn't run out the welcome mat for him.

This morning she'd wanted to be brave and tell her mother that if Dallas Parker wasn't going to be at Miss Peters's, she wasn't going to attend, either. She wanted to tell her mother, too, that she'd asked Dallas to teach her to barrel race her pony this summer. Wanted to speak with pride of his growing achievements in junior rodeo. But what she'd said, instead, was that she didn't want to go to any school that was going to gussy her up like one of Big Daddy's prize heifers for show.

It had been the wrong thing to say, and she and her mother had argued bitterly.

If she was going to have to suffer the mother-daughter uglies, she'd feel a lot better about herself, knowing she'd at least stood up for Dallas. She hadn't. And that thought, combined with the likelihood of Miss Peters's summer reign of terror, made her downright miserable.

"Hey, hey, pigtail girl!" The sound of Dallas's voice floated across the field.

Julia could not describe her feeling of joy. Her friend Dallas had come at their prearranged signal. Together they would straighten out this mess....

From the window seat in her Boston apartment, twenty-eight-year-old Julia Richardson reeled in thoughts of her younger self. Secret meetings and summer plans gone awry. How simple her childhood worries seemed in retrospect. Her present problems—far greater than the hated and long-gone prospect of Miss Peters's school—could not be solved with a pebble in a tin can, a climb in a sheltering oak and a long talk with Dallas Parker. But how she wished they could be.

In the ten years since her graduation from high school, she and Dallas had kept in touch. Irregularly. She'd gone on to college, a degree in communications, several subordinate positions in newscasting, then to a position as news producer at a big Boston television station. He'd gone on to win three grand national rodeo championships. But there was something about their old oak-tree friendship that had lingered. Even if she didn't hear from him often, Dallas was still the only person in the world she trusted implicitly. She could count on him to listen—really listen—when she spoke and to answer her honestly. Even if he couldn't clean up her present mess, the mere sound of his deep, drawl-laced voice over the telephone would, for certain, be a better pick-me-up than the box of chocolates that lay half-nibbled beside her on the window seat.

An audacious thought now begged for attention. Better even than Dallas's voice would be his presence and support when

Julia had to break the news of her altered circumstances to her judgmental family. Could she still ask her childhood friend for such a favor?

What the hey. Despite the fact that it was well past midnight, she reached for the telephone. He could only tell her no. That he was too busy with the current rodeo circuit. She could understand that. But it was worth a try. She dialed his number.

After a few short rings, he picked up. "Parker here." Sleep seeped under the two words.

Relief flooded through her at the sound of his strong, familiar voice. "Dallas. It's me, Julia. Can you meet me at the Atlanta airport? I'm in trouble."

"I'll be there. Name the date and time." Not a moment's hesitation. Not a *why?*, or a *can it wait?* As always, his response was immediate, his loyalty unconditional.

"Tomorrow. As soon as you can arrange a flight."

A little shiver of trepidation ran down Julia's spine. She only hoped that this time the simple ties that bound them would be enough to sustain her in her present distress.

Chapter One

With his good arm, Dallas heaved the heavy western saddle off the luggage carousel at Atlanta's Hartsfield International Airport. He winced. Injuries having brought an abrupt halt to his career in rodeo, he guessed it was time to retire this baby—his lucky championship saddle. He'd brought it with him to see if the Sutters would store it while he figured out a way to reinvent himself. His nomadic life-style certainly didn't allow for anything as ordinary as storage space. He traveled light. Light and free.

And that freedom seldom saw him in this all too familiar neck of the Georgia piney woods. He wouldn't be here now if it weren't for Julia Richardson's puzzling call yesterday.

Automatically, he scrutinized the airport baggage area, looking for the usual uniformed driver holding a card with his name. This time he couldn't afford the limo. But when Julia had asked him to meet her at the airport, he couldn't see driving her to Ten Oaks in some rental compact. He had his pride and old, unsettled scores where Cannons Crossing was concerned. And his pride told him to return to his hometown in a manner befitting the three-time national rodeo champ that he was. Regardless of the forever past tense of those titles.

Even if he didn't deserve the limo, Julia did. On a good day, Julia Anabeth Richardson deserved the world on a silver platter. And now that she found herself in some kind of trouble, Dallas planned to do everything in his power to ease her burden. Even if it meant going a little deeper in the hole to get her home in style.

The scent of gardenias blossomed nearby.

"Dallas." The voice oozed honey.

He turned to see his seat partner from the plane. Darned if he hadn't forgotten her name.

With a seductive tilt of her head, she held up a slip of paper. "You said you'd be staying in the area." She blotted her lipstick on the paper, then folded it and tucked it into his shirt pocket. "Give me a call," she purred, letting her hand linger on his chest just long enough to tell him she meant business.

"Sorry." Dallas forced a slow grin to make up for the refusal. "This time around I'm taken."

Fluttering her eyelashes, she cooed, "You never know."

He watched the woman walk away undeterred and obviously secure in the knowledge of her ample charms. She had the come-hither look of every groupie on the circuit. With the prospect of seeing Julia, however, that old, familiar source of comfort seemed tawdry and most definitely unappealing.

He shook his head. Now to find Julia and their limo driver. He hoped his old friend's earlier flight had been on time. He was anxious to find out what lay heavy on her mind.

Scanning the crowded terminal once more, he was struck by a familiar face in an unexpected setting. On a pile of luggage just inside the baggage-claim area, she sat. Julia Richardson. His Julia. Even if they hadn't been boon companions all through childhood, Dallas would recognize that serious expression, that straight-back demeanor anywhere. Her picture had been in the society pages often enough. Cates County royalty. That's what one article had called her.

Making his way through the throng of travelers, Dallas allowed one corner of his mouth to twitch in a smile. Julia was probably the only Richardson who didn't appreciate the "royal" label. She'd always had plans beyond the middle Georgia aristocracy. In fact, she'd been just plain driven in those plans to leave her hometown and to make it on her own. Consequently, when she hadn't been telling him her dreams at the old oak tree, she'd had her nose in a book. Any book. Intent on winning the high-school valedictory title. On getting the primo college scholarships. The description under her yearbook senior picture read "Most Likely to Succeed." She'd done just that with a stint at an Ivy League school, then a news position for a big Boston television station. But on the phone, she'd said she was in trouble.

Now, trouble didn't generally sniff at Julia Richardson's heels. Trouble was more Dallas's erstwhile companion.

As he drew close, it became apparent that Julia was not her usual cool and publicly aloof self. She was obviously distraught. And doing nothing to hide the fact.

Dallas lowered the heavy saddle and his knapsack to the floor before her. "Hey, hey, pigtail girl," he murmured in the old childhood greeting.

She looked up, and Dallas could see that she'd been crying. There were women's tears, and there were women's tears. But Julia Richardson's tears reached out and pulled at Dallas Parker's heartstrings. Always had. Always would.

"Julia," he said gently, not quite knowing what to do. It had been some time since he'd last seen her. With each adult meeting, it took a while to recapture their childhood easiness together. "It's me. Dallas. Everything's going to be okay."

She made an effort to compose herself, then stood. "Dallas." She attempted a small, stiff smile. "It's good to see a friendly face."

Now, why did her statement make him believe she'd seen far too many unfriendly faces of late? That old protective feeling rose to the fore.

She glanced at the enormous saddle. ''You still riding the rodeo circuit?''

He scowled. That was a painful question to answer. ''Let's just say I'm at a crossroads in my career. I have some decisions to make.''

''Me, too,'' she said softly, her eyes welling up with tears.

Oh, yeah. The trouble she'd hinted at. He reached out to steady her. ''Julia, are you all right?''

She leaned a little toward him. ''I'm…I'm just very tired.''

He saw immediately that was a half truth, but he wasn't about to push her. Their friendship didn't operate with push and pull. If he let her have her head, she'd tell him her heart's unease in due time. As she always had.

''Why wouldn't you be,'' he said instead, by way of comfort, ''with all this luggage and all these folks milling around and you having to wait for my plane? Maybe you should have had your parents pick you up. I could have followed when my flight got in.''

''No!'' she exclaimed, then took a deep breath. ''No. I didn't tell my family I was coming.''

''That explains it.'' Dallas grinned in an attempt to cheer her. ''Why, if Big Daddy Richardson knew about his only child flying into Atlanta, nothing but a brass band would do as welcoming committee.''

His banter didn't hearten her. Instead, she crumpled into a small heap on the nearest suitcase and began to weep silently. ''Anyway…I need you with me when I see them.''

Whatever trouble dogged her, she wasn't handling it with the old Julia Richardson aplomb. Not if she needed him, of all people, beside her when she stepped into the Richardson lair.

''You *must* be tired.'' Dallas knelt beside her. Instinctively, he reached out and brushed the lush dark fall of hair from her face. ''Just sit here while I find that rascally limo driver of mine. Don't you worry about anything. I'll take care of it all. Whatever it is, it can't be the equal of you and me together again. We can sit back and figure everything out on the way home."

At the word *home* Julia's sobs became audible. Her face tearstained, she looked up at Dallas, her eyes pleading. "I don't…think…I can…go home."

Her unexplained pain cut him like a knife. Without as much as a thought, he wrapped his arms around her and pulled her close. "Not go home? Of course you can go home. Home is where the traveling likes of us go to think and to rest. And to heal if necessary." He inhaled the wildflower freshness of her hair. Felt her tremble in his arms. Actually, his assurances of home were mere platitudes. He had no positive concept of home. But it had always seemed important to her. He said what he thought she needed to hear.

Now, what in the world had happened to strong, capable Julia to make her not want to go home?

"Dallas, you don't understand." She pushed away from him, then looked up into his face, her expression wretched.

"Then explain it to me. That's why I'm here. To listen." He ran his fingertips down the side of her face. "Just like old times."

"Just like old times," she repeated softly, sighing. She attempted a lopsided smile. Suddenly, her words came out in an unexpected rush as if she needed to get the whole thing over with. "My family thought I'd be coming home—sometime in the near future—to introduce them to my fiancé. Instead, I'm unmarried and four months' pregnant…and the baby's father has left me." She hiccuped softly. "Not to mention that I quit my job in Boston."

Holy smoke.

Julia studied Dallas's face for signs of condemnation. She saw nothing but concern. Just as he'd said. *Like old times.* For that she would be eternally grateful. He'd been the first and only person to whom she'd spoken her entire list of troubles aloud, and the bottling up of her woes had taken a toll.

Strange, but in simply voicing her plight, she felt lighter.

Considerably more hopeful. In Dallas's arms, it almost seemed that things would work out after all.

Who was she kidding? Things might work out for someone whose father wasn't Big Daddy Richardson, successful businessman, prize-winning stockman and all too powerful magistrate for Cannons Crossing, Georgia. Pillar of the small community he was. And indisputable head of the Richardson family. Wasn't it precisely because of her doting but overbearing father that she'd set out to make it on her own? And here she now sat, actually contemplating a return home for solace and guidance. She had to be crazy.

"Julia, I've hired a limo." Dallas's voice broke into her thoughts. "Let me get my driver. I can tell we need some privacy." With a callused hand, he gently wiped the tears from her cheek. "We've got an hour-and-a-half ride to Cannons Crossing. Surely two adults can figure out some solution in that time."

"Dear Lord, what have I dragged you into?" The sheer folly of her SOS call hit her.

"Hush!" Cracking a boyish, lopsided and very endearing grin, he laid a finger on her lips. "What did we used to ask to happen if one of us didn't come when the other called?"

Warm tears fought with an even warmer smile. "May the weevils get your granny, may your dogs refuse to hunt and may the kudzu cover your bones." She sniffed and held up her pinky finger as they'd done many a time in childhood.

He locked his pinky with hers. "So how could I not come?"

Oh, he was still the sweetest.

Rising, he admonished her to stay put until his return. She couldn't have moved if she'd wanted to. Her bones felt like sponge, her muscles like energy-less goop. Her head throbbed. Her eyes stung. How had she managed to get herself into this mess? And now, how, in a moment of weakness, had she managed to involve Dallas Parker?

Of all people, Dallas Parker.

How could Dallas help smooth the family waters when Big

Daddy *loathed* him? Saw him as an affront to family values and all things Richardson.

But Big Daddy didn't know Dallas the way Julia did. In fact, lots of people in Cannons Crossing might think they knew Dallas Lee Parker, but they didn't. Not really. What they saw was his exterior wall of self-preservation. His thick outer armor.

And his outer armor was hard to miss. Flashy at times. Arrogant most of the time. Devil-may-care. Even as a teenager from the wrong side of the tracks, he'd made a name for himself in rodeo. Both in and out of the arena, he'd exhibited a wild and reckless nature. He was the kid who didn't care what happened to him. And took risks commensurate with that indiscretion. Handsome and dangerous, he made the town fathers want to pass an ordinance locking up their women, young and old, when he was around.

Despite her present difficulties, Julia actually smiled. Why, Dallas at their high-school-senior graduation party had been typical. Wearing an enormous junior rodeo championship buckle and the sexiest grin she'd ever seen, he'd been leaning against the double doors of the gym, cheerfully accepting good-luck kisses from every girl and woman with breath left in her. He stood there artlessly wearing his ego on his sleeve, and Julia had almost been tempted to stand in line to collect just one kiss. His kisses, for her part, had never been more than rumor. But there was something about the public Dallas—a brightness like that of the noonday sun—that made her step away for fear of getting burned. She felt easier when she had him all to herself—as her friend and confidant—under the old oak tree. She firmly believed that the private Dallas—attentive, intense and full of dreams—was the real Dallas. Her Dallas.

Unfortunately, if Big Daddy didn't know the real Dallas as Julia did, neither did her father know, even to this day, how close a friendship his daughter had developed with the renegade Parker. Julia and Dallas's openness today would spark a melodrama at Ten Oaks in excess of that produced by the news of her altered circumstances.

Julia Richardson, what were you thinking?

"I found him." Dallas loomed before her, a luggage cart and a taciturn uniformed driver in tow. "This is Mike. Our driver. Mike. Julia."

Mike tipped his hat, then silently began loading bags onto the cart.

"I'll take care of the saddle." Hefting the unwieldy hunk of leather, Dallas turned to Julia. "Ready?"

"As I'll ever be." She fell into step at his side, dabbing at her eyes with a lace handkerchief.

"Now, don't go folding on me, Miss Julia." He winked at her, but his steely blue eyes remained serious. "We have some brainstorming to do on the ride home."

"I take it you still like a challenge." Strange, but with Dallas on her side—and at her side—she felt better already. Hadn't that always been the case? It wasn't that she couldn't handle life's predicaments alone. It was just that... well...anyone could use a friend in difficult times.

"Me? Still like a challenge?" He scowled, and the tiny weathered lines near his eyes deepened. "Sure."

"Even someone else's?"

He chuckled softly. A chuckle that seemed rusty with little use. "Especially someone else's."

Glancing up at him, Julia noted a subtle but distinct difference in her old friend. All trace of the devil-may-care teenager was gone, buried under an attitude—the thrust of his chin, the set of his shoulders—that warned the world to back off. She sighed. It always took an increasingly long period with each reunion for Dallas to begin to let down his guard with her. She wondered what new challenges since she'd last seen him had hardened him further.

Circumstances may have changed Dallas, but he was still an attention-getter. Head-turning handsome, larger than life, he stood out in the airport crowd. Tall and muscular, with a swagger that bespoke his supreme self-confidence, he toted his huge saddle as if it were nothing, while managing, at the same time, to create an aura of protectiveness around Julia. With looks and body language alone, he easily made a path for them through the crowded terminal.

Trying to ignore the stares their little procession caused, especially among the women, Julia reasoned she could have found a lot worse knight in shining armor than a well-muscled rodeo champ with a flinty gaze and a can-do attitude. Perhaps on their ride home, they could begin to relax once more in each other's company and actually think up a logical next step to her dilemma.

Curbside, Dallas handed Julia into a waiting limo while the driver loaded her luggage into the trunk. A limo. For the first time, she was struck by the *Dallasness* of it. She did find it odd, however, that, while she had enough luggage for a cruise, he had nothing but a large knapsack and the saddle which he flung in the front passenger's seat. He'd once told her that rodeo and movin' on were his entire life. And for that reason, he'd never accumulated many worldly possessions. His lack of worldly possessions didn't bother her, but it always seemed that lasting relationships for Dallas—other than their own— had been in as short supply as his belongings. Julia did think that circumstance a little sad and empty, considering the worth of the man.

Glancing at the well-worn saddle flung in the front passenger's seat, she hoped the taciturn Mike liked the smell of horse and leather.

"Comfortable?" Dallas slid into the back of the limo, next to her.

She managed a silent nod, but comfort was not an easy feeling to come by in the presence of the grown Dallas. What had she gotten herself into? With each new meeting as adults, she found it increasingly difficult to see her old childhood friend under the austere but compellingly attractive package surrounding the man. Unfortunately, he was twice as attractive in close quarters. How was she going to concentrate on a solution to her troubles in the next hour and a half? She tried to visualize the old oak tree, the rustle of leaves, the murmur of childish conversation, but saw before her instead tousled dark hair, piercing blue eyes and a heart-stopping regard full of unasked questions. The man looked for all the world like a fallen angel.

And she had been away from him far too long for this to be a good idea.

In the spacious limo, Dallas crossed one booted foot over his other knee. "You ready to talk?"

The protective tilt of his head, the soft deference in his words, brought fresh tears to her eyes. She wasn't normally an overly emotional woman; however, her pregnancy-augmented hormones were certainly wreaking havoc with her composure today.

Swiping at her damp lashes, then forcing a smile, she said, "Sure. Let's get it out in the open." She raised her chin defiantly. "Let's give it the old Richardson-Parker treatment."

He was glad that, despite all the problems facing her, she could smile through her tears. It showed strength of character. Oh, he'd known all along about Julia Richardson's strength of character. What he freshly observed as they sat in awkward semisilence was that strong and studious Julia had grown into one hell of a gorgeous woman. Glossy dark hair. Tawny eyes the color of ancient gold coins. And skin so smooth it begged to be stroked. Now, that little observation made his ears burn.

"Can we be honest with each other?" he asked at last, trying to return to the business at hand. Julia's present dilemma. Not his awakened awareness of her beauty.

Her dusky golden eyes grew wide. She nibbled self-consciously on her lower lip. The sensual movements made more than his ears burn. Staying on task just got more difficult.

Dallas frowned and cleared his throat. "I was sincere in my offer to help you see your way free of your troubles."

She cocked one eyebrow and stared at him a long time before speaking, as if she weighed her words carefully. "Perhaps I shouldn't have called. I don't want anything from you,

Dallas…the fact that you're here is more than enough…but I would value your opinion at this point.''

Why had she prefaced her acceptance? They were old friends. They went way back. There had been a time when they could share anything. Anything. Had she forgotten who he was? Had she spent too much time in the big city, to the point where every offer of assistance was suspect? Or was she now so independent she felt the need to set the record straight from the get-go? Well, hell, he wasn't about to horn in on her life. He'd simply responded to the call of the one friend who'd always been there for him. Knowing the extent of her troubles, he most definitely wasn't going to leave her alone to face an uncertain future—especially the as-yet-unrealized part when Big Daddy Richardson was to hear his only child's news. Even Dallas, with all his trophies attesting to the danger and excitement in his rodeo life, wouldn't like to arrive at that show-down without some backup. No, he wasn't trying to horn in on her life, but he wasn't about to simply listen and leave, either. Not until he knew she'd be all right.

''Can we be honest?'' he asked again. ''If I'm going to offer an opinion, I need to know the whole story. Painful details and all.''

''We've never been anything but honest with each other.'' She looked down at her hands in her lap. ''What do you want to know?'' Her voice was low, but even and lined with an unmistakable strength.

''This fellow who…had a hand in your predicament. Does your family know him?''

''No. Not even his name. He was a co-worker at the Boston station.''

''So your folks have no expectations where he's concerned?''

She shook her head sadly. ''Except that I told them I'd met someone and thought marriage was a *possibility*. Their meeting him was supposed to be a big surprise.'' She inhaled sharply. ''The surprise turned out to be on me.''

''He didn't view marriage as seriously as you did.''

"In retrospect, I'm not sure I viewed marriage seriously. The possibility, however, was like the promise of a shiny new toy." She frowned. "The excitement came more from finding that connection with a man who shared my professional interests. A man I saw as combining passion *and* staying power."

"But he left you."

"Yes. Marriage, for him, was never ever an option."

"He left you when he learned of the baby." An old, bitter taste filled Dallas's mouth. A nightmare flickered at the edges of his memory.

She raised her head and looked directly at him. Surprisingly, her eyes remained dry, her gaze filled with a steely determination. "When he learned of the baby, he left me, yes. He was—I learned too late—already married."

Dallas flinched. There were some replays in life that should be outlawed.

She scowled. "Do you feel you can judge me?" Obviously, she'd misinterpreted his winced reaction.

"Julia." Her name on his lips was a plea to remember the extent of their friendship. "Of course not." Instinctively, he reached for her hand. "There's not a saint without a past, nor a sinner without a future. I figure I have enough black marks on my record without worrying about those of others." Although, he added mentally, I'd like to get hold of the SOB who did my Julia wrong.

Damnation, but the world was one screwed-up place. A man had to buy a license to fish, to drive, to own a dog. But he could freely litter the landscape with broken hearts and unwanted children. It was an old, sorry story, and one that cut too close to Dallas's boyhood experience for comfort.

Julia allowed her hand—soft, small and very still—to remain in his. "I wouldn't feel half so witless if I hadn't broken cardinal rule number two."

"Which was?"

"I let *him* push *me* out of my job."

"How so?"

"I was so disgusted with him for lying—and with myself for being so gullible—that I couldn't stand the thought of running into him every day. I quit my job without giving notice." Her hand tensed. "I burned my bridges in Boston. And then some."

"So what do you want now, Julia Richardson?" He knew what he wanted. He wanted a moratorium on fathers abandoning their children. Hurting the women he cared for.

She didn't hesitate. "Space. And time to think ahead." She looked up at him with an expression that begged for his understanding. "You have to believe that I'm not a weak-kneed ninny. I can handle being jilted. I can handle a child out of wedlock. I can handle quitting my job. It's just that—"

"All three together require some space and time to think things through," he finished for her, giving her hand a gentle squeeze. "That's understandable." He sent her a wink, meant as much to relax himself as her. "And for the record, I never thought of you as a weak-kneed ninny. If I recall, you had a wicked roundhouse punch when you were in pigtails."

"Perhaps I was stronger then." Her words hovered above a whisper as she shook her head ruefully. "How do I react to my present situation? I get an old friend to disrupt his life. Convince him to meet me at home. Home. The one place no one will give me either space or time."

"How much time and space were you looking for?" Dallas looked deep into those tawny eyes. "We've got approximately an hour and fifteen minutes now before Mike sets us down in Cannons Crossing."

She forced a small smile. "I suppose that's more of a breather than many people get before plunging back into their lives."

It's more than my ma ever got, he thought, his anger rising. He released Julia's hand to run the limo window down. The atmosphere suddenly seemed airless. In a brusque effort to reach the lever, he twisted his bum arm and let out a grunt of pain.

"What's wrong?" Julia's response was immediate, laced with concern.

"It's nothing." Nothing except the end of his career. "Just an injury that's slow to heal," he added, trying to make his words nonchalant.

"Is that why you had some time in your schedule to help out an old friend?"

"Yeah." He'd had plenty of time to spare lately. But for all of that, he still hadn't figured out what in blazes he was going to do with the rest of his life.

To collect himself, he stared hard out the window at the scenery flashing by as he massaged his stiff arm. He needed to get his mind off his own problems and back to Julia's.

"So..." Scowling, he settled back in the seat and concentrated on keeping the conversation on Julia's dilemma. "Now that you have limo time and space, what do you see as your next step?"

"A big one. To find a job so that I can support myself and my baby."

"In Georgia?"

"Yes. Maybe not in Cannons Crossing, but somewhere in Georgia." Her features relaxed. "Despite its quirks, despite my unpredictable family, this is home. I've come to realize that in my travels."

Home. He'd never known a real one.

Dallas knit his brows and glanced reflectively out the window again. Cannons Crossing was where he'd grown up, but he didn't harbor any affectionate delusions that it was home. Home had to be more that the hardscrabble existence his mother had eked out for the two of them before she'd died and the charity the Sutters had extended thereafter. Home should encompass some degree of community acceptance. But, aside from Julia and the Sutters, Cannons Crossing had never opened its heart where Dallas Parker was concerned.

He'd liked to have come back and shown it and its sancti-monious citizens a thing or two. Liked to have returned at the peak of his career. In triumph. A star. Three-time national champion. Somehow, in all the headiness of rising to the top, he'd put it off. Perhaps, knowing that Julia Richardson was no longer there to share his success made the daydream pointless. Now he came home an *ex*–rodeo champion. Rodeo had been his life. Had defined who he was. He didn't quite know how to pick a future without it.

Julia noticed the troubled shadow that passed over Dallas's expression. As a celebrity in a high-risk career, he probably had his own concerns, and didn't need to be thinking of solutions to her situation. She tried to make her voice light. "Actually, there's a tiny, inconsequential step before the job search." She observed him carefully as he swung his gaze back to her. As he seemed to struggle to focus on her. "Facing Big Daddy." She rolled her eyes and pulled a face to emphasize the potential comedy of the situation. Life with Big Daddy Richardson was one part melodrama, one part farce. Who knew which would prevail today?

Dallas whistled through his teeth. "Lordy, girl. You are surely in for it."

"Oh, thank you, Dallas Lee Parker, for that bit of encouragement."

"Sorry." He grinned. A far too melancholy grin. "I was just remembering the time I had to come up before your daddy as magistrate. A couple of older kids I hung out with had toilet papered the high-school principal's property before the homecoming dance. Of course, I was the first to get blamed. Hell, I wasn't even with those guys that night, but that didn't stop Big Daddy from finding me guilty, too. Guilty by reputation. He meted out swift punishment to all three of us. 'Community service,' he called that month we were beholden to principal Jenks. 'Indentured servitude,' we called it. The other two boys—the ones who'd actually done the deed—got off after a week. Their fathers took care of it."

He left unspoken the fact that he'd never known a father. And his mother had been too busy working to put food on the table to "take care of it."

"I'm sorry for the way Big Daddy treated you," Julia replied, her words escaping softly. "He always took his position as defender of small-town values a tad too seriously." Too, he'd always been unduly hard on Dallas.

"Don't worry about it. It made me tough." Dallas shrugged and forced a smile. "I'm sure he'll go easy on his daughter, though."

Julia wasn't at all sure.

Dallas reached out and chucked her gently under the chin. "Oh, come on. With all his bluster, he loves you as if you hung the moon." His voice gained renewed energy. "What's the worst that could happen?"

Julia didn't want to think of the worst that could happen. "He may love me," she began, "but he loves propriety and the Richardson name even more."

"But you're his daughter. His only child."

"Yes. And because of that, he had great plans for me. Graduation. A prestigious job. Preferably a job he'd engineered for me near home. A marriage proposal from a man of social substance. A wedding. And a family that included a male heir." She straightened her back for emphasis. *"In that order."*

"As if he never made a mistake."

"Well, if he did, it never went public."

Dallas rubbed his chin thoughtfully. "You think it's appearances more than anything that's going to bother him?"

"Absolutely. Privately, he'll be pleased as punch that I'm back home under his roof with a grandbaby he always wanted." She sighed. "Right back home under his control, living by his rules, as if I were sixteen years old."

"I could always tell Mike here to turn around and take you back to the airport."

"Don't joke."

"I'm not joking." He took both her hands in his. "You're a strong woman, Julia Richardson. You don't need to come home to think through the next step in your future. With your qualifications, you could start fresh anywhere in the world."

Truth time. "But you said earlier that there's nothing like

home to help me rest and heal if necessary." She saw clouds gather in the changeable blue of his eyes. "Deep in my heart, despite the temporary pain it might bring to me and to my family, this is where I *belong,* Dallas. This is where my baby will belong. Even if we move on elsewhere in Georgia, Cannons Crossing will provide our roots."

"You speak of the baby as a given." A shadow passed over his expression. "You've definitely decided to keep it?"

"Definitely. Yes." She thought of the difficult, lonely choice she'd had to make. A choice no one could make for her. "For me, I know it's the right thing to do."

"Then we'd better use the next hour to figure out how to make the transition from Boston to Cannons Crossing as smooth as possible."

Oh, this was her old Dallas.

She reached out and touched his cheek with the tips of her fingers. "You don't have to figure out anything. You've given me a ride and moral support. You don't need to go any further than that."

"No?" Dallas turned his head and nipped playfully at her fingertips. She wondered if, deep inside, he felt as self-assured as his expression. "If I don't see you safely home…and peacefully settled in…who knows what kind of community service Big Daddy will have you performing?"

"Don't you worry. It won't be community service. Too public." She actually smiled. "It'll be banishment to the north tower until my child is twenty-one."

"Hey, I'm sure he'll let you keep cable TV and all your major department-store credit cards."

Julia harrumphed.

"It's not as if you plan to live under your daddy's roof indefinitely. How long do you think you'll stay with family?"

"Long enough to tell them of my altered circumstances. No more. Overnight would be good."

Dallas frowned. To his mind, despite how he personally felt about the Richardsons, that wasn't long enough. Julia needed to get her bearings, renew her sense of self and purpose, and that took some time and thought…and help. Without a doubt, she was a strong woman, capable of creating her own fulfilling and successful future. But he and his ma had been where Julia and her unborn child were about to go. It wasn't an easy place. Not even in the nineties. Not even for a Richardson.

She might think he was a meddling fool, but he couldn't let her set out in the unknown without an experienced guide. An audacious idea pushed itself to the forefront of his thoughts. If he dared act upon it, it might just prove to be the one absolutely right thing he'd ever done in his life.

Chapter Two

In an hour-and-a-half ride, they hadn't settled Julia's immediate future to Dallas's satisfaction. They'd talked. Julia now seemed outwardly calmer, but he worried about her stubborn independence. She'd called him for help, but hand-holding was all the help she seemed to allow him. Hell, it wasn't in his nature to sit around and just hold hands. He needed to fix the problem.

With mixed feelings, he gazed out the window at the long tree-shaded lane that curved up the hill to the enormous white-columned Richardson homestead. Mansion. Ten Oaks. By the time they reached the front door, the whole family and staff would have spotted the limo. Would line up on the veranda in small-town curiosity. Wondering who had come calling in such fashion. Richardsons or not, they'd be there. This was Cannons Crossing. Too little happened here to miss even a tick changing dogs. Let alone a long black limo.

Dallas glanced at Julia. Elegant and refined Julia. To the manor born. As unlike him with his dusty, wandering soul as cool moonlight was from the harsh sun of noonday. Unlike in more ways than that.

He wondered if she had even given a thought to the fact that this would be the first time he'd ever set foot in her home. When she was a girl, she'd invited him, sure. But he'd always laughed and told her that the old oak tree by the railroad tracks was good enough for him. He'd known, even back then, that Big Daddy hated him, for whatever reasons. Had known that if the boy Dallas had come through the front door, the man would have kept his daughter out of reach for certain and forever. No, the old oak tree had been secluded and safe and secret. It had preserved a hidden friendship that had kept Dallas going until he'd found rodeo and a way out of Cannons Crossing. He may have blown the dust of this town off his heels, but he'd never let the friendship out of his heart.

He owed Julia a debt she might not even know existed.

"You can back out even now," Julia offered bravely, breaking into his thoughts.

"Me? Not on your life. Not unless *you* tell Mike to turn around." He wasn't about to let her hang out to dry alone, especially not in the winds created by her blowhard father. Instead, he put his arm around her and pulled her close beside him. "You called me for moral support. And I plan to stick by your side until you break the news to your family and pick yourself up from the fallout."

"Don't remind me of the fallout." With a tiny groan, she snuggled more closely under his arm.

It always amazed him how *right* she felt by his side. Even after the initial awkwardness that accompanied their infrequent reunions. That feeling of rightness against all the odds, more than the upcoming scene they had to play before Big Daddy Richardson, gave him a sudden case of stage fright. Dallas Parker, he mentally chided himself, you've ridden the raunchiest bulls before sellout crowds. You aren't about to let a mere a wisp of a woman—even an extremely attractive woman—and her look-down-their-noses family members throw you for a loop. For pete's sake, she's a *friend*. The rightness you feel holding her is *friendship*. Nothing more.

And you owe her big time.

As Julia nestled even closer against him, he felt his insides buck like a bronc despite his rationalization.

He glanced out the window again. Sure enough, a small knot of people, headed by the imposing Big Daddy, stood on the deep front veranda. Even at this distance, Dallas could see the formidable man's handlebar mustache. No matter what the county magistrate wore, Dallas always pictured him wearing a Panama hat and a white suit with a black string tie. Cool and in control. Cannons Crossing law and order. Keep that image in mind, Dallas silently cautioned himself, and not the one of the hotheaded, overprotective father cleaning his legendary shotgun collection.

With his own brand of protectiveness, Dallas tightened his grip around Julia's shoulder as Mike pulled the limo to a stop before the front steps.

Nothing but tinted glass protected them from the curious stares of the Richardson household. The members hadn't changed since Dallas was a kid. Red-faced Big Daddy. Elegant Miriam, his wife. Auntie Ouidie, still spry although she must be pushing a hundred. Martha the housekeeper, who looked as if she'd defected from the East German weightlifting team. Mary Louise the birdlike cook. And Hiram Ledbetter—a man who never went by one name alone—the sun-dried and nearly fossilized gardener.

All gathered in the heat of an Indian summer sun to determine who in the blazes could be arriving at their doorstep in a long black limousine.

"Let the games begin," Julia whispered.

"It'll work out fine." Dallas gave her shoulder a gentle reassuring squeeze. "I promise."

Julia rolled her eyes. "You've obviously never spent time in the Richardson household."

"Hush!" Dallas could see Mike's shadow as he reached for

the back-door handle. "Put on your prettiest smile, my friend. It's showtime."

The door opened.

The Richardson ensemble bent as one to peer into the back seat. The stunned silence was quickly followed by an audible collective gasp.

"Julia?" Miriam was the first to move. "Is that really you, baby?"

"Mama!" Within moments Julia was in her mother's arms.

Dallas slowly uncoiled his lanky frame from the limo's interior. Big Daddy eyed him with suspicion. Auntie Ouidie and the others didn't budge. They obviously recognized a story brewing.

Reaching for Dallas, Julia drew him toward her side. "Y'all remember Dallas Parker."

"Not without a toilet-paper roll in his hand," Big Daddy muttered.

"Daddy!"

The look Julia shot her father did nothing to quell the man's gimlet gaze, but slowly he extended his hand to Dallas. "I assume I have you to thank for giving *my daughter* a ride home."

Dallas didn't miss the possessive emphasis. Nor the big man's decidedly limp handshake.

"Yes, sir." Wary himself, Dallas wasn't about to give the old man any immediate ammunition with a reckless attempt at conversation.

Clearing her throat, Julia glanced quickly at Dallas, then at her father. "Actually, it's a little more than a ride from the airport." Color stained her cheeks.

Big Daddy's mustache quivered. "How much more?"

Julia slid her hand down Dallas's arm. Entwined her fingers with his. He felt her tremble. He'd help her as soon as she directed the topic. But she had to be the one to speak the words first.

"I came home because I have all sorts of news to tell."

She tilted her chin resolutely. "I asked Dallas to meet me—as a friend—for old times' sake."

The silence deafened as each family member, in turn, glanced at Julia's and Dallas's clasped hands.

"Oh, goody!" Auntie Ouidie exclaimed at last with a cackle. "A visiting hunk. Isn't that what you girls call them these days, Julia?"

"Yes, ma'am." Julia looked up into Dallas's eyes, a small smile playing at the corners of her lips.

Dallas wasn't sure that this was any time to let down their guard.

He was right.

Julia, for her part, failed to anticipate her father's long memory and short fuse.

"Has all this time spent away from your family," Big Daddy snarled, "made you lose your sense of propriety?" His words were for her, but he aimed his black glower at Dallas.

"Big Daddy only means," Miriam interjected nervously, "that you didn't tell us you were coming. Let alone that you were bringing a guest."

"I don't need an interpreter!" Big Daddy bellowed.

Julia sighed. The Richardsons hadn't changed one iota. She threw her hands into the air. "That's it! I'm leaving." She turned back to the limo. "Come on, Dallas. We'll put up in the Battlefield Inn for tonight."

"A hotel!" Her father looked apoplectic. "With this rodeo bum? The only thing worse than a Parker under my roof is one in a hotel with my daughter!"

Narrowing his eyes and clenching his fists, Dallas took a step toward Big Daddy, but pulled himself up short when he remembered he was here to support Julia. Flattening her gasbag father, although certainly satisfying, wouldn't further Julia's cause. He inhaled slowly and deeply. Forced his fingers to uncurl.

"Now, Big Daddy, I'm sure this is Julia's idea of a joke." Fluttering about her husband, Miriam Richardson cut her daughter a withering glance. "Julia…your father's heart…" she hissed.

"Daddy…Mama…" Julia pleaded wearily, "could we all just act like the civilized family we pretend to be?" She'd chosen her words carefully.

Miriam's eyes widened. If there was one thing her mother took pride in, it was the family's perceived standing in the community. Its grace. Its manners. Its hospitality. In this light, public family bickering and rudeness to a guest—even Dallas Parker—was anathema. Julia counted on this fact to bring her mother, if not over to the cause, then at least politely in line.

"Perhaps the Sutters would take us in," Dallas said, his features expressionless.

Julia suppressed a grin. Dallas might not know it, but he'd just clinched room and board with the Richardsons. Miriam might be shocked at the idea of a Parker as a guest, but she most certainly wouldn't forfeit her chance to remain at the center of unfolding events. Morever, she wouldn't let it be said around town that her hostessing skills had slipped one iota.

As she cleared her throat delicately, Miriam dug her bright red nails into Big Daddy's arm. "Although we weren't expecting you," she offered with careful, well-modulated words and a nod of her head toward Dallas, "Ten Oaks always has room for another place at the table, another guest under our roof."

"*Not* a P—!" The long red nails cut Big Daddy off.

"Mr. Parker, as my daughter's friend, welcome." Her mother's eyes belied her sincerity, but Julia blessed her for the effort.

"Thank you." Dallas seemed to hold his tongue in check. A muscle twitched near the corner of one eye. He appeared to ball and unball his fists with great deliberation.

Julia reached out to touch his arm. She hoped she hadn't made a grave error. In asking for his support, she'd conveniently forgotten his legendary temper while worrying about Big Daddy's.

"My, my." Shaking her head, Mary Louise muttered, "I'd better hightail it back into the kitchen and put another chicken in." She rubbed her hands on her apron. "The afternoon's waning, and it looks like this boy can *eat*."

Martha turned to follow Mary Louise. "I'd better see to the spare bedroom." She lowered her voice. "The one furthest down the hall from Miss Julia's."

At that, Auntie Ouidie gave a derisive snort. "As if that would stop a hot-blooded couple," she muttered, giving Dallas an appraising once-over, her gaze finally falling on Julia's hand still resting on Dallas's arm. The old lady reached out bony fingers and affectionately pinched Julia's cheek. "I'd better take my nap now, sweetie, if you're going to regale us with your news. At dinner perhaps?"

"I think dinner would be a good time to catch up, Miss Ouidie." Turning to Julia, Dallas looked as if he could use a stiff drink and a couple hundred miles between him and the Richardsons. "How about it, Julia? Can your news wait?"

"How much do you have to tell that it requires rehearsal time?" Big Daddy stepped forward, menace in the quiver of his mustache.

"Oh, lots," Julia replied, trying to make her tone of voice light. Dallas's presence strengthened her. With him in her corner, she'd let her story unfold in her own way. In due time. She wouldn't let her family push or harry her. She'd been right to ask him to accompany her. "It can wait, however, till we've washed away this traveling dust." She reached out with her free hand and touched Dallas lightly on the chest, knowing it would make Big Daddy's blood boil. "My news can wait for dinner."

Hiram Ledbetter began to back toward the side of the house.

"Hiram Ledbetter, you old tattle!" Big Daddy fairly exploded. "You call any one of your legion of flappy-mouthed relatives and I'll boil you in oil! Do you hear me?"

"Yes, sir." Hiram's eyes looked ready to roll back in his head.

"There will not be one word about this to anyone," Big

Daddy continued in a voice that brooked no argument. "My daughter has come home. There's absolutely no gossip in that."

Julia felt a reassuring pressure as Dallas slid his big hand once again around her own.

Big Daddy froze. She had him. She was, after all, his only child. His daughter. His pride and joy. Home again. And as much as Dallas's presence surely galled him, her father would hang in there until he'd heard her news. Until he'd figured a way to manipulate it to his ends.

As for now, he scowled. He sputtered incoherently. He glared at his wife for assistance.

"So," Julia said with no small degree of satisfaction, "we don't have to put up in a hotel?"

"Of course not, darling," Miriam cooed. "How silly. You'll stay right here." She raked Dallas with her brittle regard. "So that we can better comprehend this new turn of events…whatever it might be."

This new turn of events. Obviously, her mother meant Dallas's presence.

Dallas. Bless his heart. So far he'd handled her situation and her family perfectly. He'd let her hint at the subject of the new events in her life. Had let her unravel it slowly. Her way. He'd then stood up to her father by not letting the old man bait him or rush her. And he'd stood by her side. Like a rock. Feeding her with the strength of his touch and his unspoken encouragement. Just as he'd promised. Just as he'd always done in the past. Only this time his support wasn't hidden amid the foliage of the old oak tree. This time it had been right in front of her family. In front of a clearly hostile Big Daddy. That took courage on Dallas's part, she noted with pride.

They'd survived round one. It might take a strong glass of Mary Louise's sweet tea to face round two, but together Dallas and she would do it.

"Oh, by the way," Big Daddy added as he turned to enter

the house, his voice low and vaguely menacing, "we Richardsons dress for dinner."

"I wasn't planning on showing up in my Skivvies." Dallas stiffened his stance. "Say what you will, *sir,* my mama took my upbringing seriously."

Big Daddy's eyes made tiny slits in his face, wide enough only for the exasperation to show through. Julia had to admit that Dallas was handling her father in the only way possible: by showing no fear. By showing a Parker pride to match that of any Richardson.

As her family proceeded into the house, Julia turned to face Dallas. "I know this is no picnic," she whispered, "but thank you for coming. For sticking by me."

"Don't thank me yet. You haven't really told them anything." He ran a finger lightly down her cheek. "Although, by making them wait, you may force them to imagine worse news than you bear." He winked, and the hint of a smile played about his lips. "Julia Anabeth, I always did peg you for a smart one."

At his touch, a shiver ran down Julia's spine. She tried to focus on their friendship. If she had to handpick a friend, she couldn't have picked a finer one than Dallas Parker. Strong. With both a physical strength and a strength of will. And loyal. With an ironic outlook on life that seemed to make him invincible.

She could learn a lot from this cowboy.

She slipped her arm around his waist and smiled up at him. At the feel of his well-muscled body beneath her touch, a little thrill of danger—wholly foreign to her heretofore well-planned life—ran through her like heat lightning.

Dallas had let Julia wash up and take a nap while he'd gone for a solitary walk in the woods behind the house. The fine antique furnishings in the spare bedroom, the smell of money and social standing had made him edgy. He'd known he'd need to store up on fresh air and wide-open spaces for the challenging evening ahead.

He'd been right, although the dinner to this point had been a mostly silent, brooding affair.

He now sat across from Julia at the Richardson's long, elegantly narrow, highly polished dining-room table. The candlelight became his childhood friend to the point where he was distracted enough to imagine them the only two people in the entire world.

Too soon the illusion was shattered.

"I didn't realize you two were friends." At least Auntie Ouidie's statement held no obvious malice.

"Goodness, Auntie," Julia replied lightly. "We were neighbors for eighteen years. We went all through school together."

Big Daddy grumbled almost inaudibly, but even that small noise was cut off by what seemed to be a swift kick under the table from Miriam.

"And have you kept in touch since then?" her mother asked, a decided look of surprise on her perfectly made-up face.

"We met again—" Dallas and Julia began, then stopped together.

"We met again," Dallas repeated, reaching across the table and laying his hand gently atop Julia's, "when I performed an exhibition in Boston. Julia covered the event for her station."

"Yes." Julia grasped the story and continued. "I recognized a fellow Georgia expatriate and called and asked him to dinner."

"Are the women so forward in Boston?" Miriam's expression registered shock.

"Mama…the Parkers are part and parcel of Cannons Crossing. Dallas and I were in the same class in high school."

"Oh, that class," Big Daddy snarled over his sweet-potato pie. "The one where you were valedictorian and Dallas here mopped up the bottom of the roster?"

"I admit I had more interest in ponies and rodeo than I had in books." Dallas actually chuckled. The old windbag wasn't going to get a rise out of him. He had nothing to lose. He was here to deflect flak away from Julia. Period.

"And it paid off," Julia added, admiration clear in her voice. "Dallas has won the national all-round championship three years running."

Surprised that she remembered as much, he nonetheless wished she wouldn't bring it up. That part of his life lay in ruins. Rodeo wasn't who he was anymore.

Big Daddy harrumphed loudly. "Can you make a living at it?"

"Yes, sir," Dallas replied evenly. He'd made a good living at it, although he failed to mention that his earnings were now gone. Gone to pay medical bills.

The old man harbored a malicious glint in his eyes. "When do you go back on the road? *Tomorrow,* perhaps?"

The five around the table fell silent.

Dallas didn't mind drawing flak for Julia, but this flak cut painfully close to his own dilemma. What would he be doing tomorrow and on into the future? He pushed the remaining dessert around on his plate. Sometimes the best defense was a good offense.

He began deliberately, ignoring the older man's loaded question. "Perhaps you'd share with me what you did for a living…sir…when you were my age."

The tips of Big Daddy's mustache jerked up and down. If Dallas didn't know better, he could have sworn they began to curl inward. Yes, indeedy, with the first try he'd touched a sore spot.

"Why!" Auntie Ouidie exclaimed. "If I remember correctly, my brother Norton, when he was about your age, was wild to marry Miriam. But he had nothing to offer but the family name, the clothes on his back—" she grinned wickedly "—and an amazing gift of gab."

"Ouidie!" Miriam placed both diamond-encrusted hands flat on the table for emphasis.

"True's true, Miriam." The elderly lady would not be deterred. "The Richardsons were an old but genteelly poor family. We had name but nothing else. Now, your family, sister-in-law, had money but no name to speak of.'' With an airy wave of her hand, she dismissed Miriam's expression of undisguised horror. ''But look at the two of you now. At the pinnacle of Cannons Crossing success. Both financially and socially. Perfectly crossbred.'' A tiny flash of irony crept into Auntie's sharp gaze.

''Ouidie, that's enough.'' Big Daddy snorted. ''I courted Miriam as a gentleman. With respect. Not like the kids of today. Running amok. Falling into bed before marriage. 'Hormones' is what I call it.''

''You must have had 'hormones' at least once…sir.'' Julia jutted her chin defiantly. Dallas didn't like the pugnacious glint in her eye. ''You and Mama had me.''

Easy, girl.

''Child, you will not speak to me that way!'' Big Daddy thundered, half rising from his chair.

Julia rose completely to her feet. Her eyes sparkled angrily. Her cheeks grew flushed. ''I'm not a child. I'm an adult. I ask—respectfully—that you treat me as one.''

''I'll treat you as one when you behave as one.''

Dallas rose, too. ''Julia, I think it's time we called it a night.'' This period of transition had taken about as much stress as it could tolerate. It was time to retire even without telling Julia's news. He'd underestimated the obstacles to coming clean in the Richardson household. The less said the better at this point.

''You rhinestone cowboy!'' Big Daddy staggered to his feet, bumping the table and rattling the remaining china. ''Stay out of this family discussion!''

Instinctively, Dallas clenched his fists. He'd been called worse. Had been ordered around by better men. He wasn't about to back down, but he wasn't about to start anything ugly. For Julia's sake.

Miriam rose, as well. ''Big Daddy. Your heart.'' Her hands fluttered helplessly to her throat.

''Norton's heart's only in danger when he's crossed,''

Auntie Ouidie muttered from her seat. She appeared determined to remain seated and unexcited, as if she'd seen all this before. On more than one occasion.

Tennessee Williams couldn't have scripted a more colorful family reunion. If Dallas hadn't seen tears form in Julia's eyes, the situation might almost be funny. But the pained expression on his best friend's face warned him that the time had come to leave. Immediately.

Julia seemed, however, to have different plans. "Father or not, don't you talk to a friend of mine in that tone of voice," she warned, her cheeks aflame.

Dallas was becoming truly concerned for her well-being. Both emotional and physical. He reached his hand across the table to her. "Hush, Julia. It doesn't matter. Don't trouble yourself." He mouthed the last words, *Not in your condition.*

Saints alive, but Big Daddy must have been a lip-reader. "Condition!" he bellowed. "What condition?"

Julia placed her hand protectively over her stomach. Her tawny eyes flashed defiantly in the candlelight. "I'm carrying your grandbaby," she replied slowly and with great dignity.

With an unladylike plop, Miriam landed in her chair, her mouth and eyes forming three perfect O's.

Big Daddy suddenly looked as if he were a tower of gelatin. He began to quiver from head to toe, his already florid complexion bordering on purple. Dallas worried that Miriam's talk of a heart condition might in fact be true.

When Big Daddy spoke, it was in an undertone far more threatening than any bellow. "Has there been a wedding we failed to attend?"

"No, sir." Julia, bless her, stood firm.

"Will there be?"

Julia blanched.

Not about to let her stand alone, Dallas strode around the table to her side.

With each step Dallas took toward his daughter, Big Daddy's eyes grew larger. "Sweet suffering Samuel!" he declared with contempt. "That's why you dragged this... this...this rodeo bum home. He's the father!"

Obviously flabbergasted, Julia opened her mouth to speak, but Dallas cut her off with the plan that he had been mulling since the limo ride.

"I intend to marry your daughter, sir."

He hadn't meant for his blossoming idea to come out this way. He'd meant to propose it to Julia first. But he'd seen enough of Richardson family dynamics to want to protect Julia from its turmoil. He'd formed the idea in the ride from the airport, but now having spoken it aloud, it seemed *right*.

His words hung in the air above four stunned adults. Julia seemed unable to breathe.

Big Daddy reacted first. "You're going to marry my daughter?" The man slammed his fists down on the head of the table. "What do Parkers know about marriage? What could you possibly know about fatherhood, you bastard!"

Bastard.

Dallas had been waiting to hear that word from the moment they'd crossed the town line into Cannons Crossing. Even anticipated, it cut as deep and as painful as yesterday.

If this man weren't Julia's flesh and blood, Dallas would have laid him out on the floor. No one called him a bastard anymore and remained conscious. But for Julia...

He glanced to one side to discover her gone. In an instant, he knew where. With Big Daddy's words ringing in his ears, he followed.

"I'll have you wiped out of my daughter's life so fast your head will spin! I know people clear up to the Supreme Court!" Big Daddy roared. "Annulled! I'll have your ass annulled!"

Despite the weakening evening light, Julia found her way easily to the old oak tree. In the dinner dress she wore, she couldn't climb it, but she pressed her whole body to the rough and reassuring trunk. Flung her arms around its girth. Laid her cheek against its cool bark. Let the tears flow.

How could she have imagined she would find at home the

peace and support necessary to forge her future? Moreover, in her wildest dreams could she ever have anticipated Dallas's bombshell?

Marriage. To Dallas Lee Parker. His declaration was too much to comprehend.

Hearing the grass swish behind her, she turned to find Dallas, a look that begged for her understanding on his face.

Well, she wasn't about to try to understand any more than the fact that he'd tried to railroad her back there in the dining room. Hadn't trusted her to handle her own affairs. Had come crashing in to rescue her.

"I know what you're thinking," he said softly.

She turned her back on him. Good. Then she wouldn't have to tell him.

"I meant to talk this idea over with you first, but your father—"

"My father badgered you into a testosterone match." She whirled to face him. "And you rose to the bait. Both of you trying to see who could control my life more."

"That's not it at all." He appeared hurt by her words. Truly hurt.

"Then you tell me how it is." Crossing her arms tightly in front of her, she suppressed a shiver while desperately straining to see her old friend in the waning light. Wasn't this the familiar sheltering oak tree? The site of their steadfast childhood friendship. Try as she might, however, she saw a stranger standing in Dallas's stead. A stranger who'd completely pulled the rug from under her with his astonishing announcement back in the dining room. She felt unsteady. Out of her element.

"Julia." Her name on his lips sounded like a plea. "We're friends—"

"And friends don't bushwhack friends." She threw her hands in the air in exasperation. "What did you think to accomplish by that little white lie in there? Did you think you'd pour calming oil over troubled waters?" She waggled her forefinger under his nose. "What you did, in fact, was pour gasoline on smoldering embers."

"It wasn't a white lie," he said softly.

"Come again?" Unable to read the look in his clouded blue gaze, she paused in midwaggle. "I don't believe I heard you."

"It's the right thing to do. I can feel it in my bones."

"What's the right thing?"

"Marriage."

"Whose?"

"Yours and mine."

"Have you taken leave of your senses? We're *friends!*"

He performed a lopsided grin. "My point exactly."

"Dallas! Back up! I swear I don't understand a word out of your mouth. Are you suggesting, in all seriousness, that we marry?"

"Yes."

"You're crazy."

"You asked me to help."

"I asked you to give me moral support."

"That's what I'm offering."

She exhaled sharply, blowing a wisp of hair off her forehead. The man was pure provocation. Marriage. Indeed. "But we're friends," she repeated, unable to come up with a more cogent rejoinder. "We've never even…you know."

He sidestepped her implication. "I know we've shared a lot over the years. More than most engaged couples. I know we respect each other. Trust each other. I know two heads are better than one."

"But, Dallas…" His offer coming from their long years of friendship overwhelmed her. "It's not your problem."

His handsome face broke into a soft smile. A real and rare smile. "Since when? Since when did we ever divide and assign our problems? If I remember correctly, yours were mine, and mine were yours. We were best friends."

"That was so long ago…but marriage. Even to your best friend. Your rodeo career, your life-style doesn't leave room for a wife and child."

"Perhaps it's time for a change." Turning from her, he reached out and stroked the oak's trunk. Darkness had now completely fallen. He was silhouetted by the enormous rising harvest moon.

Tentatively, she reached out and rested her hand on his outstretched arm. Felt his young strength simultaneously with the tree's ancient power. "I will forever treasure your offer. But I'm strong enough to go this road alone."

He turned to her, his face hidden in the shadows. "You may be, yes, but have you considered the child?" His words came out a strangled whisper.

"What do you mean?" She tightened her grasp on his arm.

"Didn't you hear what your father called me?"

Bastard.

Shame for her father filled her.

As she had done many times in their childhood, she stepped forward and wrapped her arms around Dallas. Laid her head on his shoulder. "For that, I'm deeply sorry. I'm sorry for my father's small-town ignorance. Sorry. So very, very sorry. It's meaningless ignorance, plain and simple." She clung to him as if the act itself would make the epithet go away.

Slowly, he embraced her. Cupped her head in his big hand. Slid his fingers through her hair. Sighed deeply as the surrounding field crickets played their melancholy concerto. "I have no doubt you've grown into a strong woman, pigtail girl. I have no doubt you can handle anything life throws your way." He planted a gentle kiss on the top of her head. "But the baby…the baby needs to know a mother and a father. Trust my experience on this."

"Oh, Dallas. My situation doesn't have to mirror your experience."

"No, it doesn't." He stroked her back. "But do you want to chance it?"

She said nothing. Dallas could feel her rapid breathing against his neck. He had no intention of frightening her. Had no intention of suggesting that every single-parent home was unhappy. But he could only advise from his own experience. And his own experience had been unhappy.

"I never knew my father," he said, repeating the words

she'd listened to time and time again. He needed to say them one more time. "Never knew who my father was. I only ever asked about him once. My ma said he couldn't marry her because he was already married. A sweet-talking traveling salesman passing through town. I never asked again. I didn't need to. The townsfolk made it their business to keep the guessing game alive."

This was his litany. This was the fact that had colored his boyhood in Cannons Crossing, where everyone knew everyone else's business. That he'd moved beyond his fatherless boyhood, had shed the dust of this judgmental small town, had made a success of himself didn't diminish in the least the pain of his growing up, on the very few occasions he let his memory revisit it.

Here with Julia, in this place, he couldn't avoid it.

He stepped back. Cupped her trusting face in his hands. "Julia, if your child hears the word *bastard* or *illegitimate* only once, it's too much."

"There are no illegitimate children, only illegitimate parents," she answered bravely.

"I'm asking you to consider an alternative."

"But you've always told me you live light and free. A wife and a baby would change that."

He traced the outline of her silky soft cheek with the back of his hand. "I sometimes think my rootlessness is the result of my own isolated upbringing."

"Your mama did what she could, Dallas." He heard a murmur of rebuke in her words. Sweet Julia. Defender of the dispossessed.

"I wasn't blaming her. She worked hard and made herself old before her time. She put food on the table and clothes on my back. And she had blessed little strength left over for affection. Perhaps she was trying, in her way, to toughen me."

"She and I are different. I have a skill that pays well."

"But time…will you have any more time? Or energy? Or support? Will you and your child come home to a house that's any less empty?"

He heard a raw sound catch in her throat. "You don't fight fair," she whispered huskily.

"Life isn't fair," he replied, pulling her to him.

"This is so sudden. So unexpected. What can I tell you tonight?"

"Tell me that you'll think about it."

She didn't answer for what seemed a long time.

Then she said, "Dallas?" Her voice rose ghostly in the dark.

"Yes."

"What do you expect to gain from saving me?"

His heart constricted. He hadn't anticipated this question. They'd never—*never*—questioned each other's motives. But never had they been evasive or dishonest in answering each other.

"Perhaps," he replied with complete candor, "you're saving me."

Chapter Three

Dallas couldn't sleep. Too many conflicting thoughts tumbled through his mind. Julia's plight. His knee-jerk reaction to it. This too formal house and the Richardsons—Big Daddy, especially—who regarded him with contempt. This unforgiving town.

This town.

Who would have guessed he'd willingly return? Ever.

He hated this town as much as Big Daddy hated him.

So why had he put himself under Cannons Crossing scrutiny once again by proposing to marry its most celebrated daughter?

In irritation, he paced the length of the spare bedroom.

He'd done the right thing in suggesting a marriage of convenience to Julia. Hadn't he? She was his best friend. Always had been. With unconditional encouragement, she'd seen him through the worst part of his life, and now she was in trouble. Needed his support. It wasn't even a matter of her alone. She bore a child. No matter that this was the tail end of the twentieth century, if Julia chose not to marry, the wags in Cannons Crossing would always snicker that the child was illegitimate. Because it would be Big Daddy's grandbaby, the gossip would surely be more muted than the talk that had trailed Dallas and his mother, but it would be there all the same. No matter where Julia chose to live, her baby's roots would always be snarled with small-town controversy.

Dallas couldn't allow that to happen to his childhood friend. She meant too much to him. And to his surprise, the happiness of her unborn baby meant too much to him, as well, because it was in his power to make a difference in that baby's life. Strange, but the fact that his life wasn't what it had been six months ago gave him the freedom to take any direction he wanted.

And he wanted to help Julia.

Maybe she was right when she'd said that not every single-parent situation had to turn out like his mother's. Maybe Julia was stronger than Rhetta Parker. More skilled. More determined. Maybe she could make it just fine on her own. Without him or his help.

But considering the misery of his own youth, he simply couldn't risk it.

He rubbed his head in frustration. Overthinking the whole damned situation could give a man a major headache. In the ten years since Julia and he had graduated from high school, Dallas had filled his life with action, not thought. Physical challenge and pain. He'd achieved success in a rugged, mostly male, highly nomadic world. A year ago, he'd been on top of that world. A year ago, he could have offered Julia his achievements and his continuing prospects, at least.

Massaging his injured arm, he winced. What about now?

Now he had a cardboard box full of trophies and an uncertain future. And a reputation in Cannons Crossing for being a traveling salesman's bastard son. What kind of sales pitch was that to throw at a prospective bride? Especially a woman as deserving as Julia Richardson.

Even so, considering Julia's situation and his regard for her, he still thought he'd been dead right to offer to marry her. That didn't mean the marriage would ever work out, however. Tomorrow, in the clear light of day, he needed to have a long, hard, honest talk with his best friend.

Julia pummeled the pillow on the high tester bed in her childhood room, then slipped farther under the puffy comforter. Regardless of the hot bath and the flannel night-gown, she'd be lucky if she didn't catch her death of cold from traipsing outdoors earlier in the brisk October evening air. Hiking about in nothing more than a filmy dinner dress and a cloak of startled indignation. Indignation at Dallas's heavy-handedness after dinner.

She hugged herself to stay warm.

What a day!

She'd come home to break some rather startling news to her family, only to be upstaged by Dallas's wholly unantici-pated bombshell. Marriage! He'd suggested they marry, for pity's sake. No, not for pity's sake. For the sake of conve-nience. Necessity.

The idea flat out wouldn't work. Why, after supper Big Daddy had left to sleep in his office at the lumberyard rather than spend a night under the same roof with "that Parker boy." Dallas didn't need such in-laws. If Julia even considered his offer, her family would try to make her choose between him and them.

And what of the offer itself? What made Dallas dream up a scheme that was patently unfair to him? An old childhood loyalty? Julia shivered. She doubted that even their longstand-ing and unique friendship could prove strong enough to over-come the fact that Dallas had not fathered the child she carried.

She'd promised him she would think carefully about his proposal, but she could think till the kudzu completely covered Georgia without coming to a different conclusion. A marriage of convenience between Dallas and her wouldn't work. Period. There was no use postponing her answer.

Flinging the bedcovers to one side, she slid to the floor,

then paused. Why did the thought of rapping on the spare bedroom door make her hesitate? She needed to talk to Dallas. *Dallas.* The one person in the world who made her feel easy in his company. The one person in the world for whom she needn't sugarcoat the truth. The one person in the world…who had changed right before her eyes at dinner. Who had altered the very nature of their friendship with a crazy proposal of marriage.

It didn't help matters that long, long ago she'd harbored a crush on the rebel teenage Dallas. Had girlishly fantasized about his declaring his love and sweeping her away to happily ever after. Opening the door to her bedroom, she tried to suppress the memory. Such thoughts of the past would only complicate her present decision making.

The long upstairs hallway was deserted, all doors besides hers tightly shut. Good. The last thing she needed was another confrontation with either her mother or her aunt. Tiptoeing toward the spare bedroom, she felt every inch the naughty child. When she reached Dallas's door, she paused before knocking, having to remind herself that it was Dallas Parker, her *friend,* on the other side. It still took a muttered prayer and several deep breaths before she could bring herself to lower her knuckles to the door's surface. She needed to tell him tonight that she truly appreciated his support so far, but that marriage was out of the question. He would probably be much relieved.

In response to her knock, the door swung open, and Dallas stood before her. Tall in the shadows. With an unfettered, lanky grace. Barefoot. Shirtless.

And shirtless, he was magnificent. With buffed muscles that rippled easily in the half light of the hallway. This was no childhood friend who stood before her. This was a strong, elemental, very attractive man. A stranger. Compelling and a little frightening at the same time.

Julia took a step backward.

Silently, he cocked his head in question, and in trying to avoid his eyes, she noticed the scars.

Scars like fine silver etchings along his side. Down his arm.

She knew that rodeo life was dangerous. But the public always seemed to concentrate on the spectacle, the glamour, the fame. She imagined a rodeo hero didn't stay a hero long if he didn't hide his injuries well.

Dressed, Dallas had certainly hidden his injuries well this afternoon.

Tonight, however, mixed with his usual natural grace and obvious strength was a physical vulnerability Julia had never before associated with the man. That discovery made a warm pool of protectiveness well deep within her. The stranger faded into the background as she suddenly regained her childhood friend.

"I came to give you your answer," she whispered, gathering courage.

"I told you to take your time," he answered softly. "As long as your family thinks the marriage is on, the pressure's less on you, more on me. I can run interference while you decide for real."

"Oh, Dallas, this isn't real for anyone concerned. My family thinks you're the baby's father."

"So?" The expression on his face was unreadable. "Would you have a problem with that?"

With Dallas as the father of her child? Never. But she didn't want him to feel trapped. Ever. "Sooner or later, the lies will trip us up. We need to tell the truth."

"The truth?" He leaned forward and skewered her with a penetrating blue regard. His voice was more growl than whisper. "You look Big Daddy in the eye and say, 'I'm home. I'm out of work. And pregnant. Unmarried. The father's back in Boston.' Now the ball's in your father's court. What's he going to do?"

Julia was too stunned by Dallas's confrontational tone to reply.

"I'll tell you what he's going to do," Dallas continued, his face drawn into a scowl. "He's going to get his twelve-gauge. He's going to climb into his Cessna. He's going to fly to

Boston, where he's going to turn that town inside out just looking for the sumbitch—excuse my French—that defiled his daughter.'' He looked hard at her. ''Am I too far off the truth?''

No. Not at all.

''What's going on?'' Auntie Ouidie's plaintive voice wafted from several doors down. ''Julia? Is that you and your beau?''

Reaching out, Dallas wrapped his arm around Julia's waist. Pulled her into his room. Firmly closed the door behind him. They stood absolutely alone, facing each other in the soft light from the bedside lamp. Far too aware of his state of undress, Julia felt the pulse at the base of her jaw throb a frantic rhythm.

''I still don't think this is going to work,'' she murmured, trying to keep her mind on the task at hand. Trying to ignore the frisson of pleasure she felt at his touch.

''Why not?'' Dallas slowly released her, too aware of the womanly warmth of her in his arms.

She tilted her chin resolutely and looked him right in the eye. For a minute, he saw a flicker of uncertainty. Was her refusal from the heart? Why did it bother him?

''Because I've made a habit of independently making my way in life,'' she said, although he could have sworn she was thinking something far different. ''Even the idea of coming home—of asking you to accompany me—was out of character. I usually take care of my problems on my own.''

So she claimed her proud and independent nature made her resist his marriage proposal. He admired a free-spirited woman. But he didn't believe for a minute she was being totally honest with him or with herself. Furthermore, she had an unborn child to consider. Surely that fact should influence her decision.

''I know you don't want Big Daddy running your life,'' he agreed, stepping away from her so that her femininity wouldn't distract him. ''But this plan takes care of that.''

Why was he pushing so hard? He had nothing to gain from her acceptance of his proposal...except knowing that he'd

done the right thing when Julia Richardson had needed someone to help her. It was obvious to him that she needed help,
immediately, whether she recognized that fact or not. And Dallas was the only likely knight on the horizon.

She blinked, emphasizing those tawny eyes framed with
thick, dark lashes. "Don't you see? I'd just be substituting one
man's control for another's."

It was his turn to blink. And stare. Hard. "You think I want
to control you?"

"No…I didn't mean…" Flustered, she backtracked. "It's
just that you'd be involved up to your neck in a situation that's
none of your worry."

None of his worry? Funny, but from the first moment he'd
seen her sitting alone and desolate on her luggage at the airport, he'd worried about her. Felt a protective tug at his heartstrings. Wanted to help in any way he could. Hell, he couldn't
explain the feeling other than childhood friendship and en-
during loyalty. But he couldn't ignore it, either.

"Julia, you're looking at a man who loves a challenge," he
offered as explanation, trying to make his words convincing
but light. He didn't want to scare her off with serious intentions. "A man who doesn't care to know what the next moment in his life is going to turn up. Who flat out loves surprises
and the spice those surprises bring." He leaned toward her
until he could smell the subtle scent she wore. "Now, don't
you think that this little proposal is just tailor-made for a man
like me?"

She inhaled sharply. "Frankly, I was more concerned about
a woman like me."

He reached out and gently brushed an errant wisp of hair
away from her face. As he did, he touched her cheek with the
back of his hand and felt skin so smooth and soft, it begged
to be kissed. "Tell me about the woman I've proposed to,"
he murmured softly as if to a skittish filly. It struck him that
he knew all about the girl, next to nothing about the woman.

She relaxed just a little. "Unlike you, I'm not comfortable
with surprises."

"No?" He pretended to find another strand of hair that needed repositioning.

"No." Lowering her gaze to the floor, she nonetheless inclined her face slightly toward him. Leaned into his touch. "I've always liked my life planned in detail. That's why this—" she placed her hand protectively over her stomach "—this radical change in plans seems to have knocked me off center."

"It seems to me," he offered gently, "that this radical change requires a radical solution."

She looked at him then with genuine worry in her eyes. Worry that turned their usual tawny color to that of burnished wood. "The problem with this radical solution is that I feel out of control. I won't know from one moment to the next how the scenario will play out."

He felt an overwhelming wave of protectiveness toward her. "That's where I come in. I'm the one who loves surprises— the spice of life. Remember? And I'll be right by your side."

She strongly suspected that the spice Dallas Parker brought to life would be nothing less than jalapeño hot. "Dallas Parker, you were a wild and crazy kid, and you're a wild and crazy man."

His eyes glinted mischievously, an inkling of her rebellious childhood friend resurfacing. "I've been called worse. That shouldn't make me an unfit husband, however."

An odd little thought crossed Julia's mind. "Have you had practice at this husband routine? A circuit wife you forgot to tell me about?"

"Me?" He looked startled, but recovered quickly. "I admit to loving women, but I've never been in love to the point I tied the knot, if that's what you're getting at."

Now, why did that admission give her a reinvigorating little lift? As if it meant that he and she would be starting out fresh. She arrested that wayward romantic notion by reminding herself that whether she accepted his proposal or not, the situation was a marriage of convenience from beginning to end.

"Dallas?" In the whirlwind that had been their day, she'd

barely allowed herself time to think. Now the questions began to crowd her thoughts. "Why did you come when I called you?"

She could see shadows in the depths of his eyes.

"Because you needed me."

"As simple as that?"

"You're going to find I'm a simple man."

She didn't believe that for a minute.

"But I'm not going to take a simple *no* for an answer." He reached for the doorknob. "Go back to bed, Julia Anabeth. Give me your answer when you've given yourself some time."

Julia turned to leave. Instead of opening the door, Dallas reached out for her with his free hand, then slowly pulled her up against him.

"Sleep tight," he urged, kissing her lightly on the top of her head.

The bare skin of his shoulder seemed to sear Julia's cheek. Unnerved, she responded, "Don't let the bedbugs bite," then blushed at the absurdity of the childhood response.

She tilted her head to look up at him and found his lips hovering above her own. If she stood on tiptoe, she could kiss him. Full on the mouth. A tiny thrill trickled down her spine at the same time she saw a startled awareness spark in the cool blue depths of his eyes.

With a fleeting scowl, he released her, opened the door and gave her a gentle push. "I'll see you in the morning."

Before she could answer, she heard the snick of the door latching behind her. He'd refused to accept her refusal, a wholly unexpected turn of events. Now what?

Instead of clearing matters up with this confrontation, she'd seen new challenges stacked on top of old with a heightened awareness of a physical nature. She couldn't deny that an electric energy hummed at their touch just now. To be aware of Dallas as a husband, as a lover, upped the emotional ante of her situation considerably. Adding a physical attraction to their relationship could only spell trouble.

With her brief visit to his bedroom, she hadn't eased her old worries; she'd intensified them with new distractions.

Her cheek still burning from the feel of his bare skin against it, Julia absently made her way back to her room, wondering, despite the specter of trouble, what it would be like to be truly desired by Dallas. Not simply saved.

Dallas flicked off the bedroom light and stared into the darkness. He could still smell Julia's scent on his skin. Wildflowers. Soft. Subtle. Provocative. Like the woman herself. He wished he hadn't sent her away. He wished he were in bed with her, holding her in his arms.

And he puzzled over this feeling.

He'd been attracted to other women before. Attracted with a raw physical yearning that inevitably led to bed. But with Julia, it was somehow different. He couldn't explain it. He could only sense it. The yearning he'd earlier felt for her when he'd looked into her eyes went beyond the pleasure of an old and familiar relationship certainly. But, too, it went beyond a casual lust. It was a double-edged sword that pricked his heartstrings. Swiped at his emotions. Adding to the complications was the new, purely physical quickening of his loins he'd felt. For Julia, his old friend. An arousal. Unmistakable. Unforeseen. And much too disconcerting.

He tried to replay their conversation in his mind. Tried to ignore the memory of their body language.

She'd asked him why he'd come when she'd called him.

Why? Because, in the end, he wanted to be near her. It was as simple as that. And as complex.

"Why did you call me?" he asked the darkness. "Of all people."

He almost opened the door to follow and ask her motivation, but in the silence that met his question, he thought of Julia in her bed, exhausted by the day's events. Thought of the new life she carried. Remembered how he'd heard that pregnant women could fall asleep in seconds. Of course. They needed their strength for the miraculous journey ahead of them. What a journey to have to face alone.

He couldn't let her face it alone. Abandoning her would be unconscionable. He tried to brush aside his earlier doubts. It wasn't that their meeting just now had allayed his unease. In fact, the opposite had happened. A whole new set of complications had arisen. Disturbing physical complications.

In her soft, old-fashioned nightgown, she'd felt so good in his arms. So warm. So feminine. So alluring. And, surprisingly, so right. He'd wanted to kiss her. And kiss her thoroughly. Passionately. Having sensed a reciprocal yearning in her gaze, he'd found it dangerously easy to fantasize that they were lovers.

But even if he could put up the emotional collateral necessary for such a highly charged relationship—which he wasn't prepared to do—they weren't lovers. They were friends in need. And if Julia accepted his marriage proposal, it would be because she saw the practicality of it.

He could handle practicality.

Renewed conviction filled him. He would protect her. To the best of his ability, he would protect Julia and the child she bore. And he would try not to let the new attraction he felt for her get in the way.

Dallas maneuvered Miriam Richardson's Mercedes over the rutted lane leading to the Sutter farm. Julia, uncharacteristically quiet, sat in the passenger's seat. She hadn't spoken since breakfast when she'd begged Dallas to leave with her on the next plane out of Atlanta.

The problem had been her family. Again.

After a night spent on the sofa in his lumberyard office, Big Daddy had returned home more wrathful than ever, bellowing about nunneries and restraining orders. His tirade interrupted Miriam's snowballing plans for a gala wedding with a cast of thousands. The promise of a glittering society event had obviously eased her initial shock and rallied her flagging spirits.

Dallas had needed little urging to abandon breakfast, borrow

the keys to Miriam's car and head out for less-chaotic surroundings. He'd used the excuse that he needed to see Aaron
and Helen Sutter about keeping his championship saddle.

He'd planned all along to drop in on the Sutters and to ask
them the favor, but originally he'd planned to do it alone. The
reunion with his foster family was not an event he wished to
share. Not even with Julia. Perhaps *especially* not with Julia.

The Sutters were good people. Simple country folk. They'd
always been kind to Dallas in a no-nonsense way. Unaccountably, Aaron Sutter had offered Dallas part-time work back
when no one else in town would give the teenager the benefit
of the doubt. Then, after the death of Dallas's mother, Aaron
and Helen had seemed to assume that Dallas should stay with
them until he'd sorted out a more permanent future. What may
have been heartfelt generosity, the pained young man had seen
as charity. He couldn't help but think that the Sutters viewed
him as little more than a burden. This period of his life had
been so difficult and filled with such bitter yearnings on his
part that Dallas hadn't fully appreciated the couple. Since leaving the farm, he'd kept in touch sporadically and sent a little
money when he could, but he hadn't been back to see them
since he was eighteen.

Because he didn't know what kind of reception awaited
him, he preferred to make this visit alone. At breakfast, Big
Daddy, with his outrageous display of temper, and Miriam,
with her out-of-control wedding fantasy, had altered his original plan. Dallas simply couldn't leave Julia in her family's
clutches. To give her the decision-making space she needed
and to keep his own temper in check, he'd opted for a change
of scene. For both of them. He'd asked her to come with him
when he visited his foster family. If he could count on nothing
else, he could at least count on the down-to-earth Sutters to
behave rationally.

Now, however, the closer he came to their farm, the more
Dallas wondered how taciturn Aaron and plainspoken Helen
would get on with Julia. As Dallas had never set foot in the
Richardson home during his growing up in Cannons Crossing,

neither had Julia ever visited him at the Sutters'. This would be a new experience for all four adults, and Dallas was uneasy about how it would shake down. He hoped for a brief but cordial reunion that would reveal little of his emotional vulnerability.

"What are we going to tell them about us?" Julia's voice cut into his thoughts.

"We should keep things simple. Simple and consistent." Despite his attempt at absolute calm, Dallas's pulse gave a hop as he spied the Sutter homestead through the trees. "We tell them what we told your family. That we're getting married."

"That we're *thinking* of getting married," she amended, laying her hand briefly on his forearm.

"Okay. That we're thinking of getting married." Her touch, warm and fleeting, reminded him of their encounter late last night. During their earlier, easier friendship, she'd touched him often. He'd always found the gesture reassuring. Now, after his proposal, after the physical awareness that had sparked between them in his room, matters had changed dramatically. Now, he didn't know exactly how Julia felt about him. Or more to the point, how he felt about her.

Pulling Miriam Richardson's Mercedes in front of the familiar log cabin, Dallas almost wished that Aaron and Helen were in town for the day. If so, he could leave his saddle and a note, then head out with Julia for a long, time-consuming ride in the countryside.

Homecomings were tough when you'd never fully developed a sense of home.

Julia stared at the little woman who had come out onto the log cabin's front porch. "Are they expecting us?" She had only a nodding acquaintance with the Sutters, and thus thought formality the better part of reason.

"No." Dallas's curt answer warned her that he was in no mood for small talk. He cut the engine, then got out of the car slowly, almost, it appeared, reluctantly.

Curious, Julia followed. She knew little about Dallas's foster relationship with the Sutters. By the time he'd reached his teens, he'd begun to hold back information and emotions even from Julia. His life on this homestead had been clearly off-limits to her. She wondered that he'd allowed her to come with him today.

Helen Sutter wiped her hands on her apron but didn't move from the porch. "As I live and breathe," she drawled softly. "Is it Dallas Parker?"

"Yes, ma'am." He took a step forward, then stopped. A palpable awkwardness hung in the air.

"And your lady friend?"

"You remember Julia Richardson. From Ten Oaks." He stepped to Julia's side, draping an arm across her shoulders. "My fiancée."

The woman on the porch quirked one eyebrow, but otherwise showed no emotion one way or another.

Julia bridled under the protracted silence. "Perhaps 'fiancée' isn't quite accurate," she said. "We're thinking of getting married."

"What's to think about? You're either going to marry the boy, or you're not." The twinkle in her dark eyes belied the brusqueness of her words. "Come on in. I just started a second pot of coffee." She turned as if their appearance were an everyday occurrence, then entered the house without waiting to see if they'd follow.

Dallas slid his hand to the small of Julia's back. "Ready?"

"More to the point, are you?"

"What's that supposed to mean?"

"I'm only asking if you're okay with this visit. You seem tense."

"I'm fine." His fingers on her back applied a rigid pressure in contradiction. "Let's get a cup of coffee, drop off the saddle *and leave.*"

"Won't they be curious about your plans to marry me?"

"Julia, I don't know if they even care whether I'm dead or alive." He nodded his head toward the front steps. "Are we going to do this or not?"

"Of course." Sensing his nervousness, Julia walked briskly across the small patch of neatly kept yard, then climbed the steps. Dallas didn't need her giving him a hard time by stalling. A mockingbird perched in a flame red dogwood tree near the stoop shrilled a cautionary tune in a minor key. Julia scowled at the bird as if it could read her thoughts. She wasn't about to probe further into Dallas's thoughts. As tense as he now was, she barely recognized the man. With his proposal yesterday, the attraction that had sparked between them last night and now her inclusion into his relationship with the Sutters, they were clearly entering uncharted territory. She didn't need a little bird warning her to tread lightly.

Stepping into Helen Sutter's kitchen, she felt herself enter an earlier time, a simpler life. The bunches of dried herbs hanging from exposed rafters evoked an existence more in harmony with nature than any she'd previously experienced. This was certainly not Boston. Nor Ten Oaks.

"How do you like your coffee?" The older woman had already poured three cups.

The thought of coffee actually turned Julia's morning-queasy stomach, but she opted for courtesy. "Cream. No sugar. Thank you."

"Sit." Helen patted a place at the large, scarred farm table. "We don't stand on ceremony here." It was obvious, too, by her no-nonsense bustle that she wasn't going to let any ten-year absence on the part of her star boarder phase her.

"Is Aaron with the stock?" Dallas sat stiffly across the table from Julia.

"He is." Helen eyed Dallas intently. "Bought three new heifers at auction. You still interested in that sort of thing?"

"Yes."

Julia didn't know if this terse conversation between the two was normal or the result of unexpected reunion.

"Aaron still checks in with me every morning about now." Helen's features softened into a half smile. "Wait till he sees Dallas Parker sitting in my kitchen, large as life." Her eyes grew wide as she looked at Julia. "With a woman who's 'thinking about' marrying him. My, my."

Julia couldn't resist. "Who's to say it's not Dallas causing the holdup?"

Helen chuckled. "True enough. You wouldn't be the first gal to chase him round the barnyard."

"Ancient history, ladies," Dallas growled in warning.

"Are you fixing to stay long?" Helen's features grew still as she paid an inordinate amount of attention to stirring her coffee. "I'm not trying to pressure you, Dallas. It's just that I've turned your old room into a sewing nook. There's a fold-out sofa in there, though—"

"We're staying with my parents," Julia said gently. She had the impression that Helen Sutter was uncharacteristically timid about the simple act of asking after Dallas's plans. "We dropped by to say hello."

"What does Big Daddy think of Dallas Parker marrying into the Richardson clan?" The woman didn't pull any punches. "Got his boxers in a bunch, I just bet."

"He'll get over it," Dallas replied, grim faced.

"He the reason you're 'thinking about it'?"

Julia tried to keep her voice light but firm. "Among other reasons."

"What else?" Helen was not about to let them off the hook.

Julia glanced at Dallas and received a cautionary scowl. "Our jobs are very different. Our life-styles, too," she said.

Helen harrumphed disdainfully. "You kids and your life-styles."

Julia didn't know how to read the blunt Mrs. Sutter. But she could see that, without a doubt, Dallas was having difficulty with this visit. His history here being obscure, it wasn't exactly obvious why. She determined to hang in and give him whatever support she could.

"Marriage is a big decision," she said simply.

"You two in love?"

Julia inhaled sharply. Was Helen Sutter always so straightforward, or was this her way of needling Dallas for his prolonged absence?

"We're friends." Dallas reached for Julia's hand.

Surprisingly, Helen placed her weatherworn hand on top of theirs. "Then it might work out." Her eyes grew misty, her voice gentle. "If you're honest with each other. If you each ask yourself the right questions."

"The right questions? Such as?" Julia felt compelled to ask even as she bridled at a stranger poking around in her most private affairs.

"Such as, what do you stand to lose by letting yourself fall in love?"

Julia started at the directness of the question.

"Such as," Helen continued, "can you love and allow yourself to be loved, flaws and all?"

Dallas felt his scowl reach into his heart. Damnation, but Helen Sutter always cut to the chase. Always made him look hard at his motivation. At his fears. Perhaps that was why he'd been so reluctant to return to her homestead with Julia at his side. It was bad enough when he wrestled alone with an emotional dilemma; he didn't need Julia witnessing his private struggle and perceiving him in any way as weak.

He found himself wishing for the quick return of Aaron Sutter and a simple conversation consisting of farming practices and stock management.

"What do you expect of marriage?" Helen persisted.

"You always did ask the hard questions." Dallas pushed his chair back then stood. He walked to the sink. Stood with his back to the two women. Stared out the small window at the brilliant foliage outside. Tried to tell himself he could marry Julia without any of this painful introspection. He could marry her because she needed him. It needn't be any more complicated than that.

If he was going to ask himself any questions, the first would be how, with his rodeo career in ruins, was he going to support a wife and child?

He turned to face Helen Sutter and changed the subject.

"How have things been for you and Aaron these past years? Since I left."

"Can't complain." She eyed him thoughtfully, then smiled, her face transformed by soft wrinkles. "Though we never found a better hand with the stock than you."

"Make me an offer."

With a wave of her hand, she dismissed his words as an idle remark. "We couldn't afford the salary for a three-time world champ."

Julia suddenly seemed to relax. "So you've followed his career?"

"Who in Cannons Crossing hasn't?"

Dallas tensed.

"You, Miss Richardson, and Dallas here are the town's rising stars. I guess it's not unusual that the two of you should find each other eventually."

Julia blushed, and Dallas felt her discomfort. They might have been rising stars, but circumstances had changed drastically for the both of them. Too soon the town gossips would have a field day.

"Oh, I've known Dallas since before he was a rodeo star." Her voice a velvety caress, Julia looked at him with unmistakable admiration in her wide, tawny gaze. "He was my own personal champion long before the world knew how special he was…is."

Dallas felt that old, familiar surge of wonder at her unconditional loyalty.

"Is that a fact?" Helen cocked her head, the gesture birdlike. A softness of expression played about her mouth. "Just how long have you and Dallas been friends?"

"Since he wandered onto Ten Oaks when we were five. He was looking for leaves for a kindergarten project, and he came across my secret hiding place." Julia grinned. "I pelted him with acorns, trying to scare him away."

"Did it work?"

Dallas never took his eyes off Julia. "No. It just made me

give up school projects as a painful waste of time.'' He'd taken on Project Julia instead.

"Dallas Parker!" Aaron Sutter's voice boomed from behind. "What makes you think you can waltz back in here and drink my coffee after ten years of being too long gone?"

Dallas turned warily as all thoughts of a brief and unrevealing reunion with his foster parents slipped into the realm of impossibility.

Chapter Four

Julia didn't know whether Aaron Sutter was going to embrace Dallas or hit him. In the end, he did neither.

His features stony, he turned to Helen and said, "Have you saved a cup of coffee for me, or has this cowboy drunk it all?"

It was then that Julia caught the fleeting twinkle in the older man's eye.

"Julia Richardson," he said, accepting a steaming mug from his wife, "the last time I saw you, you were in pigtails. Perched on the stockyard fence at an auction while Big Daddy bought that prize stallion. Beezle, I think his name was."

"That was a long time ago." Julia ran her fingers through her salon cut hair. "The pigtails are gone, and so, thank goodness, is that stallion. 'Beezle' was short for 'Beelzebub.' And he was an unholy terror."

"A terror with a bloodline that a breeder's dreams are made of." Aaron cracked a gruff approximation of a smile. "Even by the time Big Daddy sold him, though, that horse had never been ridden, if I recall.''

"Oh, he'd been ridden.'' With an involuntary blip of gut-level alarm, Julia did recall. "Once.''

"Oh?'' Aaron looked ready for an explanation.

Julia glanced at Dallas but got no reaction. With his legs crossed at the ankles, he leaned against the kitchen counter near the sink, his handsome face impassive. Hard and honed, his body spoke a language that was packed with attitude. Attitude and distance. Why had he even bothered to return to the Sutters' if he was going to keep them at bay emotionally? Keep her at bay, too, while she was with them. He'd shown more warmth in the face of her hostile family.

Well, they were all in this sticky situation together, and now Julia had the opportunity to unravel a little of the mystery that was Dallas's unspoken past. She could do it by talking to the Sutters about him and by judging their reaction. She would do it because he'd asked her to marry him, and as things stood, despite their childhood friendship, he was an enigma.

She wasn't about to marry an enigma.

Helen Sutter broke the silence. "Dallas rode him on the sly, I bet.''

"You're right.'' Surprised that Helen would suspect as much, Julia wrapped her fingers around her still warm coffee cup. "Big Daddy was at a stockman's meeting. Miriam had taken a sleeping pill because of a sick headache. Dallas and I sneaked to the paddock after dark. We were all of thirteen.''

"Hot damn!'' An unmistakable look of pride crossed Aaron's face. "You rode him, and you broke him.''

Dallas shook his head and passed a large callused hand over his face. But Julia had seen the glimmer of a smile at the corner of his sensuous mouth.

"No,'' he said. "That only happens in the movies. I rode him. For all of several seconds—''

"That's our boy,'' Helen breathed appreciatively. Her possessive tone of voice made Julia take notice.

"Then he threw me.'' Dallas's face showed more animation

than it had since they'd arrived at the farm. "And I broke my wrist. The pain alone should have warned me off, but I'm afraid that's when riding rough stock became an addiction."

Aaron cocked his head, a shadow of understanding flickering in his eyes. "You were working afternoons for me at the time. You told me you broke your wrist in a fight at school."

"Yeah." The vitality left Dallas's features as quickly as it had appeared. The unreadable mask returned. "People would've rather believed that of me."

"We weren't just 'people,'" Aaron contradicted, his voice a low rasp.

Dallas looked over his shoulder out the window. "No, you weren't." The admission was almost inaudible, but it was there, just the same. A step in the right direction.

Helen stood to refill the coffee cups. "I remember the frustration Dallas barely kept in check on account of our stock. Nothing like Big Daddy's prizewinners."

"Too tame?" Sensing Dallas's discomfort, Julia strained to turn the conversation onto safer ground. Discussing stock would be familiar and less treacherous territory than discussing past relationships.

"A herd of milk cows, two work horses and a cantankerous mule did not feed a young rodeo dreamer's fantasies." Aaron scratched his head and smiled.

Dallas's gaze had returned—softened—to the Sutters. "I was young."

"But you were good with my stock even so." Aaron narrowed his eyes. "You can tell a lot about a person's character by the way they treat animals. By the way animals respond to them. You were good, Dallas Parker, despite the fact that you thought they were duds on the excitement scale."

Julia eyed the three adults before her. This had not turned out to be the Dickensian foster situation she'd always imagined. The Sutters were plainspoken, yes. Gruff at times, too. But the level of tolerance, the undercurrent of genuine warmth, exceeded anything she'd experienced in her own upbringing under more sophisticated circumstances.

"Dallas Parker!" Helen gave him a mock stern swat on his chest as she made her way back to her seat at the table. "You've let us go on about the past and haven't said two words to Aaron about your future." She beamed at her husband. "Dallas and Julia are getting married!"

The look in Aaron Sutter's eyes was nothing that Julia had expected. Instead of disbelief or shock, she saw instant, frank joy. And the hint of moisture. "Here you let me go on about stock," he sputtered as he put down his coffee mug to offer Dallas his hand. "Congratulations."

The older man turned to Julia, welcome clearly written on his lined face. "This does my old heart good. I wish you all the best." He cleared his throat a couple times as if something were lodged there.

Julia thought of telling Aaron the same thing she'd told his wife—that Dallas and she were thinking of getting married. But somehow the words wouldn't come. The simple optimism with which the Sutters had met the announcement—so unlike the reception at Ten Oaks—warmed Julia's heart. Made her believe, for the moment, that Dallas's marriage proposal was not only practical but the happiest of events.

Dallas studied Julia's face. He couldn't quite believe she hadn't offered Aaron her thinking-about-it disclaimer. In fact, her smiling acquiescence to Aaron's congratulations was only one unbelievable event in the long list that Dallas had been accumulating since their arrival at the farm.

Right from the start, he'd been surprised at the ease with which Aaron and Helen had accepted Julia. The Richardsons, although highly respected, were not noted for their approachability. And so they were kept at a distance by all but their tight social circle.

Moreover, Dallas had been stunned by the seemingly effortless way with which Julia drew the usual crusty Aaron into her storytelling. Oh, Dallas had always known that Julia was a born storyteller and a charmer. That was part of what made her a television success. It was the subject of her tale—him—and the Sutters' response that had startled Dallas. The Beezle-riding story had been told—and received—with an unnerving open affection. Julia had always championed him, true. But had the Sutters truly cared for him as their appreciative response had indicated? Had they seen him as more than a ward of the state? Had they actually taken pride in his pranks and his accomplishments? If so, Dallas had been such an embittered young man that he'd been blinded to the outstretched hand. The depth of feeling.

That possibility was an eye-opener.

"Dallas?" Julia's presence at his elbow shattered his shadowed introspection. "Aaron says he has an engagement present for us."

A gift? This wasn't happening. This was what happened in families. Real families.

"How could you have an engagement present already?" He tried to keep his words even. Devoid of the conflicting emotions that had begun to snowball.

Aaron grinned broadly as he reached for a set of keys on a hook near the kitchen door. "Oh, I've had this present for a long time. Ten years, to be exact." He extended his hand.

Slowly Dallas accepted the keys, knowing by the old, familiar feel what they unlocked. His '59 Caddy convertible. His long-ago pride and joy. As a teenager, he'd bought it used with the money he'd earned from the Sutters. Had repaired, restored and detailed it lovingly. When he'd left Cannons Crossing for good, he'd given it to Aaron to sell as partial compensation for his foster care.

"You were supposed to have sold it," he murmured.

"Couldn't." Aaron's voice cracked. "I knew you'd want it when you returned."

How could Aaron Sutter have known he'd return? Dallas stared at the keys in his hand. He hadn't even known so himself.

"It's in the barn," Helen said. "Take Julia for a ride."

"It still runs?" Unbelievable.

"Like a charm." The older woman reached out and patted her husband's arm affectionately. "Aaron's kept it in tip-top running order."

"For ten years?" Dallas's amazement expanded.

"Well, that's how long it took you to get home."

Home. Dallas flinched. This wasn't home. He had no home. Not even a notion of one. He looked around the small kitchen at the only three people in Cannons Crossing who had ever offered him a degree of respect. If he ever developed a concept of family and hearth, however, it would look damned close to the scene before him.

"So do I finally get a ride in the infamous Coupe de Ville?" Julia's voice held girlish expectation and a hint of naughtiness. She looked directly at Dallas, and once again he was struck by the strength and beauty of her golden gaze. "Put the top down and drive me right past the lumberyard. Let's see if Big Daddy's mustache curls."

Helen chuckled. "You've caught a live one for a fiancée, Dallas Parker. She deserves a ride in the red monster." She made a shooing motion with both hands. "Go!"

Emotion threatening to overtake him, Dallas stalled. "I really came by to see if you'd store my saddle. It's on the back seat of the Mercedes—"

"I'll take care of it." Aaron's words were brusque, but the expression in his eyes showed a genuine warmth. "You go introduce your gal to that caddy."

It took a while for Dallas's feet to work. Julia helped by slipping her hand into his and tugging gently.

As they went out the back kitchen door, a low, fragmented conversation followed them. "...found someone to settle down with..."

"...prayers have been answered...give me a hug...."

Had the Sutters worried about his well-being these past years? His happiness? Stunning.

Dallas and Julia walked to the barn without talking. Pulling her with him through the open doorway, he stepped from the sunshine into the shadowed interior and shivered with the change in temperature. The reaction mirrored his entire experience of the past twenty-four hours. Just being with Julia since their arrival in Cannons Crossing yesterday had proved to be a constant condition of running spine-tingling hot and bone-chilling cool.

Despite his jumbled emotions, Dallas inhaled with satisfaction as the smell of animals, hay, old wood and hard work filled his nostrils. This barn, like the old oak tree, had once been his refuge. It had a quieting effect on him even now.

Releasing Julia's hand, Dallas strode to the farthest end of the barn, to the double stall that held his tarpaulin-covered 1959 Cadillac Coupe de Ville convertible. Aaron Sutter had kept the car for him. In anticipation of his return. The implications, amazing as they were, hadn't fully sunk in

He gently lifted the tarp so as not to scratch the paint. In the light dappled by the chinks in the barn walls, the flawless red surface winked up at him. He rolled the protective covering completely off.

"Fins!" Julia's breathy voice behind him was tinged with delight. "I'd forgotten that it had such enormous fins!"

Suddenly jubilant, Dallas turned, then swung her up in his arms. "All the better to swim with the sharks!"

She wrapped her arms around his neck. "I used to love seeing you drive through town in this thing. In all the years since, I could never picture you driving anything but. Certainly nothing ordinary."

Her words were light and musical. Her body soft and warm against him. Distracting him. Making his pulse race far more than was usual. She, too, must have felt the electricity because she lowered her gaze and suddenly grew very still.

"Dallas Parker, you make it difficult to stay on task."

"Which is?" He released her slowly.

She bent and picked up a piece of straw from the barn floor. "I'm supposed to be plotting my future." Intently, she examined the straw in her hand. "And what have I done today?" She cocked her head and leveled that disconcerting tawny gaze at him. "I've relaxed in Helen and Aaron's kitchen and talked about your boyhood follies. And now I'm...I'm...'' She smiled with enough wattage to light up the barn's dim interior. "What exactly am I doing?''

"You are examining the prettiest little Caddy in all of Cates County.'' An unaccustomed happiness lifted his spirits. "And for whatever reason, Aaron's kept it in top form.'' He opened the driver's-side door, reached in and turned the ignition key to the accessory position. The radio came to life with a soft country ballad. "See?''

Julia began to sway to the rhythm of the music. The look in her eyes became dreamy. Faraway. "It's so peaceful here. Did you ever think of leaving the world behind and escaping to this barn?''

He'd done just that. On more than one occasion. Unlike humans, animals had never judged him and found him lacking.

"Yeah.'' Crossing his arms across his chest, he leaned back against his car and watched as she executed an uninhibited waltz step in the straw. For him, this barn with its work and animal smells had been a place of quiet, thinking solitude when he was a boy. A place totally devoid of pressure or bitterness. He certainly would never have imagined, however, its appeal to the formerly bookish and still very elegant Miss Julia Richardson.

It was simply astounding how the road of life dipped and curved unexpectedly. As he'd told her last night, he'd come to savor the little random pleasures, the surprises life sometimes dropped in his lap. Such as this moment.

When the song on the radio came to an end, Julia turned in a complete circle, then curtsied low, the expression on her face one of utter contentment. "You should find a way to bottle and sell the feel of this barn,'' she said reverently, "and you'd never have to ride another bull again.''

He tensed. He, too, had forgotten to stay on task. The task of determining his own future. A future beyond rodeo. A future that required he reinvent his entire identity. A daunting task. One that he had no heart for.

Another song, slow and sexy, began on the radio. Julia

stepped to his side. Touched his cheek so that he had to turn to look directly at her. "Hey." Her voice was warm and husky, her eyes knowing. "You look like you could use a dance, cowboy."

No. If he danced with Julia in the quiet of this old barn, he might just lose himself completely. He scowled and shook his head.

He didn't count on her determination. The very same that she'd shown as a girl when she'd invariably pull him out of some black mood.

She uncrossed his arms from his chest. Took one hand. Coaxed him away from the side of the Caddy. Drew him out into the wide walkway between stalls. Never let her gaze drop from his. Silently compelled him to pull her into his arms. To begin the steps of the bittersweet country waltz. Steps that led him farther and farther away from the worry that furrowed his brow.

At first they danced as the kids used to dance in grade-school gym class—stiffly, with a mile of daylight between them. But as Dallas relaxed—as he began to *feel* Julia in his arms—he drew her closer. The dusty light in the old barn, the nostalgic smells now mixed with a new scent of wildflowers, the muted, melancholy music wrapped him in a spell.

Not to mention the feel of Julia.

Dallas had to restrain himself from uttering a heartfelt *Aaaaaahhhhhh.*

How different this dance was from those in the honky-tonks on the road. Those rhythmic embraces after long, painful days in the rodeo arena were with women who wanted a part of Dallas Parker, champion. His allure for them was in his reputation. Those dances were games, plain and simple.

This was different. A gift, it seemed, from Julia to him when she'd seen something in his expression that revealed he, too, needed comfort.

And, yes, he took comfort from holding her in his arms.

His friend, she was beautiful and womanly soft in an unsettling, provocative way. There was no denying her physical allure. But more than that, she held a promise of bright and fresh opportunities—a new life. As a mother-to-be, she was all that was right about the future. And holding her in his arms for the length of a country song, he could touch that promising future and, for a few moments, silence the past.

Closing his eyes, he lowered his cheek to her hair.

Julia's heart reacted with a little hop to his change in position. Although she'd initiated this dance, his heightened closeness made her inarticulate.

Too aware of their altered relationship, would she ever get used to the feel of him? Ever get used to the sound of his deep voice and the sight of his too-seldom smile? Or his scent—like fabric washed in a mountain stream and dried in the sunshine. It appeared she couldn't be in the same room with the man now without being thoroughly disconcerted by his larger-than-life presence. By their past skewed with his recent proposal. By their uncertain future hampered with this new, unsettling attraction.

As Dallas held her, thoughts of her obstreperous family vied for attention with her pregnancy, which vied for attention with the unexpected visit with the Sutters, who vied for attention with this niggling physical attraction that kept cropping up for Dallas.

Who held her tightly and rested his cheek on the top of her head.

Nonplussed, Julia was glad he couldn't see her face. Mentally, she upbraided herself. She was going to have to get a handle on her perpetually off-balance state. Where was the imperturbable professional woman who had her future mapped out in iron-clad detail?

Gone.

That calm, businesslike woman had gone with her ex-lover and her high-profile job. Gone with the advent of the new life within her. And with Dallas's surprise proposal. Now every moment was a trip into uncharted territory. An emotional adventure as highly charged and soul-searching as the country ballad that wound down on the car radio.

She sighed.

"A penny for your thoughts." Dallas stopped their slow dance and took a step back.

"You'd need a Swiss bank account to pay for the knot my mind's in."

"I may be short of cash, but I'm long on time and sympathy."

Julia glanced up at him, only to find him watching her intently. She felt color rise to her cheeks as she mentally scrambled to hang on to her train of thought.

"I'm…I'm not normally the at-a-loss, blushing kind," she stammered finally.

"Hormones."

She scowled. "Why do men always assume women are ruled by their hormones?"

"Are you or are you not pregnant?"

He had her there.

"I'm torn." She tried again. "When I start to relax, my thoughts are suddenly interrupted by a baby who's not quite real to me yet. Then, when I'm trying to sort out the baby's and my future, I'm distracted by family dynamics that are all too real." She didn't mention the unnerving attraction she felt for Dallas. "It seems I'm always operating on half power. Pulled every which way but loose."

He frowned. "And I put more pressure on you by suggesting you marry me."

"Yes and no." Stepping away from him, she tried to concentrate. "Your proposal has been the sweetest offer I've received since my life turned upside down. Your loyalty means the world to me."

"But?"

"But marriage is such a big step, Dallas." Didn't he feel that way, too? Or were relationships so casual and so transient in his nomadic life that his proposal was just the beginning of another temporary stop in his wanderings? Easily begun, easily ended.

"We can take that step." His gaze flinty, he seemed undeterred. "If we make up our minds to do it."

"Easier said than done. At least for me."

He reached out and ran his curled fingers over the outline of her shoulder. "What's holding you back, Julia?"

She stepped even farther away from him. His touch made her thinking fuzzy. "Shall I start a list for you?"

"Sure." One corner of his mouth quirked upward. "I'm not in any hurry to leave this barn."

She wasn't, either. Here, for the very first time since her arrival home, she felt safe. "The Sutters are at the head of the list."

"Helen and Aaron? What do they have to do with us?"

"*They* are what marriage is all about. You can't be together with them for more than a few minutes before you feel the respect. The commitment. The genuine partnership. Take the way they were happy for us. It was as if they wanted us to know what they have."

He was silent.

"Were they like that when you lived with them?"

"I don't know." He looked away. "I was so angry at the world, I didn't see much beyond myself."

A chilling thought came to Julia. If he still couldn't see much beyond himself, could he ever accept another man's child? She felt tongue-tied when it came to broaching the subject. He'd proposed to her, knowing her condition. How, then, did she ask a proud, stiff man to further explore his feelings on such a matter? Perhaps she wouldn't have to. Even without mentioning the baby's paternity, there was a long list of hurdles to clear. In fact, since they'd returned to Cannons Crossing, they seemed to have created far more challenges than they'd overcome.

"Aren't you a little in awe of the institution of marriage?" she asked at last.

"We're not dealing with an institution." He turned to look at her, his eyes blazing with intensity. "We're dealing with us. You and me. And I'm not afraid of us."

His blunt declaration put the cap on the sincerity of his offer to help. But what did she—pregnant with another man's child—have to offer him in return for that help?

"What about rodeo?" She knew it was his whole life. Asking him to give up any part of it would be unfair. "Marriage and a family would tie you down."

Dallas looked at her lovely face, shadowed with concern and unmade decision. "It's time I told you the truth about me and rodeo."

"The truth?" She crinkled her nose in question. "You're a superstar in a business that has no roots. I know the unvarnished truth, Dallas."

"Not all of it." He swallowed hard. What he was about to tell her, he hadn't spoken to a soul. Hell, he'd only half admitted it to himself. "I'm finished with rodeo. Injuries have caught up to me. I guess it's time for the kids who've been clawing at my heels to have their day."

"Finished with rodeo?" Julia pursed her lips and exhaled slowly. "What are you going to do?" More than disbelief, worry showed clearly on her face.

Sweet Julia.

He tried to pick the tone of his words carefully. "I thought I'd marry you, if you'd have me, get a regular job, settle down and raise a family."

Her eyes wide, she stood in a golden shaft of light that had found its way through an opening in the barn roof. But he was the one who felt caught in a searchlight. Admitting to his best friend that he was no longer wholly the man she'd always known made him feel exposed and vulnerable. Even so, he'd never before held the truth back from her. He wasn't about to start now.

"Dallas, I...I don't know what to say."

"Don't say anything yet. While we're dealing with the truth, there are a few more things you ought to know."

She attempted a weak smile. "I'm afraid I've reached my surprise quotient for today."

"No more surprises. Just a recap of stuff you already know.

Considering the circumstances, it bears repeating." Restless, he began to pace. "I admit I'm a man with more than his share of wanderlust. Worse yet, my history makes me clueless when it comes to the real meaning of family." He smacked the palm of his hand against the crude side of the stall. Damn, this wasn't coming out the way he intended. He turned to look at Julia, who stood absolutely still, watching him.

"I want you to get an honest picture of the man who wants to marry you," he said, "but I don't want you to think my proposal's the result of my problems. From the minute you told me about your—"

"This isn't your problem," she whispered.

"No, it isn't." He reached for her hand. Her touch strengthened his resolve. "It's my best friend's problem. But I can be part of the solution. I can do the right thing."

For maybe the first time in his life.

"I'm tempted to say yes, but—"

"I've just told you I don't have a job. I know that's got to bother you."

"You forget I'm unemployed, too." She rolled her eyes. "Even so, that's the least of our worries."

"What then?"

"Big Daddy, for one."

"I'm not marrying your father."

"Two, I'm very independent."

"Okay. We each get our own TV remote."

She stuck her tongue out at him, and looked every inch his pigtail girl. "You're not being serious."

"I'm dead serious." He lay his hand across his heart. "Trust me."

Abruptly, she turned her back on him. "If there's one thing that's been constant in my life, it's that I trust you, Dallas Lee Parker," she murmured so softly he thought he'd imagined the words.

Moved, he wondered once again exactly what he—out of work and out of favor—had to offer her in return for that trust.

"Julia?" He reached out and touched her shoulder. "Look at me."

Turning as if it pained her, she looked him in the eye but remained silent.

"Why would you consider marrying this guy from Boston after you'd known him—how long?—a few months at most, when you won't consider marrying me—the friend you've known all your life? It makes no sense."

She averted her gaze. "That affair started out such a madcap adventure. I was caught up in the moment. Now—" She clasped her hands in front of her until her knuckles showed white. "Well, the baby changes everything. For his or her sake I need to exercise the utmost caution. I can't live in the moment. I need to think of the future."

"And I can't be part of that future?"

Without looking at him, she reached into the Caddy, then turned the key in the ignition, turning off the radio, which had been playing a soft accompaniment to their discussion. "It would be a shame if Aaron's ten years of caring ended in a dead battery."

He touched her firmly on her upper arm until she faced him. "It's just a battery." The undisguised confusion in her eyes pained him. "Talk to me. There never was a thing we couldn't solve by talking."

"We were kids. Anything was possible."

"Anything *is* possible." He felt a small, unaccustomed smile warm his heart, as well as the corners of his mouth. "That's what you told me every day of my life in Cannons Crossing. You seemed so sure I couldn't help but believe you."

"The Sutters seem to think a marriage between us is possible."

They had. Much to Dallas's surprise, they certainly had.

"They always were sensible people," he said.

"If we were to marry—" she raised a finger in the air "—*if* we were to marry, we'd still have to be friends. I wouldn't want a marriage of convenience to ruin our friendship."

He agreed wholeheartedly. "Our friendship's what's going to make it work."

"Because if it didn't work out, I'd hate to go our separate ways and lose our friendship."

"Julia, I have to be honest with you." He paused to choose his words carefully. "I don't want to get married, thinking about divorce."

She looked at her feet. "I don't, either. But we have to be realistic. Practical." She raised her head and gazed straight into his heart. "This would be a marriage of convenience. I have no illusions. We know each other too well. Perhaps that's why I hesitate. Shouldn't a relationship fuel just a little mystery?"

Even as he agreed with her, he scowled his discontent. There were moments—like the dance in the barn just now, like the good-night embrace in his room last night—when he wanted the illusion that mutual attraction had fueled his proposal. And her acceptance.

Considering his history in Cannons Crossing and his shaky future, he wouldn't blame her for refusing him. But a refusal would be a mistake. He felt it deep down inside him. Despite the obstacles the world threw up before them, they were best friends. They needed each other. An unborn child needed the two of them. They could make a marriage work. If only she'd take the first step and say yes.

"Remember when we'd sneak to the quarry for the very first time in early summer?" he asked. The old quarry had been abandoned when workers had struck a spring, filling the deep rock pit quickly. The result had been an alluring and dangerous swimming hole. The first swim became a daring yearly ritual for the young Julia and Dallas. He reached out to her now with his words, using the only tools of persuasion he had. Their shared history. "Remember standing on the edge for the very first time each season?"

"Yes." She smiled. "Afraid of the cold. Afraid of getting caught. Not wanting to jump, but afraid of being called chicken."

"There was never any real thought of turning back, though. At some point, we held hands, closed our eyes and jumped."

Julia looked up into Dallas's ruggedly handsome face. His clear blue gaze seemed to dance with satisfaction at his attempted analogy. "Nice try, cowboy," she said, feeling somehow lighter because he had tried.

"It's the same idea." He seemed unwilling to let the matter drop. "Take my hand. Close your eyes if you have to. And say that you'll marry me."

Julia laughed softly. "This is crazy."

"What?"

"Us. Contemplating marriage."

"Why?"

Focusing on the tip of his nose in order to avoid his eyes, she screwed her courage to the sticking place. "Because I'm probably the only female in Cannons Crossing whom you haven't kissed."

A lazy smile lifted the corners of his mouth. Crinkled the edges of his eyes. Raised one eyebrow. "I can remedy that." He took a step forward.

Her pulse suddenly pounding, Julia took a step backward. "I was just joking."

"I wasn't."

How could two little words make her cheeks burn?

He reached out and gently cupped the side of her face. He had the good grace not to mention her hot blush. Lowering his head, he brushed her lips with his, then straightened and released her before Julia could wholly relish his touch.

Sadly, his kiss had not lived up to the promise in his eyes.

It was that promise, coupled with the barely suppressed yearning in his words, that made Julia bold. She slid her hand behind his neck, stood on tiptoe, then kissed the corner of his mouth, lingering to inhale his clean male scent, to savor his warmth, to allow herself a small *What if?*...

With a ragged moan, he turned his head and softly moved his lips over hers. As he wrapped his arms around her, enveloping her in his strength, she struggled to hold on to the idea that they were friends. *Friends.* Kissing her now, however, he felt like a lover.

Her body responded even as her mind resisted.

She closed her eyes and leaned into the kiss. How surprisingly easy it was to lose herself in Dallas for the moment. Tall, strong, heart-thumpingly handsome Dallas. Suddenly the teenage girl with the crush on the rebel boy emerged from the past to push the last of Julia's inhibitions out of her consciousness. She wrapped her arms around Dallas's neck as he deepened the kiss.

When his tongue met hers, she could taste the longing. His and hers.

This was pure madness. She threaded her fingers through his hair. Felt her normally cool exterior melt beneath his heat. Dallas had always reminded her of the noonday sun. Staying out in it too long could lead to delirium. He moved his hands down her back. What sweet delirium. She fought to hold on to the last shred of sanity. They were best friends.

With a tiny, reluctant cry, she pushed away from him.

His steely blue gaze held her still. "Julia Anabeth," he said, his voice gruff, a small, ironic grin tugging at the corner of his mouth, "I'd say we have a hell of a lot to learn about each other."

That very possibility scared her witless.

Chapter Five

Julia drove her mother's Mercedes back to Ten Oaks, and Dallas followed behind in his '59 Caddy, with the top down. In the aftermath of the kiss, he was glad to have time alone in the cool, reviving air.

That kiss. A good idea run out of control.

He'd meant to kiss Julia to reassure her. But then she'd kissed him with an unexpected intensity, and he'd responded in kind. Hell, they were friends. Where did these sparks between them come from?

The only thing that he could figure was that they were both in a vulnerable spot in their lives. The attraction they felt had to be some kind of rebound effect. Julia was pregnant, unwed and out of work. He was out of work, out of a future in the work he loved and cast out from Cannons Crossing's polite society.

In what was fast becoming a typical overturning of expectations, even that last assumption wasn't completely true.

The Sutters were polite society. Not upper-crust. But genuine, down-home polite. And they'd welcomed him and included Julia as if they were both family. The thought of it still bewildered him.

This notion to rescue his best friend had backfired. He'd totally failed to take into account emotional involvement. From any corner. Least of all from his own.

As the huge Richardson house came into view, Dallas spied Big Daddy, his feet planted on the top veranda step, his arms crossed over his ample chest.

"Now, what does that old man have up his sleeve?" Dallas muttered aloud. It didn't seem as if the day would be getting any easier. A room at the Battlefield Inn looked better by the minute.

Pulling the Caddy to a stop behind the Mercedes, Dallas took some pleasure noting that Big Daddy's mustache actually did quiver at the sight of the red monster. Dallas's amusement, however, was short-lived.

He hadn't even opened the door before Big Daddy lumbered down the steps, jabbed his index finger in the air Dallas's way and bellowed, "You upstart! I had you investigated this morning! You can't hide from me!"

The man moved pretty fast for an overweight codger tightly wrapped in blue serge. "You're washed up in rodeo, Parker! Haven't a dime to your name!" He yanked the driver's door wide open. Might have yanked Dallas right out of the car had Dallas not leveled a mean glare at the angry old man.

Big Daddy backed up a full step but continued to shout. "You think you can save your sorry ass by knocking up my baby and living off the Richardson fortune?"

That did it.

His fists balled, Dallas climbed out of the car in a heartbeat. He wouldn't let anyone spout vulgarities about Julia's situation. Not even her own father. He drew back to flatten the sputtering reprobate.

"Stop it, you two!" Julia flung herself between the men. "I will not tolerate fighting!"

"The man's a wastrel, honey." Big Daddy's puffed-up cheeks looked ready to explode.

"Hush!" Julia, dwarfed by her father, nonetheless stood toe to toe with him. The fiery glitter in her eyes seemed to surprise the old man and certainly did the trick in silencing him.

"If you do not cease badgering Dallas," she warned in a voice barely above a whisper, but every word crystal clear, "I will leave this house, never to be seen again. I will take your grandbaby to the far ends of the earth where you will never— I repeat, *never*—see him or her."

Big Daddy deflated like a leftover birthday balloon.

"I know about Dallas's lack of a job," Julia continued. "We've discussed our present situations honestly. Openly. Like two mature adults. Whatever we decide is between us." Running her hand over her stomach, she squinted at her father. "And if you wish to know the heir to Ten Oaks, you'll respect our decision. Do I make myself clear?"

Big Daddy's mumbled reply sounded vaguely like indigestion.

Julia turned to Dallas. "As for you, cowboy, this is not the Wild West. Not even the rodeo arenas of North Carolina."

Dallas stood in awe of her righteous indignation. "I—"

"You'd better be getting ready to say 'I'm sorry.'" Her eyes widened. "I warned you that I don't want to trade one hotheaded male for another. Did I fail to make that point clear?"

"No, ma'am."

"Don't patronize me, Dallas Lee Parker."

"I'm sorry." He hoped the smile that settled around his heart never made it to his mouth. He had no intention of patronizing her; he was too busy admiring her. The fact that Julia seemed hell-bent on respect made him even more determined to win her respect for himself. She was quite a woman.

"Sorry doesn't put food on the table." Obviously, Big Daddy hadn't been cowed into total submission.

Julia glared at him. "We're adults. We'll work this out without your interference."

"We'll find work." Dallas had no intention of showing even an ounce of uncertainty before Julia's disapproving father.

"You'll work for me," Big Daddy growled. "In the lumberyard office."

Together Julia and Dallas turned to stare at the red-faced old man. This had to be a trap.

"*Who* will work for you?" Julia looked from her father to Dallas. "Me? I know nothing about the lumber business."

"No. Parker."

Julia's eyes grew wide. "He knows just as little."

"Less." Dallas shook his head in pure amazement. "You had me investigated. You were about to go a round with me in your own front yard. And now you're offering me a job." Julia's family or not, these Richardsons were crazy. "Why the about-face?"

"It's certainly not to save your sorry hide." Big Daddy's little black eyes glittered. "It's for my daughter and my grandbaby."

"I'm perfectly able to take care of your daughter and your grandbaby."

"Hold it just one minute!" Her voice perched on the edge of explosion, Julia raised both hands. "*I* can take care of myself and my child."

"Of course you can, darlin'." Big Daddy glanced at her dismissively, then turned to glower at Dallas. "But no daughter of mine's going to marry a man who isn't gainfully employed. That would go against the natural order of things. The Richardson way."

"I think I'm the one to decide whom I marry." The red streaks across her cheeks showed Julia to be following in her father's footsteps in the temper department. "You cannot manipulate me." She inhaled sharply. "And while we're on the subject of manipulation, who's to say we're even thinking of settling down in Cannons Crossing?"

"Do either of you have jobs elsewhere?"

"No, but—"

"When's the baby due?"

"In four months. Plenty of time to—"

"Four months is barely enough time to prepare for a baby." Big Daddy sniffed delicately as if he were an expert. "Let alone enough time to plan a wedding *and* look for jobs. Your mother will take care of the wedding. You take care of yourself and my grandbaby. I'm offering Parker here a job."

Julia scowled. "This is outrageous."

Dallas saw the glint in Big Daddy's eye and knew the old man was testing him. Baiting him. Trying to scare him off. A job in the lumberyard office, indeed. Julia's father could have offered Dallas a job at something he was good at—such as handling Ten Oaks's prize livestock. But that would have shown some respect for Dallas's talents. Allowed him to succeed.

Big Daddy didn't want Dallas to succeed.

For all his talk of wanting security for his daughter and grandchild, it was plain Big Daddy didn't want Dallas to provide it. So he'd offered a shirt-and-tie, nine-to-five desk job— just the kind of job Dallas had absolutely no inclination for— in hopes of belittling him.

Dallas set his jaw. Big Daddy hadn't counted on the fact that his future son-in-law was a survivor. Moreover, this survivor wasn't just looking out for himself; he had Julia's best interests at heart. And those of an innocent unborn child.

"I'll take that job," he said with grim determination.

"Dallas! Are you insane?" Julia cried as Big Daddy smirked like the cat who'd just seen the mousetrap snap shut.

"In fact, I'll start tomorrow." Somehow he'd beat Big Daddy at his own game at the same time he proved himself worthy of Julia.

Julia grasped Dallas's arm and shook it. What had happened to the friend she thought she knew? She watched in mute astonishment as the two key men in her life each tried to stare the other down.

"Then I'll see you in the office at seven in the morning. Seven sharp." Stroking one side of his mustache, Big Daddy turned, then ambled off in the direction of the gardens, leaving Julia with her plans—once again—in total disarray.

Only after her father had disappeared did Dallas unfreeze and look at her. Just what she needed—more testosterone in her life.

"We need to talk. Now!" she snapped, her normally polite control beginning to crumble.

"Okay." A shadow of doubt seemed to flicker over his features.

"Let's go inside before my father comes back and decides to build us a house on the tennis courts."

Dallas didn't react. In fact, he seemed lost in thought. She took his hand and the initiative in entering the house.

No sooner had the front door closed behind them than her mother's voice rang out from the upper gallery. "Julia? Is that you? We need to discuss the wedding! You've given me absolutely no information to work with!"

Laying her finger over her lips, Julia pulled Dallas through the nearest doorway, then closed the door silently behind them. Was it too much to ask for a little privacy?

"Why are we standing in a coat closet?" Dallas's muffled words, tinged with amusement, floated in the darkness.

"Shh!" She felt tears prick her eyes at the same time she felt the need to suppress a giggle. Her hormones raged. Her family meddled. And her best friend had continued to lob emotional grenades at every turn. Her body didn't know whether to laugh or cry.

"Julia, we're not kids anymore." Dallas gently squeezed her hand as he opened the closet door. "I think we can take the direct route."

"Which would be?" Miriam stood in the foyer, her face a pinched mask, the toe of one tiny shoe tapping double time.

"Miz Richardson," Dallas said before Julia could regain her composure. "Julia and I need to sort out several important issues before we can give you the information you need." He flashed her mother one of his rare smiles.

"But—"

"We're going for a walk. First we needed to get Julia something to cover up." From the closet he grabbed the closest thing—an old, droopy, olive green sweater that Auntie Ouidie used to garden.

"But—"

"There's a chill in the air." He propelled Julia toward the door.

"But—"

"Her condition and all."

That silenced Miriam long enough for Julia and Dallas to make a clean getaway. Julia was beginning to recognize the power 'her condition' had over the Richardsons. Even Big Daddy.

"Now that I've lied, you'd better put this on." Outside once again, Dallas draped the limp, unattractive sweater over her shoulders. "Let's walk to the oak."

Despite the brisk air, Julia simmered at the thought of being mothered. By Dallas Parker, of all people.

"You're not happy." He waited for a response she wouldn't give. "Talk to me."

She didn't want to talk. She wanted to push him into that outrageous red monster he called a car. She wanted to shout at him to get lost. To tell him he'd ruined her simple plan to come home for a few days at most, make her announcement, then leave for another area of Georgia to look for employment in her field. Instead of lending support to that simple task, he'd added chaos to her already derailed life. In addition to her state of pregnancy and unemployment, she faced a wedding inspired by Cecil B. DeMille, a husband who worked for the father-in-law who hated him *and* now the prospect of settling down in Cannons Crossing, where her family would feel free to meddle in her affairs for the rest of her natural born days.

No, she didn't want to talk to Dallas. Picking up the phone two days ago and talking to him had quickly escalated the mess she called her life. She squared her shoulders and set out along the garden path for the field beyond. She'd walk to the oak, all right, but nothing said she had to walk with Mr. Parker.

"Julia…" Oh, he could make his voice soft with entreaty when he wanted to. "I know you think I'm crazy to accept your father's job offer."

"He's trying to humiliate you." She was angry. At Dallas, as well as at Big Daddy.

"I know that."

She stopped. "You do?"

Dallas came alongside her. "Yes. But I'm thick-skinned. And I need a job."

"There are other jobs in other towns."

"Your father and I need to…to…"

"Mark your territory like old tomcats?"

"I wasn't thinking of anything so colorful." His grin emerged lopsided. "We need to size each other up, the old man and me. Carve out some ground rules and maybe a little respect in the bargain."

Julia rolled her eyes and groaned.

"He needs to know that the man you're marrying is worthy of you. Call me crazy, but I think he has a right to know that."

"You're worthy of anyone, Dallas Lee, but I'm still thinking about that marrying part. It's sounding less and less like a good idea, what with you turning out almost as pushy as Big Daddy."

He touched her arm lightly. "Julia. Honey. Listen to me."

The earnestness in his voice calmed her.

"You know in your heart this marriage is the right decision. We're friends. We respect each other." Pain appeared in the depths of his eyes. "The baby is going to need two parents."

She sighed heavily. "I know." At times the thought of her situation, her unsure future, overwhelmed her. It was a difficult admission to make. "But all I wanted to do was tell my parents that I'm pregnant and that I'm going to change jobs."

"You thought you could do that and be in and out of Cannons Crossing in twenty-four hours?"

She forced a smile. "Something like that."

"The Big Daddy show alone takes longer than that."

Too true. Feeling chilled despite the old sweater, she crossed her arms over her chest. "Did you know that I'm a great disappointment to my father?"

"What are you talking about? For him the sun rises and sets with you."

"He's proud of me, yes. But proud as you'd be about a pretty possession. An expensive rug. A rare painting." She made a face. "A prize heifer. The disappointment comes because I'm not a son."

"Hey, he's not my favorite person, but I can see that he loves you."

"He loves to manipulate me. And my mother. And Auntie."

"I'll be the first to admit the Richardson dynamics aren't perfect. But they make a family."

"The price of belonging is submitting to a stronger will. I don't want to do that anymore."

"You don't have to." He took hold of her arms. "You're an adult now. About to start your own family. Stand your ground. Show your father that you're strong in your own right. His equal." He looked hard at her. "You have to deal with the past before you can build a future."

"But in Cannons Crossing?"

"In Cannons Crossing. That's where your past has the strongest hold."

She didn't like that answer. Stepping away from him, she picked a mum from one of Hiram Ledbetter's elaborate fall flower beds. She twirled the stem absently. Let the wild, burned scent carry her away as she collected her thoughts. "Considering how you feel about Cannons Crossing," she said at last, "it wouldn't be fair to ask you to stay."

"I'm not suggesting forever. Just until the baby's born." He stared into the distance. "I have my own ghosts to deal with. You talked about the price you had to pay to belong...no matter what I did, I never belonged anywhere."

Julia winced at the hollow ring to his voice.

"That's why I think we should stay here until the baby's born," he said. "He or she needs a sense of belonging. Roots. You and I need to make peace with old ghosts."

"Even if it means you work for my father in the lumber-yard?"

He looked at her, his expression plainly determined. "I can handle Big Daddy and the lumberyard."

Oh, she believed he could do just that. But could he handle taking on the stay-at-home life with a wife he didn't love and another man's child?

He put his arm around her and began to walk out of the garden toward the field and the old oak. "And you can handle showing your parents that you have a life of your own now. That you're strong. That you love them but don't need them."

Maybe she could. But another disturbing thought popped into her head. Dallas had been nothing if not take-charge since their return to Cannons Crossing. He'd always been a presence to reckon with, and she couldn't envision him changing any time soon. The real question seemed to be, could she handle two controlling men in her life?

They walked in silence, the glorious blue and gold of autumn surrounding them. Dallas breathed more easily when they left the highly manicured garden for the natural simplicity of the surrounding field with its tawny grasses and rose broom-sedge. They followed a primitive, overgrown truck track, one of many that crisscrossed the Richardsons' vast and mostly undeveloped estate. These tracks had been the means during their childhood for Julia and Dallas to quickly meet and to just as quickly separate should an adult come onto the scene. It felt strange to be walking openly on this property with his arm around Julia's shoulder.

Strange, but increasingly right.

Even stranger.

He didn't want to stay in Cannons Crossing any more than Julia did. The idea of working for Big Daddy, at a desk job, set his teeth on edge. His attempt to convince Julia that they needed to stand their ground and confront the past was an attempt to convince himself, as well. He'd just as soon forget his past. For ten years, he'd pretty much done just that.

But now career-ending injuries had disrupted his present and had endangered his future. He was faced with the task of reinventing himself. The way he saw it, he had to figure out who he'd been and where he'd come from to determine what he could be. Where he could go. That, unfortunately, involved scraping away at the hurtful past.

He'd argued to stay in Cannons Crossing until the baby was born for several reasons. Yes, the baby needed a sense of roots. Yes, he—Dallas—needed to prove to Big Daddy that he was worthy of Julia. But another reason for staying had begun to harry his thoughts.

His own nameless, faceless father.

Perhaps if Dallas dug around a bit in their stay in town, he could track down information on his father, or at least the man's identity. Roots and family were important to Julia despite the Richardson pyrotechnics. Perhaps knowing his own paternal history—good or bad—would ease his nagging sense of rootlessness.

On the other hand, it might just blow his chance for happiness with Julia right out of the water.

In the dusty lumberyard office, Dallas yanked at the borrowed tie. Even loosened, the damned thing strangled him. He glanced at the clock. Eleven-thirty. It seemed that he'd been following Big Daddy around for years not hours, touring the operations, meeting workers and outside contractors, trying to differentiate among the endless types of forms and absorb the lumber-business jargon that sounded too much like a foreign language. Would this day never end?

For the moment, his future father-in-law stood at the water cooler, his back turned. "I'm going to give you your first assignment as my personal assistant," the old man growled. "A ticklish little matter. Warren Biggs and a workman's-comp application. His third this year."

"Isn't this a job for your insurance company. Or your law-yer?"

Big Daddy turned. Dallas didn't like the predatory glint in his eyes.

"Warren Biggs has been a thorn in my side since he hired on."

And now Dallas would inherit the problem. A problem he was ill equipped to deal with. A worker he didn't know. Definitely a lose-lose situation. For the worker, as well as for him.

"What do you want me to do?"

"He needs workman's comp like I need a hole in my head. The way I see it, Biggs is running a health scam here." Big Daddy's expression grew dark and thunderous. "Use your muscle. Get him to drop the grievance. Maybe suggest that he's better suited for work elsewhere."

"You want me to lean on one of your workers?"

"I want you to ferret out the truth."

"The truth as you see it." Dallas might have to work for Big Daddy, but he wasn't about to gloss over his kind of self-centered logic.

"Look, Parker, don't forget who's the boss." The boss leaned forward, his stance vaguely menacing. "I'm leaving for a lunch appointment. Biggs will be in this office any minute now. By the time he leaves, I want either the workman's comp case dropped or Biggs looking for a new job. Do I make myself clear?"

"As glass." Watching Big Daddy stomp out of the office, Dallas shook his head. No matter the fancy title of personal assistant, he'd been hired as a Richardson goon.

He'd barely had time to let this nasty little thought sink in before a knock came at the door. He looked up to see a slight middle-aged man waiting in the doorway. Although the man wore a standard-issue black back brace, his stance was crooked.

"Biggs?"

Warren Biggs nodded.

"I'm Dallas Parker. Come in."

The worker took one step into the office, then halted. He eyed Dallas suspiciously.

Dallas blew his cheeks full of air. There was nothing to do but jump right into this mess. "Tell me," he said, "about your workman's-comp applications."

"You insurance?"

"No. I'm working for Mr. Richardson. In the office. I guess you could call me the clean-up detail."

"Ah." Biggs's wry look said he understood perfectly. "You'll be the one sweeping me under the rug or out the door."

"Not necessarily. But you've got to fill me in on these three claims." He nodded at the man's brace. "Your back?"

"Yeah. Slipped disk."

"All three times?"

"All three times. After the first, I applied for a new job within the yard."

"What's your work?"

"I drive a delivery rig."

Dallas rubbed his hand over his jaw. He didn't mean to stereotype or belittle Warren Biggs's capabilities. But if ever there was a man physically suited for the arduous work of handling a big unit on the road, this diminutive man with the bad back wasn't him. After the first comp claim, why had Big Daddy sent him out on the road again? Driving was one of the worst punishments for Biggs's injury. Dallas knew. He'd seen similar circumstances on the circuit. Only there, management made the effort to get the injured party a different job. Rodeo had been a family of sorts. They'd taken care of their own.

"You mean to tell me there isn't something else open in this yard?"

"Oh, there always is. But once Richardson's hired you, he doesn't move you around. Might make him look as if he'd made some kind of mistake in the first place." Warren Biggs narrowed his eyes. "And we wouldn't want that, now, would we?"

Irritation rose at the thought of Big Daddy's enormous ego. He might know business, but he didn't know people from hardwood. On the other hand, during his passage through the school of hard knocks, Dallas had come to make people his chief subject of study.

"Level with me." He stared intently at Warren Biggs. "What kind of a worker would you consider yourself?"

"A good worker." The man squared his shoulders. "I have a family. I want a fair shake at providing for them."

The unwavering look in Biggs's eyes led Dallas to believe him.

He walked to the office door. "Mandy?" Mandy was the lumberyard's general secretary and bookkeeper. She usually occupied a desk in the large office Dallas and Biggs stood in, but she'd conveniently run an errand in the adjoining warehouse to give Dallas privacy for his hatchet job.

"Hold your horses!" The young woman's voice rang out nearby. It was amazing how close her errand had been to the office.

If Dallas were the suspicious sort, he might even think he'd been spied upon.

Mandy appeared in the doorway.

"Biggs here is going to get a new job," Dallas said.

With a satisfied smile, Mandy headed for her desk. "I'll process his severance papers right now."

"A new job in the lumberyard," Dallas countered.

The secretary looked puzzled. "But Mr. Richardson clearly wanted—"

"Me to encourage Warren Biggs to look for another job."

"Yes…but…"

"We are hiring, aren't we, Mandy?"

"You know we are, Dallas Parker," Mandy replied, her voice low but filled with warning.

"Then I'm leaving Biggs in your care. You two figure out something that will require more brain than brawn." He looked at Warren Biggs. "Come find me when you've reached an agreement."

"What about the workman's-comp claim?"

"Yes." Her eyebrows raised sky-high, Mandy stuck her fists on her hips. "What about that claim?"

"Process it," Dallas ordered without a qualm. "Once we get Biggs into a job that doesn't cripple him, I doubt there'll be other claims. Right, Biggs?"

"Absolutely." A new look of admiration had crept over the small man's features. "I have a family to feed."

Dallas headed for the door and some fresh air. "And, Mandy?"

"Yes?"

"You can report to Mr. Richardson that I followed his orders exactly as stated." The old coot had ordered him to get Biggs to drop the claim or make sure the worker was looking for a new job. Well, he was looking for a new job.

Her attention riveted on her files, Mandy said nothing.

Dallas stepped out into the enormous warehouse. No, this nine-to-five, shirt-and-tie job wasn't his cup of tea, but that didn't mean he couldn't mold it to his own simple code of honor.

Julia stepped out of her mother's car in front of the lumberyard warehouse. She needed to find Dallas before she changed her mind about the decision she'd reached just now.

What a morning!

She'd finessed her way into an unscheduled visit with an obstetrician. While in the waiting room, she'd scoured the local papers' want ads, then had made a late-afternoon appointment for an interview as a news producer with a Macon radio station. After the doctor's exam, she'd driven to a real-estate agency. Right now she had in her purse the key to a small rented cottage halfway between Cannons Crossing and Macon.

And none of that had anything to do with her presently racing pulse.

She needed to find Dallas quickly before her courage gave out.

Making her way gingerly around trucks and heavy machinery, Julia entered the warehouse and inhaled the pungent wood smells of Big Daddy's domain. She harrumphed softly. What, in Cannons Crossing, wasn't Big Daddy's domain?

The more she thought of it the more she felt certain that the cottage outside the town limits would provide a start in the right direction.

"Julia Richardson!" The sweet, high voice rang out behind her.

Julia turned to see the yard secretary approach. Drat. Julia didn't wish to waste precious time and tenuous momentum chatting with Mandy Quaid. Quite frankly, under the best of circumstances, the woman's ingratiating manner rubbed Julia the wrong way.

With great familiarity, Mandy took both Julia's hands in her own. "My, my, but you look positively radiant! The North must agree with you."

"It does." Julia forced a smile. The always curious employee was not going to get any more information out of her.

"Are you looking for your daddy?" Mandy didn't take a second breath before she rattled on. "If you are, could I have a word with you first?"

It didn't appear as if Julia could stop her.

"Usually, Mr. Richardson shares everything about the yard with me." She took a moment to savor her self-importance. "But this morning he most certainly dropped a bombshell. In he walks with Dallas Parker." She flopped her hand across her heart. "Dallas Parker, of all people."

Julia raised one eyebrow in response.

"Then your daddy tells me that Dallas Parker is going to be his personal assistant. Personal assistant! Your daddy created a new job just for him." She rolled her eyes. "Now, Dallas Parker may be drop-dead handsome, and he may be Cannons Crossing's one true star, but what, I ask you, does he know about the lumber business? And where does his hiring leave me?"

Ah, another domain threatened. Julia shook her head in silence.

Mandy squeezed Julia's hand. "What was your daddy thinking?"

"Perhaps he was thinking to train his future son-in-law," Julia replied coolly.

Mandy's mouth dropped open.

"Excuse me." Julia extricated her hand. "I have to see my fiancé now."

Walking briskly across the warehouse floor toward Dallas, she could only imagine Mandy's expression. It didn't take much to predict the domino effect this little bit of news would have in the Richardson lumber empire. Whether or not Julia's announcement would salve Mandy's hurt professional feelings was beside the point; Julia had given the secretary a juicy scoop. It was evident Big Daddy hadn't told a soul, not even his trusted secretary, about Julia's return, her situation or her proposed relationship with the town bad boy.

Dallas stood with a small knot of workers. Rough and elemental, he looked at ease in the warehouse amid the laborers. He did not, however, look comfortable in that tie. Knowing how he hated working indoors, hated regimen, hated anything that inhibited movement and personal freedom, Julia's heart swelled at the thought that he'd reined in his wild side, even temporarily, for her and her child.

He glanced in her direction and smiled. As his regard softened with genuine welcome, her pulse picked up at the idea that he appeared glad to see her.

"Excuse me," she heard him say to the men. He closed the distance between him and her. "Suppose Big Daddy will parole me for lunch?"

She gazed up into his rugged face, a tiny part of her hoping that Mandy was watching. "That's why I'm here. To make sure of it."

Tell him. Tell him before you lose your nerve.

"But before we have lunch…" She hesitated, unsettled by her decision. "I want to go to the justice of the peace and get married. That way we have problem number one—wedding plans—off our backs."

As the words poured from her, she fumbled in her purse for the cottage key. She'd made this decision for Dallas. Surely, if he were serious about his proposal, he didn't want to be subjected to Miriam's designs for an elaborate ceremony. Not for a marriage of convenience.

"I've rented a house outside town," she continued quickly. "If we got married on your lunch break, I could move our stuff out of Ten Oaks this afternoon—"

"Julia! No." With a commanding look on his face, he wrapped his hand around her hand that held the key. "I'm not about to get pushed into marriage this afternoon."

Not marry her? What had caused this about-face?

Chapter Six

Julia looked at Dallas in amazement. Wasn't he the one who'd suggested they marry in the first place?

"You don't want to marry me?"

"Not this afternoon."

She found it ridiculous how her confidence shook at his sudden declaration. "You've decided this afternoon that you don't want to marry me? Period? Or you want to marry me, but not this afternoon?"

Putting his arm around her shoulders, he escorted her out of the warehouse—away from prying eyes and straining ears—before he spoke. "I still want to marry you. But it'd be a wrong move to take the wedding away from your family."

This was a shocker, coming from Dallas.

"Can you tell me honestly that you want to participate in my mother's circus?"

The angular lines of his face took on a pinched look. "No can do."

"Then what's the use of a marriage of convenience if you can't start it conveniently?"

Sudden amusement flecked his steely blue eyes. "Even if we ran off this afternoon, we'd still need Big Daddy's clout. In bribes, to hurry the paperwork."

"It's no joking matter, Dallas. The back seat of my mother's car is covered with bridal magazines and library wedding-etiquette books. She's talking magnolia garlands. Ice sculptures. Doves in gilded cages. She'll have us trussed in silk and gabardine till we can't move. Then she'll have us photographed with the members of the garden club, the governor—"

"Not if we give her a *very* brief window of opportunity. A week maybe." He took a deep breath. "But you'll regret it if you run off this afternoon and rob her of any say whatsoever."

Julia couldn't believe her ears. Dallas was urging consideration for her family? And restraint? In their long friendship, she'd always been the cautious one, wary of others' opinions. Dallas had never been less than the hothead. As a means of centering her flying thoughts, she reached out and touched his arm. He was real, all right. Warm and solid. But his words hadn't come from the wayfaring cowboy she'd always known.

"Dallas, you don't have to say this because you think it's what I want to hear."

"I'm saying it because I know eloping with me would come back to haunt you."

"How could it?"

"I told you before, Julia. I'm not marrying you with an eye to divorcing you. Hopefully, this is it. If you have even the smallest hankering for lace and crinoline, the time to satisfy it is now."

"Me? A hankering for lace and crinoline?" She smiled. "You do remember Mama's attempt to get me to Miss Peters's school?"

"You know what I mean." He took her hand in his. "I don't know what you've dreamed of in a wedding...but I want ours to be it."

Julia took a long, slow breath. As her longtime friend and confidant, of course he'd know just the words to say. A small, sharp voice in the back of her head reminded her that his argument would be perfect if he'd only made it out of love, not simply friendship.

"Besides…" He hesitated, scowling. "Elopement is just the kind of thing Dallas Parker would do. Your family doesn't need to stockpile any more ammunition against me."

"Of course," she murmured. What had she been thinking? In considering her own discomfort, she'd lost sight of the difficulties Dallas faced with her family. Marrying on the sly at a justice of the peace wouldn't endear him to them.

"Parker!" A man's voice called from the warehouse. "We've got trouble in shed number nine!"

Dallas shrugged. "There goes lunch."

"Not necessarily. I'll wait here."

Dallas never did get lunch with Julia. A storage rack had collapsed in shed number nine, and Dallas had spent the early afternoon working with several employees on its repair and subsequent replacement of the lumber it held. Julia finally had to leave for her interview in Macon.

He was just thankful no one had been hurt on his watch at the lumberyard.

Come to think of it, it had been his watch. Entirely. From the time Big Daddy had left Dallas to take care of Warren Biggs, the boss hadn't made even the briefest appearance. But that didn't mean the decision making stopped. Paperwork. Phone calls. Customers. Workers. And Mandy, prim faced, had told him that Big Daddy had left explicit instructions to hand all problems and decisions over to Dallas for the afternoon. To Dallas, who knew nothing about the lumber business.

Trial by fire.

The old man sure knew how to apply the pressure. He probably expected Dallas's resignation before dinner. But Big Daddy hadn't counted on a rodeo rider who knew how to hang on for dear life.

Dallas had done the only thing he could: he'd ignored the fact that he knew nothing about the business, and concentrated on his knowledge of people. He dealt with each problem as it came up. When the decision involved hard facts, he asked questions. Of Mandy. Of the workers. Of the customers themselves. He paid no attention to the odd looks because he had nothing to lose. Big Daddy had set him up to fail.

But miraculously, he hadn't failed. The lumberyard was still standing. No customers had been driven away. And although Mandy treated him with thinly disguised contempt, he'd found an unexpected ally in Warren Biggs. When the worker had found Dallas again to tell him of his finalized job switch, he'd discovered Dallas involved in a convoluted discussion with a local contractor. Despite his bad back, Biggs had a keen sense of the lumber business. In his job driving delivery trucks, he'd carefully noted the needs of customers, and the operations and inventory in the yard. On the spot, he'd helped Dallas interpret the particular contractor's needs. He'd even stuck around longer than necessary to answer several of Dallas's questions.

It was amazing the rewards you reaped when you treated others with dignity. As much as Big Daddy knew about the lumber business, he could learn this simple lesson about people.

It was now closing time, but of all things he'd been asked to do, Dallas hadn't been given the authority to lock up. Since Mandy would be the logical one to do it, he now searched for her. She could be anywhere. This was a woman who, covering enormous territory in one day, had her nose in every operation, an eye to every decision-making signature and an ear to anything—relating to work or strictly personal—that happened to Richardson employees.

She appeared to be a woman with an agenda, and Dallas made a note to keep his back to the wall when she was around.

In the warehouse, Dallas came to the end of one ceiling-high row of shelving. He could hear low voices from the other side. Mandy and a man Dallas didn't recognize.

"He's a fatherless nobody," Mandy complained bitterly. "And he now has the job that should be mine."

"Three times grand champ ain't exactly nobody."

"Oh, rodeo. That's over and done with. Mr. Richardson told me so. Anyway, what's rodeo got to do with Cannons Crossing and anybody who's somebody here?" She sniffed audibly. "Dallas Parker is nobody as far as I'm concerned."

Dallas rounded the shelving at the end of the row. "I must be," he said, his voice flat and controlled. "Because you have the keys to lock up. Wouldn't want just anybody to have them. Least of all a nobody."

Mandy's face flamed scarlet. The worker standing next to her suppressed a grin.

"Make sure you do lock up, sugah," Dallas drawled. "Show yourself to advantage every chance you get, that's what I always say." Turning to go, he looked the secretary right in the eye. "Of course, showing how responsible you are in front of a nobody like me is kind of wasted effort, don't you think?" He spied the name tag on the worker's shirt. "Perhaps Mike here would be good enough to let Mr. Richardson know how efficient you are." He narrowed his eyes. "Night."

Lord help him, but the day had finally gotten to him.

Steamed, he walked to his Caddy parked in front of the warehouse. He didn't mind being judged on performance, but he was damned weary of being tried and sentenced by a past he had no control over.

Despite the evening chill, he put the top down, then drove the long way back to Ten Oaks through town. Just to prove to himself and anyone who happened to see him that he had as much right to be in Cannons Crossing as the next person.

The only bright spot in an otherwise stressful day had been Julia's visit. It struck him just now that, in an unexpected way, she'd said yes to his marriage proposal. The thought of her waiting for him made the muscles in his neck and shoulders relax. Made his pulse race and the corners of his mouth curl upward. Despite his bad day.

Was this what it felt like to be a family man heading home? If so, the warm feeling that washed over him might be able to take the edge off his sharply curtailed freedom. His return to a hostile environment.

The image of Julia burned brightly in his thoughts.

Could he ever be as steady in his support of her as she'd always been in her support of him?

The early dark of fall had settled as he pulled up the Richardson driveway. Lights from the big house winked from behind the trees. He saw the silhouette of a lone figure standing outside on the veranda. He hoped it was Julia watching for him. Hoped, even as he wondered at this new pull she exerted over him. He didn't look forward to an evening with her family, but he sure did look forward to being in her company.

He drew up to the front steps behind several unfamiliar cars, and the figure approached. Julia in jeans and one of his flannel shirts. Her pilfering of his wardrobe seemed somehow like an act of intimacy. Made him feel good clean through.

She leaned into the car. "You wouldn't mind taking me for supper at the diner out by the interstate?"

He didn't mind one bit. "What about your family?"

"Oh, you don't want to go in there. One step through the front door and Mama will have you trying on morning coats. Tuxedos. Top hats. The place is crawling with wedding specialists. You wouldn't believe who all Big Daddy has paid to be at Mama's beck and call. Twenty-four hours a day. It's crazy!"

"Then hop in. I specialize in great escapes."

With a laugh, she opened the passenger's door, then slid across the front seat to nestle next to Dallas. "Ooooh!" She fairly purred. "Why did car manufacturers give up bench seats?"

Why indeed?

She was so near. Her warmth and her softness excited him. With a rusty chuckle that reached clear around his heart, he threw the car into gear, then headed for the old diner. "Want the top up?"

"No way." She leaned her head on his shoulder. "Just turn the heat on."

He did, then put his right arm around her.

Julia felt the biting wind nip her face and whip her hair. She looked up to see stars like ice chips twinkling above. The ghostly black shapes along the roadside flew by, cold and forbidding. Back at Ten Oaks, her mother and crew were designing death by ostentation. But inside the red monster, snuggled against Dallas, she felt safe and warm. This time she didn't bridle at his rescue.

She reached out and turned the radio to a soulful country station. "Want to tell me about your day?"

"Tell me about yours." The sudden tensing of his muscles told her his had been rough.

"Well…you happen to be cruising with a woman whose pregnancy is proceeding normally, thank you very much."

"You went to the doctor." He gave her shoulder a gentle squeeze. "I like to hear that."

"Also, we now have a house." She patted the key in her jeans pocket. "It's a rental and a fixer-upper, but it's ours."

We. Ours. She felt suddenly timid, speaking the words. If they sounded strange to Dallas's ears, however, he didn't mention the fact.

"This house," he said, "Big Daddy's not footing the bill, is he?"

"Not a bit of it!" Julia laughed into the night air. The freedom felt wonderful. "Your salary and mine will have to cover it."

"Your salary?"

She sat up straight and looked at him. "Meet the news producer at WMCN, Macon."

"Hot damn." He glanced at her, then back at the road. His features outlined in the dashboard lights showed pleasure. "You work fast."

"I'm good," she countered. The open car and Dallas's presence made her bold. She felt as if she could take on the world. She settled back next to him, content in her self-assurance.

In a short while, Dallas pulled the Caddy into the crowded dirt parking lot in front of the Georgia Diner. A flickering neon sign in one window proclaimed South's Best Pies, while another advertised a national beer. Julia wanted neither. Ever since lunch, she'd craved macaroni and cheese. Comfort food. Something she hadn't eaten since childhood. And she'd only eaten that in the kitchen with Mary Louise. Certainly the dish never made an appearance on the dinner table at Ten Oaks.

When she opened the door to get out, the most amazing sensation washed over her. Her tummy felt caressed by the flutter of tiny wings.

"Oh, Dallas!" She reached for him. "The doctor said this might happen soon."

"Are you all right?" Concern scraped his words.

"Yes!" Oh, yes, she was just fine. "The baby moved!"

He slid his hand over her stomach. "Can I feel it?"

"Not yet!" Excitement filled the breath she drew. "It's called the quickening. And I can barely feel it. Just a slither to let me know—for the very first time—it's there. Alive and well."

Awe descended over her. She carried a child. A living being. A part of herself.

Unbidden tears stung her eyes. With the tears came a most extraordinary feeling toward this little creature. Without a doubt, she knew she would protect it with her very life. When her child was born, she would struggle to give it the best that lay within her power. Love. Security.

Julia looked at Dallas, his strong features accented in the diner's neon glow. He'd offered to help her with the security of a second income and the support of a second parent. Having just now felt the reality of her child, she'd be a fool not to accept.

"I think this little one's going to need a daddy," she murmured.

A slow smile crossed Dallas's features. "This calls for a celebration." He helped her out of the Caddy. "What do mamas-to-be crave?"

As much love as their unborn babies need, Julia thought ruefully, reality settling once again over her.

"Macaroni and cheese," she said instead.

Brushing by Dallas to enter the diner, she experienced the by now expected physical jolt of attraction for him. She couldn't afford this one-sided feeling. He'd made his marriage proposal out of the pain from his past and their longtime friendship. He'd made it out of empathy and loyalty. Not out of any romantic love for her. Intellectually, she acknowledged that fact. But still she wondered, having made a pact to protect her child, would she be able to protect her own heart?

Dallas followed Julia through the diner's door, the warmth and noise from the big room enveloping them. He suddenly wondered if this supper out was such a good idea. With Julia's acceptance of his proposal just now, he wanted to talk over so much with her. None of which he wanted overheard by anyone in this too public place. Just the fact that every head in the room turned in mild curiosity each time the front door opened irked him, overriding his pleasure a minute ago when Julia had felt her baby move.

"It's seat yourself. So find a booth and I'll be with you shortly." A tall, thin waitress with a cheery voice brushed past Julia and Dallas, her tray laden with the kind of food that gives a cardiologist fits.

Dallas ushered Julia to an empty booth by a window. Seated at last opposite the woman he was going to marry, he discovered himself at a loss for words. The buzz of the neon sign, added to the drone of conversation in the room, made for a dreamlike atmosphere. Scowling at the clean but scarred tabletop, he traced a crudely carved heart with the tip of one finger. When he'd been in high school, the diner had been the kids' late-night hangout. Not for him, however. He'd had chores to do at the Sutters'. Any free time had been taken up with rodeo. Either practice or competition. The girls he'd gone out with had been rodeo groupies even then. He wouldn't have brought them here, where he'd have felt out of place with the squeaky-clean children of Cannons Crossing's upstanding families. It was only a diner, for pete's sake, but the romantic carvings on the tabletop reminded him how closed out he'd felt all during his growing up.

"If that's the face you wear to celebrate, this evening's in trouble."

Dallas looked up to see Julia grinning at him from across the table.

"Sorry." He tried to shake off the cobwebs of the past.

"Rough day?"

"Yes and no." It was strange that he hadn't even dwelled on his day once he'd picked up Julia. He could deal with the present. It was the past that continued to trip him up. "I can learn the lumber business as long as I don't have to wear that damned tie."

Crossing her arms on the tabletop, Julia leaned toward him. "I always believed you could do anything you set your mind to."

That she had. And every time she'd told him as much, he'd felt alive. Truly alive. The only other thing that made him feel equally alive was rodeo. Now rodeo was gone. Lost to him forever. Only Julia and her belief in him remained.

Julia.

How beautiful she looked, even after a long day. Her tawny eyes shone with a vitality that belied the list of things she'd accomplished since breakfast. Her skin, even in the harsh light and shadows of the diner, fairly glowed. Her voice slid over his senses like velvet. She'd always been beautiful, but tonight she was radiant. He couldn't quite believe, that, for whatever reasons, she'd agreed to be his.

"There must be something to the old saying that pregnancy makes a beautiful woman more so," he said.

She cocked her head, surprise and pleasure suffusing her features. "Where did that come from, Dallas Lee?"

"Y'all ready to order?" The waitress rescued him.

"Yes." Julia ran the tip of her tongue over her lips in anticipation. The innocent movement made Dallas's senses come alive. "I'll have the macaroni and cheese," she said. "And since it's my night to cook, so will he." She winked at Dallas.

What had gotten into her tonight? Away from her family, she was the Julia of his childhood. Relaxed and impish.

The waitress raised one eyebrow and gave Dallas an appraising glance. "Anything else?"

"Turnip greens," he said. He'd read somewhere that pregnant women needed extra vitamins. "And baked apples if you have them."

"We do." The waitress licked her pencil tip. "Drinks?"

"Coffee," Julia said.

"No. Milk," Dallas countered. When Julia blushed, he added, "For both of us."

As the waitress pocketed her tablet and turned to go, Julia whispered across the table, "You *mother* very well for a single guy."

"You deserve it," he replied simply. She did. It was time to pay her back for all the support she'd shown him through the years.

Suddenly uncomfortable with the well of emotion he felt toward the woman who sat across from him, he glanced around the diner. A family of four in the corner seemed to be far too interested in Julia and Dallas. Sidelong glances, whispers and laughter aimed their way, made the hair rise on the back of Dallas's neck. What about a man and a woman having a meal in public could have sparked any interest?

The adults were well in the shadows, but the boy, about ten or eleven, and his sister, about four or five, slid from their seats and approached. The boy held a pen and a napkin in his hand.

"You Dallas Parker the rodeo champ?" the boy asked as the two stopped at the end of the table.

"I am." Dallas softened just a little. "Who's asking?"

"Jeb Carleton, sir. This is my sister, Suki."

The little girl popped her thumb in her mouth and stared at Dallas with enormous eyes.

"Would you autograph this napkin, please?" Jeb thrust the

napkin and pen in front of Dallas. "My daddy said he went to school with you, but I didn't believe him."

Carleton? Dallas glanced over at the table where the man had now turned so that his face was visible. Rick Carleton. He had indeed gone to school with Dallas. Rick gave a nod. The woman next to him beamed in obvious maternal pride.

"Always believe in your daddy," Dallas said as he signed his name on the paper napkin.

"He said you were the best rider to ever come out of the state." Jeb puffed up with the enormity of his statement.

Little Suki pulled her thumb out of her mouth. "Mama said you must have been the prettiest!"

Jeb rolled his eyes at his sister. "Boys aren't pretty."

"But he is!" Suki lowered her chin onto the end of the table and smiled up at Dallas in unabashed admiration.

"C'mon, kids." Rick Carleton came over to the booth, his hand extended. "Let's give Dallas and Miss Julia some breathing room."

Dallas shook hands. "It's been a long time."

"Sure has. This is my wife, Hannah." He smiled at Julia. "We see Julia now and again, but I don't believe I've seen you since graduation."

"Haven't been back until now."

"Visiting?" Hannah looked from Julia to Dallas.

"An extended visit." Now, why didn't he just come right out and say that he and Julia were getting married? Because, even with her yes, it didn't feel real to him.

"If you have time," Rick said, ruffling his son's hair, "stop by. We live right in town in the old Miller house."

"Okay." He watched the Carleton family walk away, an odd feeling that he couldn't quite articulate nagging at him.

"You expected no one to be pleased to see you, is that it?" Julia's soft words sliced to the heart of the matter. "But the Sutters, and now the Carletons…"

"I didn't have time to make many friends. I was working so hard to scrape up the cash to blow this town."

"You didn't have time to see the people who genuinely admired you."

"Like your father?"

Julia scowled. "Daddy certainly had a few of his generation who agreed with him where you were concerned. But the kids at school admired you."

That came as news to Dallas.

Reaching across the table, Julia laid her hand over his. "Need I remind you that Big Daddy's generation is giving way to ours? You'll find your reception in Cannons Crossing may not be what you'd expected."

Could this be?

The waitress brought their dinners, giving Dallas an excuse not to pursue this conversation wholeheartedly. Always, when he listed the reasons Julia Richardson couldn't possibly take marriage to him seriously, Dallas added the fact that he'd been the town pariah. If that fact wasn't exactly true anymore, what stopped him from making Julia his more than just in name?

His fatherless state. His lack of family, for starters.

The very first night he'd been at Ten Oaks, Auntie Ouidie had mentioned the Richardsons as being poor but of good family. Family meant the world to the Richardsons. Even if she didn't admit as much, Julia respected family and roots, too. Otherwise, she wouldn't have come home at this difficult turning point in her life.

Dallas needed to identify his father. His family. He needed to offer Julia something more than his wandering rodeo soul.

Tomorrow on his lunch break, he'd begin the search.

Julia observed Dallas as he ate in silence. She wondered if he was brooding over her comments. She certainly hoped not. If they couldn't be as honest with each other now as they'd been in their childhood, this marriage of convenience was doomed from the start.

She reached for another napkin from the holder near the window. In the process, she had to move the salt and pepper and the ketchup bottle. When she did, she spied the initials scratched into the tabletop.

"J.A.R. + D.L.P."

She'd forgotten carving them.

But now that she'd seen them, that whole day came back to her in a wash of vivid memories. It was the summer after sixth grade. Big Daddy had agreed to take her and three other eleven-year-old girls to the junior rodeo competition. Miriam had pitched a fit, saying that hurly-burly was nothing little ladies should be interested in. For once, Big Daddy had sided with Julia. Of course, you could get Big Daddy to go anywhere there'd be a showing of good horseflesh.

Julia had never seen Dallas compete. Sure, she'd sneaked to watch him practice, but she'd never been present for any of the wins that were gaining him statewide recognition. Wins that seemed assured now. She wanted to see the fruition of her belief in him.

Julia had another reason in wanting to see Dallas compete, and she wasn't very proud of this reason. There was a little part of her, awakening woman who she was, that was jealous of rodeo. This roping and riding had the potential to take her Dallas away, and she felt determined to assess the strength of her rival.

The day before at the old oak, she'd given Dallas a slim yellow satin ribbon and asked him to wear it somewhere on him the day of competition as a good-luck charm. Having just recently read the legend of King Arthur, she was wild for romantic symbolism. The thought of Dallas wearing her favor into battle had stirred her blood. Dallas, however, had eyed the ribbon skeptically and, promising nothing, had stuffed it in his back pocket.

The day of the competition, Big Daddy had given the girls money for refreshments and advice to sit with a family they knew before he headed for the livestock paddocks. The girls had found seats in the crowded grandstand behind Abe Pritchard and his nephew. Abe went to the Little Shepherd Baptist Church, and although Julia knew scant more about the man and less about his nephew, his churchgoing habits recommended him as an unofficial chaperon.

Julia's insides were tied in knots as competitor after competitor went through his paces. When at last Dallas Parker's name was announced in the calf-roping event, she thought she might lose consciousness. As he and his pony hurtled into the arena, she saw nothing of his performance. Her only thoughts were for the slender bit of yellow ribbon tied in one buttonhole. He'd worn it. Before God and Cates County. He'd worn it. For her.

Her rival, rodeo, didn't seem so menacing.

Abe Pritchard had obviously watched more of Dallas's performance. He stood, whooping loudly and slapping his hat on his thigh. He looked at his nephew. "For a bastard, that boy can ride!"

It was then that Julia broke the ladylike silence concerning Dallas that she'd maintained her entire short life "Why, Mr. Pritchard! And you a churchgoing man!"

Abe Pritchard seemed surprised that anyone had cared about his comment.

Julia straightened her Richardson spine. "Dallas Parker can *ride*. Period."

When the grown man didn't disagree, when he actually looked sheepish, the eleven-year-old girl learned the power of speaking her mind.

Later, Big Daddy took the girls to the diner for chili dogs and Cokes. He let them pretend at being grown-up with their own booth while he schmoozed with acquaintances at the counter. Julia's three friends had reprimanded her for her outspokenness.

"Julia, you'll get the reputation for being brassy."

"Dallas Parker's cute as the day is long, but he's not worth stirring up trouble over."

"My mama says he comes from the wrong side of the tracks."

Julia bristled. Feeling the earlier power of speaking her mind, she recognized the need to take some kind of stand in front of her friends, too. "Hand me that nail file in your purse, Emma."

With a perplexed look, Emma obliged.

Julia took the nail file, then, glancing around to make certain no adult was watching, hastily scratched her initials with Dallas's. "There. That shows you what I think of Dallas Lee Parker. If he'd have me, rodeo champ that he is, I'd be his girl in a minute."

Her act of rebellion had been met by three girlish gasps.

Julia ran her finger lightly over the seventeen-year-old initials, then moved the sugar bowl to cover them. Time hadn't changed much. If the rodeo champ would have her, she'd still be his girl.

But as some things remained the same, others had taken on painful baggage in time's journey.

"You're really uncomfortable here in Cannons Crossing, aren't you?" she asked a silent Dallas. "Even after all these years."

She could only see reflections in his eyes. Nothing deeper. "It's not just Cannons Crossing," he said. "I've only ever felt comfortable with horses and bulls and a ring."

Her heart sighed with disappointment.

"Except when I was with you at the old oak tree. As friends."

"We're still friends," she offered tentatively, worrying that taking on the task of husband to a wife he didn't love and father to another man's child paled beside the passion that had been rodeo. Would grow old too soon.

"Let's not ever change that." Dallas reached for the bill in a gesture that ended further conversation. "Let's not mess with a sure situation."

Julia remembered one of the hard questions Helen Sutter had thrown out as a challenge. *What do you have to lose by letting yourself fall in love?*

Maybe Dallas Lee Parker, Julia answered mentally.

Chapter Seven

With her hands on her hips, Mandy stood before Dallas in the main warehouse. He didn't like the satisfied smirk that showed through her heavily applied makeup.

"Can it wait?" he asked. "I'm just about to break for lunch."

"Mr. Richardson wants you to use your lunch hour to go through old files, annual reports. Stuff like that. He left some reference books about the lumber industry on your desk." She smiled sweetly. "He says if you're to be his son-in-law, you're to learn the business."

What the hell did Big Daddy think Dallas had been doing all morning?

Irritably, Dallas smacked the dust from his hands onto his jeans. This morning he'd foregone the tie; instead, he'd come dressed for manual labor. He meant to learn the business, sure. But his way of doing it was from the ground up—working alongside the employees. Already he'd discovered several problems at Richardson Lumber. One was low worker morale.

That was no surprise. Big Daddy ran a dictatorship, not a business. Another was a spotty track record in operations and customer service. Why should employees be particularly proud of or careful in their work if the boss didn't show he was proud of them? Dallas suspected that a third problem, although he couldn't prove it yet, was worker theft. He even had some common-sense ideas on how to tackle these issues.

But Big Daddy wanted him to sit behind a desk and go through dry books and musty files—a manipulative tactic, plain and simple. Dallas had seen the look of displeasure on the old man's face this morning when he'd observed Dallas, sleeves rolled up, working alongside the men in the warehouse. It must have galled the boss to see the hated newcomer finding his own niche. His own hands-on management style, despite his ignorance of the business itself. The plan had been to humiliate Dallas. To drive him away from Julia and Cannons Crossing. Not to have him become a productive member of operations.

Well, Big Daddy could just rearrange his strategy. Dallas planned to hang in for the long and bumpy haul because he'd soon have a wife and child who depended on his tenacity.

He followed Mandy back to the office, where he found her getting ready to go out for lunch.

"I can bring you something to eat," she offered, her tone bordering on petulant.

"No, thanks." She would probably poison it.

"Suit yourself." She paused in the doorway. "Files earlier than the last few years are stored in that closet in the corner." Her smile showed fake clear through. "Just in case you run out of things to study."

A sudden idea struck him. "Do the salesmen who come through here put their names on any of the paperwork?"

"Sometimes their last names. On the order forms."

"How far back have the order forms been saved?"

"Forever. Mr. Richardson's very particular about keeping complete records. There may even be some handwritten ledgers from the previous owners." The secretary appeared vaguely disappointed that Dallas had found something to interest him. "Why?"

He shot her his most brilliant smile. "Just learning the business."

She looked as if she didn't believe a word of it, but said nothing and left, her disdain trailing behind her like perfume.

Dallas headed directly for the closet of old files. He'd learn the business by the sweat of his brow. In the warehouse and on the road with the employees. If Big Daddy wanted to keep him in at lunch like a naughty schoolboy, he would use the time to look up the salesmen that came through Richardson Lumber twenty-nine years ago.

Little did his future father-in-law know that he'd actually provided Dallas with the tools to begin the search for his father.

Dallas took a deep breath, opened the closet door and stepped back in time. The enormous closet, lit only by one bare, dim overhead bulb, housed row upon row of labeled filing cabinets. In his search for the lumberyard files the year before his birth, Dallas noticed one whole file devoted to Big Daddy's stock records. Curiosity and grudging admiration for the old man's history of breeding and showing champions made Dallas pull out the top drawer labeled Horses. He soon became lost in a fascinating world of money and strategy and bloodlines. One thing was clear upon inspection of the records: Big Daddy had won just about every award and honor you could win in this pricey hobby. Unless Dallas missed his guess, the big ego would soon be on the prowl for new territories to conquer.

"What in tarnation do you think you're doing, boy?" Big Daddy's quivering bulk filled the doorway.

"Word had it I was supposed to learn the business by going over the old files—"

"I left two books on the lumber industry on your desk."

"I always did bridle under book assignments." Dallas shook his head. "If I have to look at numbers, I want them to be real, specific numbers. Like these files." He refused to be drawn into an ugly confrontation, but he refused to be intimidated.

"The recent files are in the other room."

"If I'm to learn the business, I'm starting at the beginning." He grinned. "You *were* serious about me learning the business?"

Big Daddy reached out and snatched the folder out of Dallas's hand. "You can snoop all you want. In the business files. Just leave my stock records alone."

"You afraid that I might know something about stock, is that it?"

Big Daddy narrowed his eyes. "I'm not afraid of anything, you interloper."

"No? Then tell me why you can't stand the sight of me?" Dallas didn't want a fight, but maybe alone they could lay their cards on the table. Honesty was better than bottled-up suspicions and acrimony any day.

"Because—"

"Lordy!" Julia sneezed directly behind her father. "Have you two never heard of a lunch break?" She waved her hand in front of her face. "Come out of the closet, at least. You've loosed a dust storm."

"You sure you should be running all over town in your condition?" Backing out of the closet, Big Daddy bristled. "I thought you and your mama were home making wedding plans."

"I'm pregnant, Daddy, not sick." Julia stood on tiptoe and planted a kiss on her father's cheek. "Besides, everyone's entitled to lunch. Mama dropped me off with a picnic basket." She turned a beatific smile on Dallas. "I thought you'd drive me over to see our house. We could eat it there."

Dallas froze.

An incredible change seemed to have come over Julia. She purely radiated happiness.

"Dallas can't," Big Daddy huffed. "I have work for him here."

"For goodness' sakes." Julia rolled her eyes and laughed.

"The man's getting married in two days. To your only child. The least you can do is give him the rest of the day off. I don't even start my job at the radio station until after the wedding."

Two days. Did she say *two days?* This was the first Dallas had heard of a wedding in two days.

Big Daddy glowered. "The lumberyard's a business. A real seven-day-a-week business. Not like some pink-tea job with a radio station. We have real work to do."

Dallas waited for Julia to explode.

Surprisingly, she didn't. In fact, Big Daddy's tactless words seemed to roll right off her. "In that case," she said, her eyes sparkling mischievously, "maybe I'll make myself busy while you two do this manly work. I could, say, go out and talk union shop with your workers."

The word *union* seemed to send an electric current through the old man. "Get out of here," he grumbled, his upper lip curled in a snarl. "Parker, take the rest of the day off."

Julia patted her father's arm. "That's what I love about you. Your ability to see reason."

Dallas stifled a cough. Big Daddy might have many abilities, but seeing reason certainly wasn't one of them. His only child, however, knew how to tighten the screws—a new, formerly unseen side to Julia. Dallas wondered how much of a challenge he'd taken on with his feisty wife-to-be.

Julia glanced from her father to her husband-to-be. She knew the men had been quarreling, but she wasn't going to let that fact dampen her good mood. Yesterday the doctor had assured her that her pregnancy was off to a healthy start. And this morning the usual dreaded morning sickness hadn't materialized. She looked forward to having a picnic lunch with Dallas in their new home.

Their home.

The thought still blew her away.

"So!" She actually batted her eyelashes at Dallas as she reached for the picnic basket she'd placed on his desk. "Do we have a date?"

She detected a look of relief in Dallas's eyes.

"You do." His expression turned to one of surprise as he lifted the picnic basket. "How much food's in here?"

"Mary Louise knows you eat for six. And now I'm eating for two." Oh, how happy that made her feel today. She slipped her arm through Dallas's. "Think it will fit in the red monster?"

"Speaking of that disgrace of a car..." Obviously, Big Daddy wanted the last word. "Do you think that before my grandbaby's born, you could purchase something safe?"

"Norton," Dallas said with a grin, using the first name Big Daddy despised, "I'm thinking of installing a roll bar instead."

Julia and Dallas escaped from the office under a shower of harrumphs and snorts and muttered expletives.

"Why, Miss Julia, what has gotten into you today?" Dallas asked on the way to the car. "You positively glow!" Admiration showed in his regard even as amusement played about his mouth.

"Good health and a good friend," Julia replied. "Do you know, I think that macaroni and cheese last night had magical powers, too." She flexed her muscles playfully. "I feel terrific today. Strong."

"You look terrific."

The gentleness with which he uttered the words made her stop and turn to him.

"You do," he insisted. "There's something different about you today. You've come back to life. My pigtail girl from the old oak."

It would have been at this point in their childhood friendship that one of them would have reached out and touched the other. But an unaccountable shyness now seemed to separate them. This was no longer a relationship Julia recognized. And any physical contact only seemed to complicate matters.

She felt color rise to her cheeks. "It's the macaroni and cheese. I'm sure of it." Glancing at the ground, she scuffed the toe of her shoe in the soft red dust. Why did she suddenly feel so tongue-tied?

Dallas put the picnic basket in the back seat of the Caddy, then stood by the door, waiting and watching her, his dark hair ruffled by the wind, his chiseled features still and unreadable. Did he, too, feel these unspoken, disconcerting changes between them?

Moving to the car tentatively as if this were a first date, Julia found she could no longer even make small talk.

The top of the Caddy down, they drove in silence along the road that stretched toward Macon. The weather had turned very warm with temperatures exceeding even those of a normal Indian summer. Julia felt bathed in soft breezes and sensuous sunlight. Normally, she'd be sitting close to Dallas, chatting up a storm. Today, however, she sat against the passenger's door with an expanse of bench seat between them. She ached to snuggle up to him as she'd done in the ride to the diner last night. But today, along with the return of her good spirits, had arrived an uncommon case of reserve.

At last Dallas said, "You're going to have to tell me where to turn off."

"It's…it's not far." She was surprised her voice actually worked. "On the right. A small gray Victorian. There's a messy old magnolia in the side yard and a picket fence with roses out front." Stereotype or not, the picket fence with the roses had convinced her that she'd found the house she must share with Dallas.

He pulled into the gravel driveway, stopped the car, then sat, staring at the cottage.

"Well?" Excitement buffeted her insides. This cottage was a real find.

The muscles in his face and neck tensed. "Well, what?" His words sounded ragged.

"What do you think of the house? I know it needs work. Paint mostly. But we can do that after-hours. I just thought it was perfect for privacy. It's a fair distance from Ten Oaks, and we can barely see the neighbors up and down the road—"

"It's okay." He got out of the car.

Julia followed, not surprised at his reaction, but disappointed nonetheless. He'd never shown an interest in the homey arts...but this was going to be *their* house. "Are you angry that I didn't consult you before signing the agreement?"

"No." He hoisted the picnic basket out of the back seat, his motions jerky as if he weren't really concentrating on the task. "I'm not angry at all. I wouldn't have been any help. I haven't the slightest idea what a home should feel like."

Ah, so the domestication of Dallas Lee Parker might be more of a problem than Julia anticipated.

She decided not to push the issue by gushing over the quaint little house and its possibilities. She'd forgo telling him her plans for reviving the overgrown gardens, the ideas she had for the nursery, the thoughts she had on paint colors and maximizing the small spaces. As volatile as the Richardson household was, it had given her a sense of home. A desire to create one of her own. Where she had all that, Dallas claimed he felt a void.

With her help, however, he'd come around in time. And help sometimes meant not pushing.

Her key at the ready, she led the way up the front steps. "Mama, Martha and I spent the morning cleaning."

"Miriam cleaned house?"

"Well, she supervised." Julia opened the front door and stepped into the small front hall. "But in the end, she managed some genuine enthusiasm, so I count myself lucky."

Dallas stood stiffly beside her, surveying his surroundings with narrowed eyes.

She opted not to overwhelm him with a tour right at the start. "You must be hungry. Let's eat on the floor in the parlor. If there's time later, I can show you the rest of the house. If not...well, it's not important."

He reached out and touched her. "It's okay. You don't have to pussyfoot around me. If the house makes you happy, let your happiness show." He performed a lopsided grin. "I'm not much of a homebody, true. But if I find myself getting claustrophobia, I'll just take my sleeping bag out under the magnolia. That's no indication of the worth of your choice. It's just me."

An attempt to meet her halfway. That's all she asked. Anything was possible with mutual effort.

She linked her fingers through the handle of the basket he carried, then tugged it and him toward the sun-drenched parlor. "I think we both could use some of Mary Louise's food."

With an awkward reticence, they spread a picnic cloth on the old hardwood floor in the empty room. As Dallas settled himself, Julia noted how out of place he looked. Big and rawboned, he seemed like a giant in a dollhouse. A creature taken from his natural habitat and caged. Perhaps it was a good thing that they wouldn't be able to afford much furniture at the start. She was certain he wouldn't appreciate the confining clutter.

"Do you have any belongings you need shipped here?" she asked as she laid out the food.

"No." Picking up a hard-boiled egg, Dallas frowned. "Just the saddle I dropped at the Sutters'. How about you?"

"I have a few pieces in my apartment in Boston. I called a friend who's going to have them sent here. She's also going to see about subletting the apartment until the lease expires."

"Leases and furniture," he said almost to himself. " I've never had reason to deal with them."

He looked like a man who'd just felt the noose slip over his head, and suddenly Julia's fine mood began to droop.

"I suppose," she ventured softly, "this wouldn't be the best time to remind you that Mama declares she can have the wedding up and running in two days."

For a fleeting instant, his eyes held a wild, spooked look. She hoped he didn't feel that the hangman had just released the trapdoor.

"Two days," he murmured. "I thought I heard you say as much back in the office." Dallas hadn't quite believed it.

Julia turned her head away, but not before he saw tears gather on her lashes. He needed to get a grip. If he showed reluctance toward this marriage, how would Julia feel? Re-

IT'S FUN! IT'S FREE
AND IT COULD MAKE YOU
£600,000.00 RICHER

If you've ever played scratch off game tickets before, you should be familiar with how our games work. On each of the first four tickets (numbered 1 to 4) there are Gold strips to scratch off.

Using a coin, do just that - carefully scratch the Gold strips to reveal how much each ticket could be worth if it is a winning ticket. Tickets could be worth from £6.00 to £600,000.00 in lifetime cash (£20,000.00 each year for 30 years).

Note, also, that each of your 4 tickets will have a unique prize draw Lucky Number... and that's 4 chances for a **BIG WIN!**

FREE BOOKS!

At the same time you play your tickets to qualify for big prizes, you are invited to play Ticket 5 to get specially selected Silhouette Special Edition® novels. These books have a cover price of over £2.00 each, but are yours to keep absolutely FREE.

There's no catch. You're under no obligation to buy anything. You don't have to make a minimum number of purchases - not even one! The fact is, thousands of readers enjoy receiving books by mail from The Reader Service™. They like the convenience of home delivery... they like getting the best new novels before they're available in the shops... and they love their subscriber Newsletter packed with author news, competitions and much more.

We hope that after receiving your free books you'll want to remain a subscriber. But the choice is yours - to continue or cancel, anytime at all! So why not take us up on our invitation, with no risk of any kind. You'll be glad you did!

PLUS A FREE GIFT!

One more thing - when you accept the free books on Ticket 5, you're also entitled to play Ticket 6 which is GOOD FOR A GREAT GIFT! Like the books, this gift is totally **free** and yours to keep as a thank you for giving the Reader Service a try!

So scratch off the GOLD STRIPS on all your GAME TICKETS and send for everything today! You've got nothing to lose and everything to gain!

OFFICIAL RULES
MILLION DOLLAR SWEEPSTAKES

Here are your BIG WIN Game Tickets potentially worth from £6.00 to £600,000.00 each. Scratch off the GOLD STRIP on each of your Prize Draw tickets to see what you could win and post your entry right away.

This could be your lucky day – Good Luck!

TICKET 1
Scratch GOLD STRIP to reveal potential value of cash prize and return to find out if this is a winning ticket.
Return all game tickets intact.

LUCKY NUMBER

OJ 157905

TICKET 2
Scratch GOLD STRIP to reveal potential value of cash prize and return to find out if this is a winning ticket.
Return all game tickets intact.

LUCKY NUMBER

GL 767214

TICKET 3
Scratch GOLD STRIP to reveal potential value of cash prize and return to find out if this is a winning ticket.
Return all game tickets intact.

LUCKY NUMBER

ZH 613309

TICKET 4
Scratch GOLD STRIP to reveal potential value of cash prize and return to find out if this is a winning ticket.
Return all game tickets intact.

LUCKY NUMBER

FP 273900

TICKET 5
FREE BOOKS
Scratch GOLD STRIP to reveal number of books you will receive. These books, part of a sampling project to introduce romance readers to the benefits of the Reader Service, are FREE

AUTHORISATION CODE

193279-411

TICKET 6
FREE GIFT
All gifts are free. No purchase required. Scratch GOLD STRIP to reveal free gift, our thanks to readers for trying our books.

AUTHORISATION CODE

130107-742

YES! Enter my Lucky Numbers in the £600,000.00 Grand Prize Draw and when winners are selected, tell me if I've won any prize. If the GOLD STRIP is scratched off Ticket 5, I will also receive FREE Silhouette Special Edition® novels along with the FREE GIFT on Ticket 6. *I am over 18 years of age.*

E9II

MS/MRS/MISS/MR
BLOCK CAPITALS PLEASE

ADDRESS _____

_____ POSTCODE _____

The Reader Service™
FREEPOST CN81
CROYDON
CR9 3WZ

NO
STAMP
NEEDED

jected. Adrift. Alone. Never did he want her to experience any of those feelings. She'd struggled all her childhood to keep him from feeling those very emotions.

Never should she feel them. Never.

He'd made a vow to support her as she'd always supported him. Letting his own reservations, his own personal baggage show up and get in the way, was to break that vow. She had the greater need now.

"Two days? That's great," he said, making his words deliberately hearty, remembering his vow and his best friend, trying not to give credence to the nagging fact that he'd never before stayed in one place for any length of time.

Marriage. That would certainly root him.

She sighed. "Dallas, this isn't going to work."

"Why not?"

"Just look at you." She only half looked at him. "Your body language alone says you're ready to hit the road again."

He reached out to turn her face to him. "You forget. I have nowhere to go but here."

"Are you saying that marriage is the last-chance ranch?"

"Not at all." He ran his index finger along her chin. "I'm saying that rodeo and wandering are behind me. It's time I settled down."

He suddenly wanted to kiss her. Badly. The memory of the passion they'd shared in the Sutters' barn was beginning to fade. Despite all reason, he wanted to renew it. Needed to draw strength from feeling one with her.

Instead, he said, "It's time to settle down with my best friend."

If he mentally repeated *best friend* often enough, it should cool this dangerous, hot yearning.

Her smile was ever so faint. "Well, your best friend's mother says to be in the solarium with your tux on, six o'clock Saturday evening."

"I don't have a tux." He let his fingers trail down her arm. She was so beautiful he couldn't pull away.

"You will when the mother of the bride and her henchmen

get through with you tonight after dinner." Her smile grew stronger. "There's still time to put a ladder under my bedroom window."

"No." He drew back from her, resisted the growing physical attraction he felt. "If we're going to get married—and we are—we're going to do it right."

"What makes you so stubborn, Dallas Lee?"

He smiled at that. He'd been called stubborn from the day he'd been born. Sheer stubbornness had pulled him through too many rough spots in his life to recount. Stubbornness wasn't necessarily a bad trait.

"You should talk about stubborn," he replied. "Remember how you hauled me by the force of your mule-headed will through junior-year American history?"

"Remember! I was afraid American history was going to be able to do what no one in Cannons Crossing had done so far—tear our friendship apart."

"Lordy, but you were a tough tutor. Wouldn't let me copy one letter of your work. Made me go over and over the lessons until you were satisfied I understood." He chuckled softly. "Do you remember what you told me every time we studied together at the old oak?"

Her golden eyes sparkled as she remembered. "I said, 'If you're going to graduate—and you are—you're going to do it right.'"

"I rest my case."

The light faded from her eyes. "A high-school diploma doesn't compare to a lifetime of marriage."

"I sure as heck hope not!" He chucked her under the chin. "I would expect marriage is a lot more interesting."

She blushed prettily.

Mingled with the respect he held her in and the protectiveness he felt toward her lay deep desire. Say what they might aloud, this was no longer an ordinary friendship. Dallas felt the complications in his life increase a notch.

Suddenly, the room seemed to close in on them; he needed

to move. "Show me the rest of the house." He rose, pulling Julia with him.

"But lunch?"

"It can wait."

"But you're not really interested."

"I'm interested because you're interested."

She laughed, and the sound was as fresh and appealing as all outdoors. "Men only say that in romance novels!" She skipped lightly out of the room, her renewed happiness filling the empty spaces.

He followed although he only half noted the rooms they walked through on her energetic tour. Instead, he studied Julia. He'd forgotten how much fun she was to watch. All animation and enthusiasm. Now, pregnant, she exuded an unmistakable sensuality that startled him.

"And this is the master bedroom," she said as if encouraging his wayward thoughts.

He stared at the small, light-filled room in amazement. Call him a fool, but until now he hadn't fully absorbed the after-the-ceremony reality: Julia and he would be living in this house. Sleeping in this room. Together. As husband and wife. He was as red-blooded a man as the next, but shifting gears from best friend to lover proved unsettling. Add to his unease the thought of the baby. He pleaded ignorance in such matters. Was intimacy even healthy during pregnancy?

"We need to talk," he began, but was cut off by the sound of the front door closing downstairs.

"Julia!" Miriam called. "We need to move along, darling. The florist needs your final okay."

Dallas reached out and grasped Julia's wrist. "Do you have to go?"

"If we're going to get married in two days, yes." She smiled up at him, and his resistance crumbled. "You were the one who told me to let Mama take a part."

He groaned softly.

"Dallas!" Miriam's imperious voice rang out from the foot

of the stairs. "You let my girl go! The two of us have a million things to do."

Dallas released Julia's arm as if Miriam had been an all-seeing chaperon at a junior-high social, then shook his head in chagrin at his schoolboy reflex. "Promise me you won't give her a key to the house."

Julia stood on tiptoe, brushed her lips against his cheek and murmured, "Promise."

Had he imagined the faintly seductive glimmer in her eyes? Even if he had, he surely hadn't imagined his body's instantaneous response to her touch. Perhaps it was fortunate Miriam had interrupted their solitude. He'd grown in the mood for a repeat of the Sutters' barn. And more. Much more.

Mentally trying to list the U.S. presidential succession to cool his ardor, he followed Julia downstairs.

"Dallas and I haven't eaten lunch," she said in the hallway.

Miriam scowled. "You, my dear, can skip lunch if you're going to fit in that wedding gown. Dallas can eat—" she waved her hand dismissively in the air "—anywhere."

"Sorry, Miriam," Dallas replied, moving to the parlor. "Julia and the baby need to eat properly. We'll split Mary Louise's basket. You can eat your half on the way to the florist."

Julia beamed and patted her stomach. "My condition."

"Honestly, you two. I never saw a couple get so much mileage out of a pregnancy."

A *couple*. Dallas finished dividing the contents of the picnic basket as he let that word sink in.

"There." He'd taken three sandwiches and an apple for himself. The women could have the rest. Mary Louise had packed for an army. "I'll carry the basket out to the car for you. Julia, you'll lock up?"

As the threesome moved outside, Miriam seemed to be studying Dallas. "You could come with us," she offered tentatively.

"No, ma'am. I have a few things I need to ask the Sutters." Although her attempt to include him pleased him.

"Oh, ask them if the courier delivered their invitation," Julia said.

"I don't understand."

"Because the wedding's in two days, we've had the invitations hand delivered."

"But to the Sutters?" For some reason, Dallas had figured this would be a Richardson affair through and through.

Julia cocked her head to one side. "I assumed you'd want them, Dallas. They're your family."

He didn't argue, but he'd never thought of the Sutters as family. Despite their kindness, he'd always thought of them as the people who'd put up with him. As always, Julia had assumed the best about people and relationships. As always, she'd seen the glass as half-full where he'd seen it half-empty.

Dallas strode toward the Sutter barn. Puzzled over the events of the past few days, he needed to talk to Aaron.

Miriam Richardson had seemed to soften toward Dallas as the inevitability of a wedding became apparent. At least she'd resigned herself to the event. Big Daddy, on the other hand, had not resigned himself to anything concerning his future son-in-law's sudden appearance and unexpected stay. The old man barely tolerated the younger at Ten Oaks and seemed nearly apoplectic at his presence in the lumberyard.

Uncharacteristically, Dallas felt ill at ease broaching the subject with Julia, considering their unusual circumstances and altered relationship. But he needed to know why Big Daddy hated him so much.

Maybe Aaron Sutter could shed some light on the subject.

Dallas could see both Aaron and Helen unloading baled hay from a pickup. They paused when they caught sight of him, genuine welcome written on their faces.

"We hoped we'd be seeing more of you," Aaron said.

Helen brushed the back of her palm across her forehead. "That was some invitation came this morning."

Dallas suddenly felt uncomfortable. "I know it's late notice. If you have something else more important—"

"Nothing's more important," Helen declared. She squinted at Dallas. "Why the long face?" she asked in her usual blunt manner.

He'd come to get some frank answers to a hard question. There was no use delaying. "Can either of you tell me why Big Daddy Richardson would hate me?"

Aaron scratched his head. "*Hate's* a strong word."

"Well, it's not strong enough for the gut reaction Julia's father has for me."

"I expect," Helen offered, "it's because he sees you as taking away his only child. Lord only knows how he doted on that girl. She was the child of his late years, and the time Miriam had delivering her, he knew he'd never have another."

Dallas hadn't known that last fact. It somehow humanized Big Daddy. "But this goes back to when I was a kid."

Aaron frowned, then said something odd. "Every parent wants the very best for his child. With you living so close to the Richardson property, I think Big Daddy had his eye on this day ever since you started to shave. Your friendship with Julia may have been secret, but that wouldn't have stopped the man's suspicions and fears."

Dallas looked hard at Aaron. The Sutters were childless. But the catch in Aaron's voice when he'd said "every parent" had hinted at a deep and heartfelt emotion.

"You know," Helen added, "this whole dislike might have arisen not so much because of Dallas but because of the feud Big Daddy had with Rhetta."

This was the first Dallas had heard of a feud between his future father-in-law and his mother.

"You may be right, Helen." Aaron chuckled. "Rhetta Parker was one of the few in Cannons Crossing who never caved in to Big Daddy's will."

"What are you talking about?" Dallas couldn't believe his ears. His mother had been tough, but he'd always thought she'd avoided her neighbors, the Richardsons. The Sutters were suggesting a more confrontational woman.

"The land your house stood on," Aaron explained, "was—

is—prize bottomland. Big Daddy coveted it the way he covets anything of exceptional value. Your mama, though, wouldn't sell, no matter how much pressure old man Richardson exerted. No matter how many ugly rumors about her he spread.''

"Wait a minute." Dallas held up his hand. "I always thought Mama *rented* that property."

A shadowed look passed between the couple. "No. She owned it," Aaron said.

"But when she died, there was nothing." Dallas worried this new information. "The state people never mentioned property."

"You were a minor. They wouldn't necessarily have discussed your mama's estate with you." Helen averted her eyes. "Maybe the state took the property. Maybe it went to pay debts."

"There could have been a large debt," Aaron said softly.

The Sutters had always appeared uncomfortable discussing Rhetta Parker. In Dallas's stay with them, they'd only talked of her if he'd brought up the subject first. Dallas had never known if they viewed her with the same disdain the rest of Cannons Crossing had shown, or if they were trying to spare Dallas pain.

He was beginning to think the latter.

"After what he did," Dallas said, "she wouldn't have willed it to my father...would she?"

Aaron blanched. "What makes you think of your father after all these years?"

He hadn't told Julia of his plans because they might come to nothing, but he had to tell someone. "I'm thinking of finding my father. Or, at least, his identity."

"But why?" Unmistakable shock registered on Helen's face. "It might only lead to sorrow."

"I have to. For Julia." He leaned against the fender of the pickup. Let the cold metal ease his heated blood. "Family means so much to her. I have nothing to offer her. A name would be a start."

Aaron shook his head vehemently. "You have grit and determination and a big heart, Dallas Parker. No one could ask for more.''

"Julia hasn't asked for more. But I need to give it to her."

"You must purely love the girl," Helen murmured.

If he did, he wouldn't admit it aloud. He'd just laid too much of himself bare before the Sutters as it was.

Chapter Eight

The day before the ceremony had begun under hazy skies blanketing unseasonable heat and humidity. The weatherman had promised a storm front with cold air behind it. The approaching front brought the threat of severe thunderstorms, but tomorrow should be a glorious fall day. Cool, crisp and fair.

As much as Miriam would have dearly loved a garden wedding, she took no chances by scheduling the rite for the solarium.

Late-afternoon sun squeezed around the drapes in Julia's room, a particularly bright shaft highlighting the wedding gown hanging just outside her closet. Lying in her bed, staring at the dress so hurriedly chosen, Julia wondered if she would make it through the next twenty-four hours with her wits intact.

Not to mention keeping her friendship to Dallas Parker unscathed.

Julia rose to sit on the edge of the bed. The nap hadn't

helped. Her headache hadn't been eliminated, only smudged. She still felt tension in the pit of her stomach.

All the fragmented concerns of the past week—telling her parents about her plight, her new job, Dallas's new job, Big Daddy's continued animosity toward Dallas—had almost eclipsed the fact that Julia was about to marry her best friend.

That fact hit her now with undiluted intensity.

She was about to marry Dallas Lee Parker and settle down in Cannons Crossing. Incredible.

What had brought the two of them—two independent people with personalities as different as night and day, with nothing more than a kiss between them—to this pass?

Getting slowly out of bed, Julia had to admit that *at this point in time* they each needed the other. They needed the mutual strength their old friendship could provide. They both needed to get their bearings and plot a future from an unexpected past. Julia needed a partner in this new adventure of parenthood. Dallas needed to discover that he could make a living at something other than rodeo.

But what would happen to their marriage as the immediate need lessened? What would happen as they found their balance? As they each made new goals. As they grew and changed.

Julia crossed to her bathroom, where she began to brush her hair with rough strokes, creating static that mirrored the buildup in the atmosphere at large. The pressure—natural and man-made—rose both outside and inside the Richardson mansion. Julia felt the stress but thought only of Dallas.

Dallas had said her child needed a father. He'd been solicitous of her condition this past week. But how did he really feel about her unborn baby? Another man's baby. Would he legally adopt it? Or would he view it as a ward? An obligation. Would the support he pledged be deep and emotional, or did he think that a second income was more than enough effort?

You should ask him outright, Julia prodded herself mentally. But there was a small dark thorn lodged near her heart that warned of certain answers. In his life, Dallas had been shown a hardscrabble love and limited commitment. As much as she admired and respected him, she couldn't say for certain whether he was capable of the kind of lasting emotional relationship she craved. And the baby needed.

Furthermore, she felt it patently unfair to insist that Dallas give in ways foreign to his nature. He was who he was, and she'd always loved him for it.

"I don't believe this is how a bride-to-be should feel the day before her wedding," she muttered, heading for the bedroom door. She would find the other members of the household. Even Richardson pyrotechnics were preferable to this dark and heavy mood that dogged her.

As she descended the stairs, she could hear loud voices raised in argument. They came from the direction of the library, where Dallas and Big Daddy were to have their final fittings.

Having crossed the foyer, Julia opened the double doors to a bizarre sight.

Dressed in matching tuxedos, Dallas and Big Daddy stood, squared off, secured a safe distance from each other only by the two obviously nervous tailors who hovered about them, making the necessary alterations to the wedding suits.

So intent were the men on each other that they didn't notice Julia stopped in the doorway, her arms crossed, prepared to let her fiancé and her father work out their differences despite the pain it brought her to see them constantly at odds.

"You want me to hang myself," Dallas growled between clenched teeth. "Okay." He balled his fists tightly at his sides. "Give me the rope and thirty days. Let me make some managerial decisions. If I fail, I'm out of your hair for good."

"What you're asking is for me to give away the store." Big Daddy's face was florid, his words laden with deep resentment. "Some businessman you're turning out to be."

"I'm asking that you give your employees a discount on materials they buy from your yard. Even the mall stores give their minimum-wage employees as much."

"I give 'em decent pay," Big Daddy snarled.

"And precious little else. If you cut them a break now and again, showed them that you thought of them as human beings, you might reduce the sabotage and theft. Most of these guys do their own home repairs. They're forced to get their materials from you because—short of Macon—you're the only game in town. When they feel they're never given a break, they take what revenge they can. In petty larceny on the job."

"I can absorb what little losses you think you've observed." A smirk crossed Big Daddy's face. "What matters is, he who has the power…has the power."

"Power! You think that makes you a businessman. A man, even. You overblown egomaniac!" Dallas jerked toward Big Daddy, only to be restrained by the tailor who protested around the pins sticking out of his mouth.

"Sir! I'll be done a lot faster if you'd just cooperate."

Dallas did settle down somewhat but continued to glare at Big Daddy. "I'm asking you to do what's decent. In the long run, it'll raise your bottom line."

Julia had heard enough. Her headache threatened. She stepped into the room. "Could you two, *please,* declare a truce for the next twenty-four hours? For my sake."

Big Daddy looked sorely aggrieved. "He started—"

"Boys!" Julia held up her hands. "No finger-pointing! I haven't the strength to apply the strap."

One corner of Dallas's mouth twitched. "How was your nap?"

"Only slightly more restful than your fitting." She turned to go. "We need to talk when you've finished in here."

"You're finished," Dallas's tailor declared with obvious relief.

"Meet me in the kitchen when you've changed?" Perhaps Mary Louise could provide a quiet nook and a soothing glass of tea. Julia did need to have a straight talk with Dallas. About the baby.

"Give me five minutes." Dallas had already shrugged off the tux jacket.

"Five minutes to torment me with your presence and your plans to ruin me," Big Daddy muttered.

"Since you brought it up," Dallas snapped back, "let's talk about those half-dozen men you've let linger in jobs they're ill suited for...."

Julia refused to listen to any more. She went in search of her mother, because she knew that Dallas and Big Daddy would be at it for more than five minutes.

It seemed that Dallas had been consumed with his new job these past few days. Driven. And Julia couldn't quite put her finger on the reason why. Was he trying to prove himself—to her and to her father? Was he trying to forget rodeo? Was he trying to numb the fact that he'd rashly committed to solving a problem that wasn't his?

He didn't have to marry Julia.

He could walk away at any time. Hadn't he just told Big Daddy that if he failed in the lumberyard, he'd be out of the way for good? What did that mean? If he could walk away from the job, could he walk away from Julia? What was his tolerance for failure? In a job. In a relationship. Even the best of marriages hit rocky patches. Would their childhood friendship be strong enough to guide them? Or would Dallas finally realize that he didn't have to stick with a woman he didn't love and a child he hadn't conceived?

"Lordy, what an ugly mood you're in, girl," she muttered to herself. And this time she couldn't do the one thing that always cheered her up—call her best friend for unbiased advice.

"Julia!" Miriam stepped out of the solarium, a genuine smile wreathing her features. "Come see!" The mother reached out and clasped the daughter's hand.

Julia stepped into the enormous, two-story, glass-enclosed room. It smelled of the tropics and of the orchids Miriam grew by her own hand. Ever since childhood, Julia had loved the adventure of this room. The stone paths. The palms. The exotic plants. The waterfall and pond. The hummingbird pair that had one year become trapped inside and that had made this their paradise ever since. Before now she hadn't looked in to see how her mother had prepared the room for the wedding because she'd been afraid that Miriam might kill the wildness of the setting with satin bows and sconces and formal floral arrangements.

To her amazement, an enchanted world met her eyes. Not changed so much as enhanced by fairy magic.

There were no white satin bows. The flowers that the florist and her assistants had been trucking in for the past few days had been tucked artistically amid the plants already growing in the gardens that lined the winding paths. The central clearing that usually held patio furniture had been reworked, the wicker and wrought iron replaced with seating for twenty-five guests. Tiny, tiny white lights winked from the palms and miniature trees as if the stars had come to earth and nestled amid the branches. The waterfall burbled. Stowaway crickets chirruped softly. An early storm-induced dusk descended outside the windows, highlighting the magic within. Making the enclosed solarium seem a refuge from the turbulence of the larger world.

Julia felt transported. And breathless.

"Do you like it, baby?" Miriam asked, worry creasing her forehead.

"How could I not?" Julia whispered. "Oh, Mama!" She turned to embrace her mother. "You're an angel!"

"I don't know about the angel part." Miriam stroked Julia's hair. "But I do want you to be happy. Tomorrow. And always."

Tears formed in Julia's eyes. She sidestepped out of her mother's embrace and took a seat on a little stone bench to the side of the pathway.

"Honey?" Miriam sat beside her. "You *are* happy, aren't you?"

Julia didn't know. She did know, however, that if she were to enter this room tomorrow, knowing that Dallas loved her, she'd be the happiest woman on earth.

* * *

Dallas hurried toward the kitchen. He hoped Julia was still waiting for him. In arguing with Big Daddy, he'd purely let time slip away.

He shook his head and grinned. Life with Julia resembled nothing of life on the rodeo circuit. Rodeo life was black-and-white: stay on the bull or bronc. Avoid injury. Earn enough money to keep the bill collectors at bay. But life with Julia—and that had to include Cannons Crossing and the Richardson family—had developed into a series of tricky grays.

Take Big Daddy.

Please.

Big Daddy seemed to be the one person in Cannons Crossing—short of Mandy—who still regarded Dallas as the bastard without a future.

But—and this was an enormous *but*—even Big Daddy's animosity had changed subtly in the past few days. Standing toe-to-toe with him just now in the library, Dallas had seen an unfamiliar sparkle in the old man's eyes. As if he actually enjoyed the mental exercise the go-arounds with his future son-in-law provided.

Surprisingly, Dallas had to admit he enjoyed the sparring, too.

As much as he prepared to settle in for a lifelong feud, he couldn't deny the grudging respect he felt for Julia's father. Big Daddy was a survivor. Like himself. Fiercest when he was protecting his own. Dallas, also, had begun to feel this elemental protective urge. Toward Julia and her baby. Moreover, Dallas could imagine that Big Daddy, as powerful as he was, feared losing his daughter's affection—or at least feared the change in affection a wedding would bring. Change could be frightening even to the strongest man. Dallas could understand that. He found himself smack in the middle of the most disconcerting altered life-style.

Too, he'd begun to realize that it wasn't easy sharing Julia's attentions.

Like now.

She'd told him to meet her in the kitchen, the one room

that would probably be mobbed with people preparing for the wedding. Had she done this to keep him at a distance? Regardless of heat and humidity, they could have talked with much more freedom out by the old oak tree. And he really needed to talk candidly about another variation of gray in their lives. The baby and to what extent Julia wanted to share the child's upbringing with Dallas.

He knew that technically this was *her* child. He knew Julia's history of stubborn independence. But just as he'd told her he wasn't entering this marriage with an eye to divorce, so too he wasn't proposing a half-baked parenthood.

He wanted to be this baby's father. The real father. But he didn't know if he'd have to argue with Julia for that right. Didn't know how much, if any, convincing she needed. The only way he'd ever ease his mind on this subject was to do what he'd always done in times of uncertainty—talk to Julia.

He took a deep breath. Talking to Julia these days seemed more and more of a challenge.

Maneuvering around workers carrying china and silverware toward the dining room, he entered the kitchen—the madhouse he'd expected.

Miriam stood nearby, hands on hips, anguish written on her face. "Honestly, Mary Louise! Lobster Newburg…and biscuits?"

"Dallas loves my biscuits." Mary Louise set her shoulders. "And biscuits aren't that much different from puff pastries. Better than the toast tips you'd get at the Battlefield Inn. Biscuits'll give the dinner a Southern flair, too."

Miriam threw her hands in the air. "Why don't we just stuff the mushrooms with grits instead of wild rice? Pour redeye gravy over the asparagus instead of hollandaise?" She turned to Dallas. "Talk some sense into her, please. She seems to idolize you."

"Where's Julia?"

"Oh…somewhere." Miriam looked around distractedly before leveling her gaze at Dallas. "The menu, darling. Talk some menu sense into Mary Louise.'' She turned on her heel and left Dallas with a flustered cook.

"Don't let her get to you," he urged. "You've never made a bad meal yet." Patting the cook's shoulder, he winked. "Biscuits, grits and redeye gravy sound good to me. If only to see the governor's reaction." He spotted Julia sitting by the window in the breakfast nook. "Excuse me."

He could barely make his way through the crowded kitchen. So many people at so many tasks. Pastry, linens and flowers competed for counter space. He thought he'd heard that the wedding party would be no more than twenty-five. Lordy, he'd seen less fuss at rodeo barbecues for two hundred. And less noise in the chutes.

At last he managed to slide onto a chair across from Julia, who sipped iced tea and absently gazed out the window. The light outside had grown eerily purple. Above the din in the kitchen, Dallas could hear the ominous rumble of thunder.

He placed his hand over hers. "Don't worry. The storm will blow over by tomorrow." He didn't like the faint circles under her eyes, an indication, surely, that the stress of homecoming and other people's plans for her future had caught up with her. Weren't pregnant women supposed to be shielded from stress? He needed to get better at his job of protecting her.

"The change in weather doesn't bother me," she said softly. "It's the change in those people I thought I knew that has me off balance."

Him. She meant him.

He'd changed, sure. As a result of both their altered circumstances. Because he'd been cut free from rodeo and because she needed him, he'd shocked her with the proposal for marriage. Shocked her further with the suggestion that they settle down in Cannons Crossing until the baby was safely delivered. Shocked her even more with his acceptance of Big Daddy's job offer.

How shocked would she be at the undeclared change within him?

They'd spoken only of the practicality of their plans based

on their long-lasting friendship. Would independent Julia turn tail and run if she knew of the growing emotional pull he felt for her? Of the physical attraction? She needed him now more than ever. She didn't need his scaring her off with feelings she probably didn't reciprocate.

"Hey," he said, "we could get out of here. Go to the cottage for the evening. It's got to be quieter than here. We can paint. Or talk. Or we can do absolutely nothing but enjoy the silence."

She shook her head wearily. "The rehearsal. You've forgotten about the rehearsal and dinner afterward."

"Well, then, let's make do. Right here. What did you want to talk about?"

"Julia! Dallas!" Miriam bustled over to the table. "The Reverend Howath is here. And so are your godparents, Julia. So we've got the witnesses. We're ready to rehearse if Martha can locate Big Daddy."

"Miriam." Dallas scowled. "Can you spare us a minute? Julia and I have something to discuss."

"Not even a second!" She tugged at their sleeves impatiently. "You have the rest of your married life to discuss. Save some of this for when conversation lags twenty years from now." She smacked the table several times in succession. "Up, up, up! Now!"

Despite Miriam's herding instincts, he would have sat in his chair, an immovable object, if Julia had shown signs of wanting to stay and talk. But she rose to follow her mother. Her face, her usually lively eyes, showed no sign of emotion. He didn't know if she'd deadened herself merely to the hoopla surrounding her...or to the thought of marrying him.

He needed to reestablish emotional contact with his old friend. And quickly.

"Julia." He reached for her hand. "I'm sorry if you feel pressured into this whole formal ceremony. I just thought—"

"Shh." She placed her fingers gently over his lips. "Your heart was in the right place. I guess I'd forgotten how overwhelming my family can be."

"Do you still want to marry me?"

"Yes," she replied, looking directly at him. She placed her hand over her stomach. "You've convinced me this baby needs two parents."

For an instant, he felt a flicker of disappointment. What would it be like if Julia had accepted his offer of marriage, not out of necessity, but because she loved him?

He should be so lucky.

"Come." She linked her hand with his. "Tonight won't be too bad. It's just the family, Mr. Howath and my godparents, Delta and Winton Macomber." A small smile raised the corners of her mouth. "Promise you won't leave my side."

Leave her? Never.

He knew she referred to the evening's events, but he had a more long-term outlook. She meant more to him now than she had at any time in his life. If he was patient, if he didn't push, perhaps she'd come to return the love that slowly but steadily grew within him despite the obstacles that faced them as a couple.

The rehearsal and most of the dinner over, Julia stood at the outer solarium door open to the gardens and fields beyond. She'd excused herself for several minutes from the dining-room table just as dessert was being served. Ever mindful of appearances, Miriam had shot her a troubled glance. Too bad. She needed air. Mr. Howath and the Macombers were almost family. Let them think she'd needed to use the powder room. Let them think she'd inherited the eccentric Richardson genes. Let them think she'd developed a case of nerves on her wedding eve.

They wouldn't be too far off the mark with that last one.

Thunder rumbled ominously close, but as yet no rain fell. Sheet lightning flared in the distance. It was difficult to catch a clear breath of air in the oppressive atmosphere.

"I came to see if you're all right," Dallas said from behind her.

Without turning, she felt his presence in little prickles of electricity running up and down her back. "I'm all right. I needed air."

He stepped to her side, then leaned artlessly against the doorjamb. "I'm the one who's supposed to crave the wide-open spaces. You're the one who's comfortable with crystal and twenty courses."

"Perhaps I'm more like you than either of us thought." She turned to face him. "Do you know that I really wanted a simple open-air ceremony—just my family and the Sutters as witnesses—under the old oak tree?"

"Why didn't you say so?"

"I don't know." She pinched the bridge of her nose to ward off a headache. "Perhaps because I thought this wedding would never take place."

"Why wouldn't it take place?"

"The entire past week has seemed so...unreal. Started by what you have to believe was an innocent phone call to an old friend. For moral support. Period."

"Why do I have to believe it was an innocent phone call? Do you think I might suspect you tricked me into marrying you?" Mischief sparked in his eyes as a lopsided grin tugged at one corner of his mouth. He was far too handsome for his own good. Far too attractive for them to ever revive the old sense of easiness that had been their friendship. "In reality, I've been plotting for twenty-three years to trick you into marrying me."

"Twenty-three years? Why twenty-three?" She knew he was just trying to distract her from her dark mood with light teasing, but at this point she welcomed distraction.

"I was in kindergarten when I first met you," he said with a simplicity that seemed devoid of distracting banter. "I'd already lost five years' momentum."

He couldn't be serious about wanting to marry her all these years. Perhaps the oppressive weather and the gravity of the upcoming wedding just made any attempt to recapture their usual light teasing fizzle.

Suddenly disconcerted by his nearness, she turned to look

out over the gardens and the fields beyond. "Do you know that you can see the crown of the old oak tree silhouetted whenever the sheet lightning flashes?" she asked to change the subject.

"Julia." He reached out and gently touched her hair. "When did we lose it?" he asked, his voice husky.

"Lose what?" She wouldn't look at him.

He stroked her hair. "The comfort in our relationship."

She did turn to him then. In surprise, that he felt the change, too.

He continued, his words soft and beckoning. "I used to be able to comfort you. Now I seem to be the one giving you grief."

"No!" How could he ever think that?

"Then why do I feel you slipping away from me?"

"I'm still here, Dallas. It's just that our relationship has become…a formal contract. I'm unfamiliar with the road we travel."

An enormous fork of lightning split the sky, followed seconds later by a deafening clap of thunder. Large drops of rain began to pelt the solarium windows.

"Come away from the doorway," Dallas urged. He stepped back into the room, pulling Julia up against him.

The electricity in the air, the sudden release of rain, the noise, all worked Julia's senses toward overload. Dallas's touch pushed her over the brink. She gazed up into his eyes and tried desperately to rediscover her old friend. Try as she might, she could only see a compellingly attractive man, a principled man who sought to help her because she was in need. A stranger who set her pulse racing. A knight in shining armor who wore her favor, but whose heart remained forever wild and free.

"Hold me," he said. "We'll both feel better."

She slid her arms around his firm waist. Leaned her head cautiously on his broad shoulder. Felt his strong arms enfold her, his soft breath in her hair. Maybe she hadn't realized it at the time, but she'd certainly been preparing twenty-three years for this moment. If only she didn't feel so restricted by this new marriage contract they'd formed. If only she didn't feel silenced by this emerging and unsure relationship. Then she'd ask him—outright—*Do you think you could ever love me?*

If only she weren't human and so very vulnerable to rejection.

Lightning raked the sky as, simultaneously, thunder rattled the solarium windows. Even as they stood back from the open door, a fine mist snaked into the room, enveloping them.

She shivered. "Dallas…"

"It'll be over soon," he murmured. "It's a fast mover."

He'd misunderstood. The weather had no power to touch her. Not here in this enchanted place. Not here in Dallas's arms. It was the wanting him that made her tremble.

The wanting him to want her.

She nestled closer in his arms and hoped he couldn't feel her wildly beating heart. "Why do things have to change? Things. Places. People…us."

"You're shaking." He moved back ever so slightly and looked down at her. "Don't be afraid. Underneath it all, it's still just you and me."

The heat and humidity had reached steamy proportions. Julia's head throbbed. A tiny trickle of perspiration ran down her spine. Dallas's midnight blue gaze held her immobile. In one lightning flash, she saw desire in the depths. Pure physical longing to match her own.

"It's just me," he repeated softly, lowering his lips to hers.

The thunder roared overhead as she clung to him.

His lips were hot, his tongue seductive. His hands pulled her close against him until she felt his unexpected hardness. One part of her heart still clung to their old relationship; the other strained to surrender to a new. She felt sadness and fear and exhilaration. But above all else, she felt exhilaration.

It happened all in a second.

Lightning so bright she could see it behind her closed eyelids. Thunder so loud her ears rang. And the awful smell of brimstone.

They pulled apart.

Framed in the open door, Julia saw a tower of flame in the distance. Just where the old oak tree stood.

"No!" The scream escaped her throat. Raw. Painful. "Not our tree!" The last tangible evidence of their innocent past.

Heedless of the pull of Dallas's hands, she fled. Through the doorway. Out into the storm. So much had been taken from her in the past few weeks. She'd borne it all. But she couldn't bear this. The destruction of their refuge. The symbol of an uncomplicated love and devotion.

Rain nearly blinding her, she stumbled through the gardens in the darkness. She must get to the tree. Perhaps it had been another struck by lightning. Not their tree.

"Julia!" Dallas said, right behind her. "Get back inside! It's dangerous!"

Yes, it was dangerous. This new love she felt for her old friend.

Brambles clawed at her skirt as she ran from the garden path into the field. Stones pushed up to hurt her feet through her thin-soled evening shoes. Lightning flashed all around her. Thunder crashed, a constant companion. Rain had drenched her to the skin. Dallas, chasing her, seemed less real.

He grasped her wrist, and she swung around with the interrupted momentum. "Come back with me!" he shouted over the roar of the storm.

"No!" Her wrist slick with rain, she pulled away from him. "Not until I've seen that the tree is okay!"

"For God's sake, Julia, it's just a tree!"

"No, it isn't. It's *us*." If he failed to understand that fact, she didn't know him after all.

He didn't argue. Instead, he shook his head and laughed into Mother Nature's furious face. "Heaven knows we've done crazier." He held out his hand to her. "Come on, pigtail girl! Let's check on our tree."

She relinquished her hand to his strong grip as they ran

together through the increasingly chill rain. He'd been right. It had turned out to be a fast-moving front. The lightning and thunder ranged farther and farther in the distance. The inky darkness left in the wake made footing treacherous. The wind had picked up, bringing them the acrid smell of charred wood. Hardwood.

Oak.

The terrain sloped upward. They had one small rise to conquer before they'd be able to see more than the oak's crown. The enormous tree grew in a sheltered dell. Climbing, Julia felt her lungs burn. Emotion pumped adrenaline through her body, however, giving her the strength to go on. Their tree would be all right. It had survived twenty-three years of their friendship, but before that it had withstood hundreds of years of violent Southern weather.

As they crested the hill, a flash of distant sheet lightning illuminated the horizon and the wreckage in the hollow.

A blackened skeleton was all that remained of the once noble oak. A faint red glow pulsed at the center of its trunk. The superheated wood gave off a menacing hiss in the steadily falling rain. The branches that had once sheltered childish dreams were gone—incinerated. Nothing remained on the ground about the base but ashes.

Uttering a ragged cry, Julia tried to run down the slope, but Dallas restrained her.

"It's still burning. Leave it."

Leave it? How could she? It had been the anchor of friendship. A symbol of security that had reached well beyond childhood. Any time, far from home, when she'd felt lonely or sad or a little lost, she'd thought of the tree. And Dallas.

The two were entwined.

No. The three—the oak, Dallas and she—were entwined. They'd been what was known, what was safe, what was supportive in an otherwise unpredictable world.

He wrapped his arms around her and pulled her close. Surely he felt the loss as deeply as she did. With the oak gone, a part of the past was gone. The familiar part that they could count on. What was left? The prospect of an obscure, contracted future shared by two strangers.

"It's gone." She moaned softly against his neck. "On our wedding eve. Why?" She shivered. Perhaps raging hormones were making her superstitious.

"There's no why. It just is."

"The oak was what I thought of when I thought of us. Strong…forever."

He scooped her into his arms and began to carry her home through the drizzle. The storm had spent its fury, leaving the landscape and Julia exhausted.

"It was us," she murmured, trying to make him understand.

"We'll make a new us," he replied, his words determined.

How could they? Their old center had been destroyed. Julia pressed her face against Dallas's cheek and sobbed.

Chapter Nine

Dallas threw cold water on his face. It was dawn of his wedding day, and he hadn't slept the entire night for worrying about Julia. He had to see her.

Last night, as soon as he'd brought her in from the storm, the Richardsons had taken over. They'd spirited her away to her room. They'd called the family doctor. Hell, Julia didn't need a doctor. She needed him.

Her fear for their future had been all too evident in the wake of the oak's destruction, and reassurance now fell to him.

He must tell her that he wasn't going to let her down just as she'd never let him down. She needed him to tell her that they were more than the sum of their shared pasts. More than friends. They were going to be husband and wife. Marriage of convenience or not, he was going to take their vows today seriously. She shouldn't have to worry that he would fail her. Sure, he'd spent the past ten years in a nomadic existence. But circumstances had changed. He didn't want her to be afraid of an uncertain future, an unreliable partner. He was as dedicated to her now as he'd been in their childhood.

More so.

He toweled his face dry, then headed for Julia's bedroom.

At the end of the hall, he could see a sliver of light under her door. He knocked lightly twice. "Julia, it's me. Dallas," he said, keeping his voice low.

The door opened, and Dallas found himself face-to-face with Miriam.

"Dallas Parker, you know it's bad luck for the groom to see the bride on the wedding day."

"Don't mess with me today, Miriam. I need to see that Julia's all right."

"She's fine. She rested during the night, and she'll rest today."

"The baby?"

"Fine, too." Miriam smiled. A surprising, genuine smile. Devoid of makeup and ulterior motive. "You and Big Daddy need to quit prowling around this door and find something to keep the two of you occupied for the better part of today. The wedding's at six. You only need to show up, dressed in your tuxedos."

"There's still going to be a wedding?" He'd worried this thought all night long.

"Why wouldn't there be?"

He wasn't sure. "I need to hear it from Julia."

From deep in the room came Julia's voice. Smooth. Even. Reassuring. "There's still going to be a wedding, Dallas."

He brushed quickly past Miriam, ignoring her clucking protest.

Julia lay propped up on pillows in the soft light of a single lamp, her dark hair feathered out around her head on the snow white linens. She looked pale, but calm and rested. Sitting gingerly on the edge of her bed, Dallas scooped up her hand in his.

"You're sure?" he asked. If she would just give him this

chance, he felt positive he could convince her over time that their marriage would work.

"For the baby, yes."

Ah, yes. For the baby. For a moment, he'd forgotten that this marriage wasn't going to be about Julia and him.

"About last night," he said.

She cast an uneasy glance toward Miriam. "I'd gotten over-tired. Emotional. That's all." She said it, but he knew she didn't fully believe that was all. Last night her emotions, down to her darkest fear, had been laid bare. This morning, however, she was back in control.

He wasn't sure he liked the armor that came with the control.

"Miriam!" Auntie Ouidie burst into the room. "What are the two of them doing in bed?"

"Talking, it appears." Miriam crossed her arms in front of her. "Don't have a coronary, Ouidie."

"Well, Norton certainly will if he sees this." The old lady descended upon Dallas, flapping her thin arms. "Shoo, young man! Shoo!"

"I'm going." Trying not to smile, Dallas rose. He bent to plant a light kiss on the top of Julia's head. "Rest well."

He crossed the room with Ouidie hot on his heels. Miriam actually rolled her eyes. "Richardsons," she muttered. It al-most seemed as if Miriam sympathized with his harried plight.

At the door, Dallas turned for one last glance at Julia. She looked small and somehow not quite as brave as before.

He was sorry he hadn't told her what he'd come to tell her. Hadn't had a chance to offer his reassurances. More than that, seeing doubt in her eyes, he now wanted to tell her how he really felt about her. A woman should know how her man felt before her wedding. But Dallas couldn't bring himself to bare his soul before Miriam and Ouidie. There were limits.

Vowing to find Julia alone before the ceremony, Dallas left to fill the hours before six o'clock.

Clutching a piece of paper with two names and addresses written on it, Dallas stepped out of his Caddy in Macon, in front of a roofing-supply wholesaler. His first stop.

There'd been no way he was going to stay around Ten Oaks, making small talk. Since Big Daddy had declared a holiday at the lumberyard, work wasn't an option. And the Sutters...well, Dallas's emotions were pulled every which way but loose today as it was. He didn't need to cope with his emerging feelings for his foster parents.

He thought he might try to track down two salesmen who'd called on Richardson Lumber twenty-nine years ago. He'd picked their names off old orders. They were the only two that had been full signatures and legible. It was a long shot, but it beat doing nothing.

He strode to the front door of the shop and pulled the handle. Locked. The posted hours gave none for Saturday.

What kind of a business was closed on Saturday?

Shading his eyes, he peered through the dirty plate-glass window. No lights. No movement. He was surprised at the disappointment that gnawed at his stomach.

He headed back to the Caddy.

With an eye on the second name and address on the paper, he reached through the car window and retrieved the map of Macon he'd bought at a gas station. The plumbing wholesaler appeared to be clear across town.

Dallas scanned the streetscape for a public phone, but came up with nothing. He had the time; he might as well make the drive. With a huge sigh, he slipped behind the wheel. No one ever said the search for his father's identity was going to be easy. Or fruitful.

Even for a Saturday, traffic was light in downtown Macon. The suburban sprawl and malls had taken care of that. Because Dallas wasn't forced to focus heavily on the road, he noticed Big Daddy, of all people, stepping out of a jewelry store.

With Mandy.

Dallas slammed on the brakes and ignored the rude gesture of the driver who swerved around him. His father-in-law-to-be had declared a business holiday, and this was too early in the year to be out shopping for Miriam's Christmas present. Now, what was the old goat up to? Dallas planned to find out. He wasn't about to have his father-in-law humiliating Julia or her mother on this day, especially.

He pulled into the next open curbside parking space, then charged out of the car. He'd let their initial reaction to his presence determine the couple's guilt or innocence.

Big Daddy had just handed Mandy into the passenger's side of his big white Lincoln Towncar as Dallas came abreast.

"Big Daddy," Dallas said nonchalantly. "Mandy."

The immediate scarlet blush on the secretary's face when she spotted Dallas told him in no uncertain terms that this wasn't an innocent business buying trip.

"What the hell are you doing in Macon?" Big Daddy sputtered, his own face becoming shiny and moist. "Why, if you're up to something Julia wouldn't want to hear about—"

"May I have a word with you...sir? Alone." Dallas stepped to the front of the long car.

With Big Daddy's smoke-screen accusation, Dallas had had a moment's hesitation over his own mission—over the fact that he hadn't as yet let his future wife in on this big-step search. But he let the flicker of guilt slide. Big Daddy, defender of family values, needed a frank review lesson from a future family member.

"This is not what you think," Big Daddy protested.

"I hope not."

"Even if it was, it's none of your damned business."

"Oh, I think it is." Dallas narrowed his eyes and stepped right into Big Daddy's private space. "For years you tried to make my mama and me feel cheap and dirty because there wasn't a man around our house. I'm beginning to look at it this way. Maybe my father took off because he knew we'd be better off without him. Maybe he took off to spare us the humiliation his cheatin' ways would have caused us. I think...sir...I'd rather have an absent father than a father who trampled on my mama's and his relationship in broad daylight." He slid his gaze to a very nervous-looking Mandy waiting in the front seat. "With a woman who's too young even to be his daughter."

"We were shopping for Miriam," Big Daddy snarled, lie written in his every nervous movement.

"I certainly hope so." Dallas remained passive. In control. "Because I would hate to see you screw up the family life you're lucky enough to have. A real lady for a wife. A daughter who loves you. A sister who depends on you." He leaned even closer. "And a son-in-law who'll be your worst nightmare if you hurt any one of them."

"You upstart rodeo bum! What makes you think you can talk to me this way? Who made you protector of the Richardson womenfolk?"

"Oh, I wouldn't think to usurp your position as head of the Richardson household...unless, of course, you prove yourself morally incompetent."

Big Daddy muttered and spluttered and cursed under his breath.

"Now, I'm not saying you need policing, by me or anyone else. Big Daddy Richardson's conscience and straitlaced ethics are renowned in Cannons Crossing. You could ask my mama if she weren't already dead from overwork and ostracism." Dallas's voice grew raw. "I'm sure you know the right thing to do." He stopped in midturn to go. "But I do suggest that if you can't keep your pants zipped, you find another secretary."

The fact that dead silence followed Dallas's walk back to the Caddy proved he'd not been wrong in his suspicions. That he'd been right saddened him.

What made a man who had the world by the tail cheat?

Dallas certainly didn't see himself as any deep philosopher, but this encounter had shaken him. He didn't try to fool himself that he'd been a saint in the hunger-and-passion department. But the thought of Big Daddy's jeopardizing a long and solid marriage angered him. And the thought of his ever risking hurting Julia in a similar fashion seemed insane. A man's word was important. And what were wedding vows but a man's word pledged in public no less?

Not to let him off the hook, but perhaps the old man had too much time on his hands. His duties as Cannons Crossing magistrate took only a few hours out of the day. The lumberyard almost ran itself. And the luster and competitive edge seemed to have worn off his prizewinning breeding program. Julia's father had accumulated every award and honor worth achieving. Maybe Big Daddy flat out saw Mandy as new territory to conquer.

Well, Dallas could surely think up a less harmful new territory. The memory of a conversation in the warehouse came back to him. Workers had been talking about a newly revived practice—logging with draft horses like Percherons and red Suffolks. Because horses could maneuver in a more precise manner than heavy machinery, the logging process became one of selection rather than clear-cutting. Lumbermen got a better grade of wood, environmentalists hailed the reduction of waste and the loggers rediscovered the satisfying bond between man and beast, proving once again that everything old can be new again. Not only had logging with horses become a small but growing business, but it had spawned new breeding techniques. New competition possibilities.

Dallas would talk to Walter Marshall, the man who seemed to have the most information on the subject, on Monday.

Driving the distance to the plumbing wholesaler, Dallas marveled at the thought that he was trying to help out a man who despised him. What did he care if Big Daddy crashed and burned?

What did he care? He never wanted to see the pain and ugliness the wreck would leave in its wake. He didn't want Julia to be hurt. Or Miriam. Or even Ouidie. Big Daddy would soon become Dallas's father-in-law. Vowing to protect Julia and her child, Dallas must overcome his own personal dislikes for the good of family harmony.

Family?

Had he just included himself in that alien concept? Hot

damn. This day was turning out with far too many unsettling surprises.

As Julia gazed in the full-length mirror, Miriam smoothed the skirt of her daughter's wedding gown, then stood back to survey the effect. "You are *the* most beautiful bride!" she exclaimed, tears welling in her eyes.

"Oh, Mama, don't cry."

"I can't help it. I don't think mothers are ever fully prepared for this day."

Julia suddenly saw her upcoming marriage through her mother's—her parents'—eyes. "I'm sorry. I haven't made the preparations any easier."

Miriam's features stilled. "Do you love him, Julia?"

Julia inhaled deeply before answering. With total honesty. "Yes, I do. Very much."

"Then that's all that matters."

"Do you really mean it? You aren't going to find fault with Dallas? Try to make me change my mind at the last minute?"

"No." Miriam shrugged. "You should have heard the ruckus my parents put up when I announced I was going to marry Big Daddy."

"They didn't approve?" Julia was shocked. Her mother had never been one to confide. Had always been one to maintain appearances, no matter what. Her maternal grandparents had been even more reserved. "You never told me this."

"I didn't see much point…until now." Miriam gazed wistfully out the window. "Your daddy and I have had a stormy marriage. I admit now that we were ill suited to each other from the start. But he loved me, and I still love him."

"And love is enough?"

"If you're determined to make it enough." Miriam giggled unexpectedly and blushed. "After all these years, your daddy still has the power to surprise me. Like this afternoon."

"Oh?" Julia had been thoroughly unprepared for this sharing. She began to see her mother—and her parents' relation-

ship—in a new light. Not from the egocentric perspective of
a child, but from the sympathetic perspective of a peer.

"Out of the blue, he brings me one perfect rose. And the
loveliest card written as a poem about the miracle of two lives
entwined…" With a sigh, Miriam's voice trailed off.

Julia felt almost as if she'd been eavesdropping on strangers. The man her mother now described was not the bellowing
father who'd ruled her childhood household with an iron fist.
She smiled to herself. So she wasn't the only Richardson
woman privy to a proud man's seldom-seen side.

With genuine emotion, she hugged her mother.

"It's time," Miriam said "Your daddy, Delta and Winton
are waiting downstairs. And, of course, Dallas."

Glancing in the mirror one last time, Julia suddenly felt like
an impostor. The gown was very real and very lovely. Simple
lines in silk and seed pearls. But Julia, wearing the gown, was
a stand-in for the woman—whoever she might be—who
should be preparing to wed Dallas Parker because he loved
her above all others.

"Sweetheart?" Miriam gently touched Julia's arm.

"I'm ready." Julia raised her chin, scooped up the hem of
her gown and, with a show of equanimity she didn't quite
feel, led the way downstairs to her waiting family, guests and
groom.

At the door of the solarium, Big Daddy stood—very still—
with Winton Macomber. Julia was struck by the subdued expression on her father's usually volatile features.

Smiling, Winton offered his arm to Miriam. "Everyone's
here. It's time for the mother of the bride."

With a little sniffle, Miriam hastily embraced Julia. "Be
happy, my baby," she urged.

Big Daddy offered his arm to Julia as Winton led Miriam
down the garden path to her seat. "It's not too late to pull
out," he muttered.

No, it wasn't. She could pull out now and know her future
for certain: she'd be the talk of Cannons Crossing polite society for years to come. An uncomfortable but manageable

future to be sure. But if she crossed the threshold into the solarium now, if she married Dallas, she wouldn't know from day to day how their relationship would play out. She would be a stranger in a strange land and could only hope for the best. Could only pray that the friendship that had bound them all these years would grow and deepen.

The harpist began to play the wedding processional.

Through the open door, Julia glanced down the path outlined with fairy lights. She could smell the intoxicating scent of exotic flowers and hothouse greenery and see the guests, standing now, waiting respectfully for the bride.

And she could see her groom. Dallas.

She inhaled sharply. How handsome he looked. How straight and strong and how calm. As if he wasn't being roped into an uncomfortable situation. In fact, he flashed her a grin—the same kind he used to send her the minute he caught sight of her at their tree.

The grin did it.

Julia gave her father's arm a gentle squeeze and stepped over the solarium threshold. As they said in showbiz, she'd passed the point of no return.

Stepping lightly in time to the music, she focused on Dallas. His unwavering regard gave her strength. Only he and she in this room full of people knew that this was a marriage in name only. A marriage of convenience.

She smiled. How convenient it would be, for today at least, to pretend that she married for love. She felt a flutter low in her abdomen and couldn't tell if it was the reaction to that giddy thought or the baby.

At the end of the aisle, Dallas stepped forward, offering her his arm. A low, menacing rumble came from Big Daddy as he clung to his daughter. But the die had been cast. Julia's future, she felt certain, entwined with Dallas Lee Parker's as her past had. Intricately.

She slipped her arm from her father's possessive clasp, then stepped to Dallas's side.

The Reverend Howath smiled beatifically down upon them. "Dearly beloved..."

Julia's old Sunday school teacher would have had conniptions if she knew how little Julia heard of the minister's words.

Dallas was the only presence she felt in the room. And she felt his presence like a pure, sweet flame.

Were all brides at the altar so oblivious to everything but their husbands-to-be? Or did Julia's conflicting emotions make her especially inattentive?

Dallas had turned to face her as the Reverend Howath began to ask the questions of the traditional wedding vows. "Do you, Julia Anabeth Richardson, take Dallas Lee Parker...?"

She did. Oh, yes, she did with the greatest trepidation. She did with a secret joy that made her nearly deaf and blind to the ceremony around her. Her response slipped out automatically. In turn, she saw Dallas's mouth move, but didn't hear his words.

"Please, join hands." The minister startled her out of her reverie.

She knew that Dallas spoke his vows at the Reverend Howath's prompt, but it made no difference. She looked into his level blue gaze and heard Dallas. Only Dallas.

He gently caressed her fingers. "I, Dallas, take thee, Julia, to be my wedded wife, to love and to cherish, to honor and comfort, in sickness or in health, in sorrow or in joy, in hardship or in ease, and forsaking all others, to have and to hold from this day forth." His voice came to her deep and true, his regard unwavering.

As she repeated her part of the vows, her own voice sounded distant to her ears. She was distracted by how *contractual* the words sounded. Practical. Realistic. No mention of romance and passion.

Julia scowled. Her great-great-grandmother had been a mail-order bride of sorts. Had built a solid marriage and had raised eight children on honor and practical realism. What right had Julia to quibble over hearts and flowers?

When Dallas shot Julia a quizzical glance, she consciously relaxed her furrowed brow.

The Reverend Howath raised two gold bands above his head. "Bless, O Lord, these rings...."

Never dropping his gaze from hers, Dallas accepted Julia's ring from the minister, then, without faltering, slipped it on her finger.

Julia had more trouble with his. His hands were big. Work roughened. Unused to jewelry or confinement. But, bless his heart, he held steady for her and sighed heartily when the band finally moved safely over his knuckle.

"For as much as Dallas and Julia have pledged themselves each to the other in the presence of this company, and have declared the same by giving and receiving a ring and by joining hands, I now pronounce that they are husband and wife."

Julia felt a hot blush creep into her cheeks as the assembled guests applauded. Husband and wife. The fact was truly unbelievable.

"Mr. Parker," the minister said gently, humor rising in his voice, "you may now kiss Mrs. Parker."

Here? In front of family and friends? Julia's heart seemed to skip a beat. Surely Dallas would balk at the convention.

On the contrary, if the look in his eyes could be believed, he relished it. Oh, he could be the consummate actor when circumstances warranted. That's precisely how he'd survived a childhood in a hostile environment.

Letting go of her hands, he slipped an arm around her waist and drew her close. It seemed that his lips descended upon hers in slow motion. Slow, sweet and heady motion. He pressed her backward to the point where she had to thread her arms around her neck and claim him as her own in public. When she did so, she felt his lips move in a sensuous smile.

And then he kissed her. Thoroughly. To a smattering of applause from the guests and a clattering in her heart.

The harpist struck up a spirited recessional.

Fortunately, as Dallas released her from his embrace, he tucked her arm securely in his. Because her knees were suddenly wobbly, she needed his support. Slightly dazed from his kiss, she looked out over the assembled guests, now standing, and felt a little like Cinderella at the ball, knowing that the gown was really cobweb and the carriage a pumpkin beneath the magic. A sham. All of it for show.

Her mother dabbed at her eyes and leaned on her father. Big Daddy glared at the newlyweds, his jaw set, his stance rigid. Across the aisle from her parents, Aaron and Helen Sutter purely beamed their delight. Aaron even sent them a quick thumbs-up.

With great dignity, Dallas led her up the aisle.

Halfway to the door of the solarium, Julia felt her baby move. More forcefully than in the past. With this reminder of the new life she harbored, her doubts of the moment fled. She had made the right decision. A choice for survival for her and her baby.

If Dallas kept his vow to honor her, she could ask for no more.

That didn't mean she couldn't secretly nurse the growing flame of love she felt for him. And tonight she could play the role of Cinderella to the hilt. Midnight was a long time coming.

Dallas and Julia made their way among the guests, saying their goodbyes. True to her word and Richardson reputation, Miriam had produced an elegant dinner-party reception. Along with Julia, she'd even tried to make Dallas comfortable among the powerful, celebrated and generally well-to-do guests.

Not so Big Daddy.

Relations had most definitely not thawed between Dallas and his new father-in-law. Their encounter in Macon earlier in the afternoon hadn't helped to ease tensions any. In fact, the old man's stare had become frostier as the evening had worn on.

Julia slipped her arm from Dallas's to embrace Helen Sutter. "I'm so glad you could be here!"

Squeezing her eyes shut, Helen gave Julia a long tight hug. "We wouldn't have missed it for the world."

Dallas didn't quite know what he and Aaron should be talking about. An awkwardness descended upon the two men.

His foster father first broke the silence. "You and Julia won't be too far from us. Come over any time to ride. I've maintained the trails. Of course, my horses aren't anything like Big Daddy's—"

"And I haven't been extended an invitation to ride any of Big Daddy's horses." Dallas shook his head. "Sometimes I wonder why he keeps any stock. He doesn't seem to derive much enjoyment from them."

"Funny, but you wouldn't think coming in first all the time would grow old."

"Do you know anything about logging horses?" The turn in subject was abrupt, but Dallas could use Aaron's advice.

"Only that my grandpappy used to get seasonal work logging. And the men worked with horses. I hear the practice is coming back. Good for the environment, the advocates claim."

"Are you talking business? On Julia and Dallas's wedding day?" Helen Sutter gave the two men each a playful swat. "Shame on you."

"Actually," Aaron replied, "I was encouraging Dallas not to be a stranger."

"I'll second that." Helen stepped forward and wrapped her arms around Dallas.

Dallas stood stock-still. Feeling ill at ease. It wasn't so much that the diminutive Helen only came up to his chest and that he could crush her if he heartily embraced her. It was that, in all his years of living with the Sutters, he'd never let either one of them touch him. As a teenager, he'd been proud of his ability to keep people at a distance and had worn his loneliness like a badge.

But now Helen didn't let him back away. He felt the small woman's warmth radiate through his tux, but still couldn't make his arms move to embrace her.

She stepped back at last, her eyes moist. "You're starting your own family, Dallas. How proud your mama would be to see this day."

Dallas started. In mentioning his mother, Helen had managed to catch him off balance twice. He could count on one hand the number of times Helen Sutter had ever referred to his mother in the past.

"Weddings!" Helen exclaimed, dabbing at her eyes. "They make a body go all to mush."

With remarkable ease, Julia slipped her arm about Helen's shoulders and dashed a kiss on the older woman's cheek.

Beautiful, sensitive Julia. His best friend. *His wife.* How absolutely unbelievable.

She turned her gaze to him and almost took his breath away.

As much as he'd felt like a fish out of water with the Richardsons' fancy reception and their high-level friends, the evening had provided a welcome buffer of sorts between the wedding ceremony and the time when Julia and he would be alone. He needed to come to terms with that prospect.

She slipped her hand in his. "Just a few more goodbyes," she promised.

He marveled at her calm, at the radiance that seemed to settle around her like a shawl. Just last night, after the destruction of the oak, he'd wondered if she wouldn't back out of the wedding entirely. She'd seemed afraid and lost.

Not so now.

Now she was warmth and composure and grace. As she said her goodbyes, her hand fluttered protectively to her abdomen. The baby. He'd heard people say that pregnant women glowed. They'd been right. His Julia was alight with an inner fire that surprised him.

Watching her, he felt a twinge of jealousy. He wished that he, rather than hormones, had ignited that fire. Earlier he'd promised to honor and comfort her. When he'd first proposed this marriage of convenience, he'd emphasized that her honor and her comfort were his motivations. But before all these assembled guests tonight, he'd also vowed to love and cherish her. Afraid that she might rebuff him, he'd never offered up those intentions to Julia in private.

But that didn't mean he couldn't hold them—a deep secret—in his heart.

"Well, my dears," Miriam piped up at his elbow. "It's time." She placed a hand firmly in the small of Dallas's back. "Now go before I cry."

"Oh, Mama!" Julia threw her arms around her mother as Big Daddy, glowering, approached Dallas, for whom the emotional intensity in the room had become unsettling. Was this what family was all about?

Big Daddy jerked his head to one side, apparently indicating he wanted to talk to Dallas in private. Dallas knew the man was still angry from the sidewalk encounter and comeuppance in Macon and hoped he didn't intend to make a scene that would upset Julia.

"You think Julia wants her mail tonight?" Big Daddy pulled an envelope from an inside jacket pocket.

"Mail?" Had the old man lost touch with reality? "This is our wedding night."

A wicked glint shone out of Big Daddy's slitted eyes. "This looks mighty important." He held the slim priority-mail envelope so that the return address was clearly visible. "A response, I think, to a letter Julia wrote earlier in the week."

"I think it can wait till Monday." Dallas couldn't get a handle on what devilry his father-in-law had in mind. Whatever it was, the expression on Big Daddy's face told him it was no good. He noticed, too, that the envelope, although addressed to Julia, had been opened.

Dallas glanced more closely at the return address. Boston. Initials and the last name, Samson. The writing a bold male scrawl. Just enough to make Dallas wonder if Julia had been in touch with the father of her child. And why.

Big Daddy's eyes widened. "Then again, it being your wedding night, perhaps mail can wait." He stuffed the envelope back in his jacket.

"Ready?" Julia's soft question at his elbow jolted Dallas.

He scowled even as he walked with her to the Richardson front door. Was he ready? How could he be when he didn't know what the future held in store? Was Julia keeping secrets from him? He felt a sudden twinge at the thought that he hadn't yet let her in on his own father search.

Less than total honesty didn't seem an auspicious beginning to any marriage.

Martha and Mary Louise stood on the veranda, smiling to beat the band. Hiram Ledbetter stood at attention next to the Caddy parked at the foot of the steps.

The Caddy.

Dallas barely recognized it. Polished to within an inch of its antique life, it proudly bore a Just Married sign between its two enormous fins. Old shoes, tin cans and satin ribbons streamed from the rear bumper. Even in the cool night air, the gardener had put the top down. Someone had ringed the back seat with magnolia leaves and white roses.

For a moment, Dallas felt as if he were watching the send-off for another couple. Strangers.

Then Hiram Ledbetter opened the passenger door, and Julia stepped easily into the car. Seated in the front, she extended her hand to Dallas. The look in her eyes beckoned with a stunning intensity.

This was his wedding. Julia was his bride. He was no longer a loner who could pull up stakes in a heartbeat. The situation would take some getting used to.

When Hiram Ledbetter held open the driver's door, Dallas mobilized his frozen limbs to seat himself beside his new wife. Felt her settle against him in the crisp fall air. As much as he'd wanted this ceremony to take place—for many practical reasons—he suddenly felt himself in uncharted territory. In convincing Julia to marry him, he'd told her he loved the twists and turns, the little surprises life threw his way.

Out of the corner of his eye, Dallas caught Big Daddy, a self-satisfied smirk on his face, staring hard at Julia and him.

For all his experience with the unexpected, this evening certainly beat all.

Chapter Ten

Julia and Dallas stood on the small front porch of their rented Victorian cottage. They were together at last, their lives now inextricably linked. And they were alone—truly alone—for the first time since their return to Cannons Crossing.

Inhaling deeply, Julia hazarded a glance at Dallas as he unlocked the door. He'd been remarkably quiet in the ride from Ten Oaks.

And she'd been remarkably nervous.

For the sake of her unborn child, she'd married in haste. She'd become pregnant in the first place because she'd acted precipitously in her Boston choice of lover. Furthermore, she saw her agreement to stay—even temporarily—in her hometown with her volatile and meddling family as a rash capitulation.

Some dowry of unthought-out decisions she brought to this marriage.

Having pushed the front door open, Dallas turned to her, his eyes clouded, his expression unreadable. With amazing strength and dexterity, he swept her up and into his arms. "For luck," he said, his voice husky as he carried her over the threshold.

Julia tensed instead of settling into his embrace—a disturbingly unfamiliar embrace. She no longer knew him. No longer knew herself in conjunction with him. The old oak tree had been destroyed, and with it the aura of their safe and abiding friendship. She didn't know what new emotions had stepped in to fill the void, although it was certain that Dallas and she could never be *just* friends again.

For luck, he'd said. They were going to need luck if this contrived and fragile relationship was going to work.

Dallas set her down gently in the small foyer. "Are you tired?" he asked.

Unable to find her voice, she shook her head.

"Hungry?"

Mute, she shook her head again.

"Thirsty?"

"Dallas…" She didn't quite know what she wanted to say, but she didn't want meaningless filler. Tonight they needed to begin to establish a new relationship. Ironically, it would be a lot easier to begin if he and she had a physical history.

This was, after all, their wedding night.

Trying to find a significant conversation starter, Julia took in her surroundings. The place that she'd chosen to be their home. From the subdued lighting in the foyer, she could see the glint of a silver ice bucket on one end of the mantel in the parlor. A bottle neck peeped over the edge. Two champagne flutes stood sentry next to the bucket, while an intricate candelabra awaited the match at the mantel's other end.

Miriam's contribution to romance.

Julia walked to the fireplace, lit the candles, then lifted the bottle from the ice bucket. Sparkling apple cider. Her mother hadn't forgotten her condition.

"A toast?" Holding the bottle out to Dallas, she attempted a smile. "For luck?"

Deftly, Dallas uncorked the bottle. With a loud pop, the

stopper hit the ceiling, leaving a distinctive ding in the finish. A rueful grin creasing his otherwise serious expression, Dallas shook his head. "It's just my luck we got in a big shipment of Spackle at the lumberyard yesterday."

He poured them each a glass of cider.

The champagne flute in Julia's hand felt awkward. The soft light in the room seemed awkward, too. As did the lack of conversation. Had Dallas and she in their long friendship ever so lacked for words?

Never.

Until this trip home.

She raised her glass.

"To the old Parker-Richardson team." He tipped his glass to hers. "Plus one."

"To new beginnings." As if on cue, the baby did its little polliwog slither. Julia smiled and rested her hand over her abdomen.

"About the baby," Dallas said, caution rimming his words. "About the baby's father."

Not knowing in which direction this train of thought ran, Julia stiffened. "What about the baby's father?"

Dallas leaned against the mantel, his features shadowed. "You've never told me if you...carry some kind of attachment to him still."

A chill ran through her. This had turned into a fine wedding-night discussion. What in the world had precipitated it? Suddenly, she felt like Cinderella just before the clock was to strike the midnight hour, bringing her fantasy evening to an end.

Dallas wanted to know if she still cared for the baby's father.

Humiliation knifed through her at the thought of her ex-lover. At his duplicity. At her gullibility. Her attachment to the cad had ended with his scorn and his betrayal. But she'd never fully discussed him with Dallas because she hadn't wanted her friend to think less of her as a result of her poor choices.

"He's married." She spoke between clenched teeth. "That's the end of it."

Dallas felt a pain thread around his heart. His mother had said nearly the very same words when, as a boy, he'd asked her who his father was. Her dismissive statement hadn't stopped the longing in Rhetta Parker's eyes, however. Against the odds, did Julia experience that same longing for a man she couldn't have? The answer suddenly mattered to Dallas. Very much.

But why?

Up until last week, he'd been unattached. Fancy-free. Reluctant to form any attachment longer than a scheduled stop on the circuit. He'd made no claims on any woman, and wanted none placed on him.

Now here he stood, caring very much whether Julia's heart remained free for the winning.

Julia placed her glass on the mantel. All semblance of ease had vanished from the room. Why had he brought up the baby's father when he hadn't thought two thinks about him since Julia had told her story at the airport?

Big Daddy and his not so subtle hints. That's why.

Removing her simple veil, Julia appeared tired. "I don't want to talk about…*him*…tonight of all nights."

Neither did he.

But the image of Big Daddy, drawing that envelope with the Boston return address from his jacket, had nagged at the optimistic mood established by the wedding ceremony. Add to the image the fact that his father-in-law, if indeed he'd read Julia's mail, *might* now know of the baby's real father, a small bit of information Julia and Dallas had carefully hoarded from the Richardsons. The extent of Big Daddy's understanding hinged upon the nature of the communication between Julia and the man named Samson.

Dallas tried not to let the memory of the envelope drive a wedge between Julia and him. Not tonight, when everything about their relationship was so new. So brittle.

Julia stood before him all in white. Beautiful except for the pain in her eyes. Under childhood circumstances, the pain would have drawn him to her; tonight it made her seem unapproachable.

"Dallas, how do we start?"

He'd been wondering the very same thing. He took a deep breath, then reached out his hand to her. "The same way we always did. By talking."

He gently drew her to the sofa, which had mysteriously arrived after Miriam had noted their total lack of furniture. It was the only piece in the room. When they sat, Julia pulled away from him. Curled up well against the farther armrest.

"I get so tired at night," she said, "and so unaccountably emotional when I'm tired. The doctor said some women react to pregnancy that way." For an instant, her eyes fluttered closed. "I don't like losing control."

"If you're tired, maybe we'd better turn in."

"No!" Her eyes flew open. Her blush was instantaneous and deep scarlet. "I couldn't sleep. Not yet. I'm still too keyed up." Her immediate unease told him sleep wasn't the real worry.

A half smile tugged at one corner of his lips. Damn, but they were neither fish nor fowl. The kiss in the Sutters' barn and the second in the solarium last night had taken them beyond friendship. The ceremony this evening had legally catapulted them toward intimacy. But were they ready to be lovers?

His body told him they were.

Watching her in the flickering candlelight, he couldn't help but want her. Couldn't help but find her desirable. If he were truly honest with himself, he'd have to admit that he'd always desired her. But Julia was no circuit groupie to be bedded in haste. She was a lady who'd been hurt. A woman made vulnerable by her situation. A cherished friend—yes, no matter what, still a cherished friend—who trusted him.

"Julia, honey—" He meant to reassure her, but a godawful caterwauling erupted outside the cottage.

Julia let out a shriek, then clapped her hands over her mouth as he rose to discover the cause. He expected to see fear in her eyes, but instead he saw amused comprehension.

"What the—?"

"Ooh, Lordy, it's the shivaree!" As if she hadn't just said she was tired, she jumped up from the sofa, flew to the mantel and blew out the candles. The cacophony outside increased.

He groaned. Shivaree. A singularly bizarre wedding-night ritual that persisted in pockets all over the South. He'd never participated in one, and he never, ever expected to be on the receiving end.

"Come! Come!" She grasped his hand and pulled him toward the foyer and the staircase. "If we don't give them what they want, we'll never get rid of them!"

"What do they want?" He balked at following her. An outsider, he'd only heard of shivaree shenanigans minus the details.

"Not much." She giggled as she hiked up her wedding dress to climb the stairs. "Just foolishness, but we'd best comply or we'll be deaf by dawn."

That was the truth. The noise combined the singular torture of fingernails down a chalkboard and hog calling. He'd do anything within reason to stop it.

At the head of the stairs, Julia turned, then entered the front bedroom. Once in the room, however, she didn't switch on a light. With darkness her cloak, she quickly glided, a ghostly white figure, to the window, which she threw open.

"What are you doing?" Following closely behind her, Dallas reached to shut the window and shut out the din, but she lay her hand on his arm to stop him. In amazement, he looked first at her, then down at the motley crew on the lawn outside.

He recognized Warren Biggs. The worker stood at the fore of the group, strumming an antique washboard and yowling to beat all. Hiram Ledbetter stood behind him, pounding an empty paint can. Others—some Dallas recognized, some he didn't—beat an assortment of household objects and sang like alley cats. One fellow actually strummed a guitar, but it appeared that real music in any form was not to conquer the evening.

When the serenaders caught sight of Dallas and Julia above them, they began a rhythmic, insistent, incomprehensible chant.

"You're going to have to guide me through this one." In confusion, Dallas turned to Julia. "What stops them?"

"This."

He felt her fingers grasp the front of his shirt. Felt her pull him firmly toward her. Felt her lips on his before he knew what hit him. Noise roared in his ears.

Instinctively, he wrapped his arms around Julia and drew her into the kiss she'd so boldly started. Hell, if they had to do this all night to ward off the shivaree, he was more than game.

A cheer went up from the small crowd below.

Just as Dallas began to warm to the reality of Julia in his arms, she pulled away. The demanding chant began anew.

"What—?"

She drew him away from the window. "They want something to prove we're on our way to bed."

"Such as?" He couldn't believe the craziness. Couldn't believe, either, the change in Julia. From the exhausted, tentative woman of a few minutes ago, she'd turned into the mischievous imp of old.

He liked the change. Yes, indeed he did.

"Your shirt!" Her fingers already flew at the buttons.

"My shirt?" In unbuttoning his shirt, her fingertips grazed his bare skin. Her touch tickled his senses clear to his toes. He'd sacrifice a shirt for that pleasure any day.

With a lovely bell-like laugh, she peeled the dress shirt from him. Could she know what her change in mood, what her uninhibited playfulness, did to him? To the physical impulses he'd been trying to keep in check all week?

He took the shirt from her with the intention of throwing it to the waiting shivaree crowd. He suddenly wanted them gone so that he could be alone with this renewed Julia.

"No!" She caught at the shirt. "The wife has to throw the husband's clothing and vice versa. To prove...something...amorous, I guess...." Her words trailed off in a soft giggle.

Whatever she had to prove, she boldly stepped to the window, then flung the shirt with a motion that would make a centerfielder proud.

A cheer went up from below.

She turned to him. "Now me!"

He was supposed to peel off an article of her clothing? He began to appreciate what had before been only a ridiculous ritualized prank.

Tapping her index finger to her chin, she paced as the still unsatisfied group below renewed its chant. "Not my veil. No jewelry. Certainly not the gown. The shoes I could dye and use again."

He had a couple more-intimate ideas.

"Dallas! No!" she warned. Obviously, his thoughts had grown transparent in the rising moonlight.

The chanting had become much louder. Certainly more insistent.

"I know!" Kicking off her high heels, she placed one foot upon the windowsill and slid her skirt up the length of her shapely leg, stopping at a frilly garter.

Dallas only marginally noticed the garter.

"Mama thought that throwing it at the reception would be tacky." She cocked her head expectantly at him. "You have to remove it...it's tradition."

And he was a traditional kind of guy.

The whistles rose from below as Dallas approached Julia. He suddenly felt in the spotlight and unaccountably nervous. "This doesn't bother you?" he asked. "This public show?"

"No." Her moon-drenched gaze locked on to his. "Shivaree is silly, yes, but it's a community's show of acceptance."

Acceptance. What a loaded word.

He reached out for the garter. Slipped his fingers under the elastic confection. Felt the silky warmth of Julia's skin. Grew deaf to any sound but that of his own breathing. As he slid the lacy band down her leg, he became aware with every smooth inch of flesh that this woman was now his wife. And no one but Julia and he knew the real circumstances of their marrying. The only restrictions to their future relationship would be ones that Julia and he designed.

Now, that thought boggled the mind.

Julia wriggled her toes enticingly as he slid the garter over her bare foot. A cheer erupted from below.

Without taking his eyes from Julia's smiling face, Dallas cast the garter sideways from the window, then drew his bride into a crushing embrace.

Old friends, they'd been flung together out of mutual necessity, but out of that need arose a compelling new intimacy. Although Dallas didn't fully understand this fresh and untested union, he couldn't resist it.

Especially with the feel of Julia in his arms.

He looked down to find her laughing up at him.

"Thanks for coming through like a champ," she said with just enough saucy mischief in her eyes to make his pulse race. "Who knew you were so good at keeping up appearances?"

Did she think he'd acted only to keep up appearances? Perhaps she needed to be shown otherwise.

He glanced out the window. The shivaree participants, satisfied, had dispersed, their laughter and goodwill still drifting on the evening air. "Do you see anyone out there I need to impress?"

"No." Her response came whisper soft.

Her eyes grew wide. Her hair, disheveled by all the frenetic activity, floated in a wild cloud about her head. Her cheeks showed the growing stain of a blush. In her white gown, she looked for all the world like an angel fallen to earth before him in this bedroom prepared for strangers.

She was his earthly angel. Real. Close. And very desirable.

In an instant, he dismissed her Boston past. He dismissed the fact that she'd accepted his proposal out of necessity. Dismissed impending parenthood. Dismissed his own, less than stellar standing in the community. He dismissed, too, the envelope in Big Daddy's jacket pocket.

One thought remained: they were alone. And he only ever felt whole alone with Julia. He needed her. Always had. He wanted her. And if his skill at reading people ran true to form, she felt the same want and need as he. Felt, too, the same vulnerability.

Vulnerability be damned tonight.

He drew her into his arms and lowered his mouth to hers.

Dallas's kiss seared Julia's senses, flinging common sense out the window along with his shirt and her garter. Desire and abandon rose strong and heady. She wrapped her arms around him and returned his kiss.

His mouth tasted of sparkling cider and childhood laughter and a new delicious, unknown flavor—faintly tart and forbidden. She didn't care. The week of suppressed truths and hidden emotions had taken its toll. Had, against all intention, stoked her passion. Had made her reckless.

Dallas and she were legally wed. The shivaree and the moonlight and this kiss suspended the reality of ex-lovers and babies and meddlesome families and an emerging relationship not properly spelled out. For Julia, fantasy reigned tonight.

Come what may, she would seize tonight against all logic.

"I want you," Dallas growled, pulling away only slightly.

She flicked her tongue over his powerful chest in answer. Ran her fingers down the taut muscles of his abdomen all the way to the zipper of his tux trousers. She felt his sharp intake of breath. Pure, mindless want washed over her.

"Julia!" He grasped her shoulders. "Do you know what we're doing?"

She looked deep into his midnight-darkened eyes. "I haven't a clue." Although a sense of absolute rightness pervaded her ignorance. Because she trusted Dallas, she felt safe. Because she felt safe, she felt suddenly free and daring. She smiled. "Do you?"

A slow, sexy grin spread over his rugged face. A lock of

dark hair fell over one eye. "We may have all hell to pay later."

"Let's let later take care of itself."

"Miz Parker, you always were a risk taker."

She slipped one hand behind his neck. "Stop talking before I change my mind."

He didn't seem to need any more directions. His kiss was swift and hot and fierce. And possessive. He claimed her with his mouth and his hands. Molded her form to his own powerful body. Made it clear that there was no turning back.

How many points of no return had they passed this week?

The intensity of his embrace—the pure, raw physicality— left her breathless. Suddenly, she didn't see her new husband as safe. Suddenly, safety faded as the furthest concern from the present.

As he pushed the fabric of her gown from her shoulders, she reached for the catch on his trousers. Her skin prickled, hot and impatient, where he touched her. Her hands longed to make him feel the sensations that pleasured her. He worked the tiny covered buttons down her back. With fumbling fingers, she released his zipper, then skimmed the last of his clothing down over his lean, angular hips.

He'd been hers—emotionally—all through childhood. Tonight he was hers—bodily—as well. When a tiny little voice warned that his heart might still be up for grabs and out of her reach, she hushed it with the urgency of the moment.

Although she was worldly wise enough not to equate sex with love, she would harvest this passion born of friendship and trust before the harsh, revealing light of reality set in with the dawn.

As her gown slid to the floor, her body responded to the cool of evening air with a prolonged shiver. She blamed the open window.

Scooping her into his arms, Dallas carried her to the big bed. Laid her gently upon the comforter. Stretched out beside her. Naked. Powerful. And visibly aroused.

He ran his index finger down her shoulder, along the curve

of her breast and over her nipple. "What about the baby?" he asked, his gaze fixed full upon her.

The baby.

Nameless, it had the power to draw them together or drive them apart.

"If you mean will we hurt the baby, the answer is no." She crossed her heart and, in the process, his hand that rested warm and poised for intimacy across her breast. "Scout's honor and doctor's word."

He seemed to hesitate. Was it because of the baby? Was it because of her past? Was it because this lovemaking wouldn't be just a one-night-stand—because this lovemaking signaled his free spirit roped and tied by the force of domesticity? Or could it be a shyness arising because of their formerly platonic relationship?

Dallas Parker, to her knowledge, had never, before tonight, been shy.

She reached out and touched him. She, who could relate to shyness, grew unaccountably fearless. She stroked his face, his chest and finally—boldly—his arousal.

He responded with a groan and an enveloping embrace.

No amount of *thinking* prepared her for the feel of him hot and hard along the length of her bare skin. She would have this night, for, if she was honest with herself, this joining had been in the stars from the beginning.

With Dallas.

Her lifelong hero and her heart's desire.

She succumbed to his caresses. Let the frissons of excitement wash over her. Rode the increasing waves of pleasure his touch produced. Twined her fingers in his hair and shamelessly guided his mouth over her body. She grew afraid of nothing.

Nothing, except his eyes.

So badly did she want this fantasy night, she avoided his gaze, afraid that she might see the truth therein. Afraid that she might see that this was sex and not lovemaking. Afraid that she might see her own reflection and—the truth?—that she needed to bond with this man to survive. To survive and protect her baby.

She didn't want to doubt her motives. She wanted to believe that her actions arose out of a shared history and a genuine caring.

She did care for Dallas. She did.

It was difficult to keep her mind focused on genuine affection, however, when her body seemed determined to blot out all but the most-primal sensations. Her skin tingled and yearned for his possessive touch. Her fingertips ached to explore the rippling planes of his smooth, hard body. Deep within her grew a hunger to have him fill her. Complete her. Consummate their relationship.

But Dallas didn't rush to enter her. Instead, he played with her body and her senses, claiming her flesh, stoking her passion, until her breathing came in short, electric pants.

He kissed her lips, her eyelids, her earlobes, as his hands consumed her, leaving her with no bodily privacy, no physical secrets. She shivered with delight to think how well his lips, his tongue, his fingers, had come to know her, to stamp her forevermore as a part of him.

If she could not have his heart, she would settle—tonight— for this physical part of him.

He rose above her, his body love slick in the moonlight.

"I am so ready for you," she murmured huskily, burying her face in his shoulder, quivering with near sensory overload.

With a deep, low, primitive growl, he entered her. She wrapped her legs around his waist, drawing him farther within, and placed a hot, wet kiss upon his neck.

His long, hard strokes drove her to distraction. His heavy breathing told her he was as close to culmination as she.

"Dallas! I'm going to—" The stars behind closed eyelids! The falling through bottomless space! The sweet, profound release!

"Julia!" Her name came ragged from his lips. He thrust deep within her, shuddered violently, then rolled to his side, gathering her tightly to him.

She lay against his chest, listening to the thundering of his heart. For an instant, he was hers. Wholly hers and no one else's. But that instant had made her inexplicably greedy for more. More of the same. More than an instant at a time. Yet more than the blinding physical need.

More of his heart.

She lay in his arms and wondered what kind of Pandora's box of longing they'd opened with this passionate consummation.

Julia awoke to chill fall morning air and the sound of migratory songbirds through the open bedroom window. Stretching, she realized that she hadn't slept so soundly in weeks and weeks and weeks.

Dallas had certainly cured her insomnia.

Rolling toward the center of the bed, she reached for him, but came up with nothing but empty, rumpled sheets. An ill feeling settled in the pit of her stomach.

Her fantasy night had officially ended.

What did morning bring in the way of truth about this new relationship?

Suddenly cold, she slipped from bed and hurried across the hardwood floor to the tiny closet in one corner of the bedroom. Martha had transferred Dallas's and Julia's clothing from Ten Oaks to the cottage the day of the wedding. Julia wrapped herself in a warm robe, slid her feet in slippers, then headed for the bathroom. Hopefully, washing her face and brushing her teeth before encountering her husband in the revealing light of a new day would allay some of the post-wedding-night jitters.

From the upstairs hallway, she could hear the low rumble of Dallas's voice on the telephone in the kitchen below. She hadn't heard the phone ring. What could be so important that he needed to make a call on the one day that they'd designated their honeymoon?

In the bathroom, Julia scrubbed her face and brushed her teeth with unaccustomed vigor. They only had one day to begin to sort out—absolutely alone and uninterrupted—this marriage. Tomorrow Dallas had to report back to work at the lumberyard.

Big Daddy had been absolutely ugly about not giving Dallas more time off.

The smell of coffee—strong coffee—wafted into the bathroom. Pregnant or not, she could use a cup. Running a brush through her tousled hair, she gave herself a cursory glance in the mirror. Friend Dallas had seen her many times without makeup. Husband and lover Dallas had not. How much should last night change her behavior?

She opted to have coffee—without makeup—with friend Dallas.

Hurrying downstairs before she changed her mind, she tried to consciously slow her racing pulse. Friend, indeed. What had one night of glorious passion done to their friendship? She didn't want to see Dallas's empty side of their marriage bed as an omen.

As she approached the kitchen, she heard Dallas discussing horseflesh. Was it rodeo come to reclaim him?

Suddenly, that old mistress seemed all too powerful.

Then she heard the words "...good for Richardson Lumber" and realized he was somehow conducting business. Business. On Sunday.

More important, on the first and only morning of their honeymoon.

When she entered the kitchen, he looked up. An uneasiness shadowed his eyes. Standing barefoot and clad only in jeans, he stiffened as he leaned against the counter. Although he didn't move from his spot near the telephone, the distance between them seemed to grow until a cool, bottomless psychological gulf divided them.

This man before her was not her old, safe friend. Neither was he the hot and reckless lover of the previous night. This man was a controlled and wary stranger. And Julia felt at a loss as to how to begin to make his acquaintance.

Dallas stared at Julia. Frankly, he'd expected her to sleep until noon.

"I'll talk to you later," he said to Aaron Sutter on the other end of the line. Hanging up, he couldn't find the words to begin the day with his wife.

Because he hadn't meant for last night to end as it had.

He'd promised himself, against all logic, that he would prove himself worthy of Julia *before* he made love to her. That, because of the baby, because of Julia's vulnerability, because of all the unanswered questions about her possible connection—still—with her ex-lover, he would take it slowly. Cautiously. For both their sakes.

He didn't want to hurt Julia in any way.

And he didn't want to leave his own heart open to hurt if Julia could never learn to love him.

For those reasons, he'd seen lovemaking as complicating matters. He'd thought he could show self-control enough for two. But self-control had clearly flown out the window with the shivaree sacrifices last night. His bottled-up longing for Julia had erased any semblance of restraint he could muster. The dam of higher motives had burst, and desire had prevailed. For all his wanting, for all his taking, Julia had held back nothing of her body. Last night that giving of herself had excited him no end. Had made him dream that maybe they could have it all. But today...

This morning, in the clear light of day, he wondered how much of her heart and soul she'd reserved. Kept inviolate and apart in the heat of the night...

The one thing—communication—that had been the strength of their friendship to this point, failed him now. Having faced rejection all his life, he couldn't bear to ask her honest feelings if her honest feelings included rejecting his love. A strong man, even hard at times, he'd always proved himself vulnerable where Julia was concerned.

"I made coffee," he said, his words brusque to his own ears.

Eyeing him thoughtfully, she moved to the stove, where she poured herself a half cup of coffee. "I'm really more hungry."

"Mary Louise left some kind of breakfast casserole in the fridge with instructions on heating it up." He nodded toward the oven. "It should be ready any time now."

They both retreated in silence to their coffee cups.

Why was conversation—the staple of their childhood—so difficult this morning?

He didn't know why it might be for Julia, but for him it all hinged on last night's lovemaking.

They had made love with the intensity of a one-night stand. They had explored each other's bodies as if neither had ever heard the words *platonic friendship*. They'd abandoned all inhibitions. They'd each all but devoured the other. It had been wild, passionate lovemaking.

Or sex.

Dallas had enough experience not to equate sex with either true love or commitment. He'd observed enough in human nature to know that even deeply emotional lovemaking sometimes wasn't adequate to cure what ailed a relationship. A physical union simply *was;* it never explained anything. And any attempt at explaining it wasted valuable time and energy.

In the past, with other women, he'd been content with that reality. Last night with Julia, he'd come away from the experience wanting more. With Julia he felt something he'd never felt before. He craved all of her. Her heart, as well as her body. And maybe even an explanation into the mysteries of life thrown in, too.

But what did he have to offer her in return?

A career in ruins and a temporary job with her father, who hated him for the restless wandering soul he'd always been. Now, those were a couple of prize wedding gifts.

As he watched Julia lift Mary Louise's breakfast casserole out of the oven, he vowed that he would make himself worthy of his new bride. He'd already mapped out the route he would take. But if it turned out that Julia's commitment to him had emotional limitations, he didn't know how to protect his own heart from the possibility of real hurt along the way.

Chapter Eleven

Unsettled by the out-of-the-ordinary dead silence between Dallas and herself, Julia ate very little of what normally would be her favorite of all Mary Louise's breakfast dishes, an herbed egg-and-cheese casserole. Slowly pushing her food around the plate with her fork, she glanced at her husband across the small kitchen table and caught him watching her.

"What did you have in mind for today?" he asked.

A loaded question.

What did she have in mind? For starters, she would like to talk and talk and talk until they'd erased this unease that lay heavily between them. She would like to sit down and discuss their feelings until they'd defined this new relationship they'd so precipitously created.

"I'd like to suggest something." A flicker of animation in his eyes, Dallas cocked his head. He began to move his hands over the table surface in a familiar restless motion. A motion he'd often used to stroke the bark of the old oak tree when he was about to divulge some new dream. Some new scheme.

"What?" Julia croaked, unable to suppress the thought that those very hands had sent her over pleasure's brink last night. Did he have more of the same in mind for today? If so—she blushed—talking perhaps could wait.

"I'm working on a new hobby for Big Daddy. You might want to get involved, too."

"You're what?" Julia sputtered. Thoughts of talk, thoughts of lovemaking, thoughts of coming to some kind of understanding, flew out the window. He had her father—*her father*—in mind on this, their honeymoon morning.

Standing up to clear his empty plate, he appeared suddenly unsure of himself. How odd. Dallas Parker hadn't exhibited signs of insecurity since his boyhood. What plan did he have up his sleeve now that made him edgy?

"Let me start at the beginning…or near the beginning," he said. He put his dirty dishes in the sink, then turned to face Julia. "Your father has about run out of territories to conquer when it comes to show stock. I have a hunch, just from observing him, that if he doesn't find a new interest soon, he might just…begin to make life for those around him miserable. Unless I miss my guess, Big Daddy's a man who needs to be kept occupied."

Julia squinted hard at Dallas. She knew him well enough to know that he'd left parts out of his narrative. But since she had no idea where his scheme headed, she couldn't sort out the pertinent information from the omissions. "And?" she asked warily. "What makes you so concerned all of a sudden with Big Daddy's welfare?"

"Who in town isn't?" Dallas shook his head, but managed the hint of a smile. "Hell. Your father sneezes, and the whole of Cannons Crossing feels the ramifications."

"The point being?"

"Julia, he's testy enough with you marrying me. With me working in the yard. He needs an outlet. Show stock isn't providing it anymore because he's scooped up every local, state and regional award there is to be had. Your daddy's a man who needs a *legitimate* challenge. Not—"

"Not?" Julia stared hard at Dallas as he averted his gaze from hers. "Are you suggesting he's in some kind of trouble?"

Scowling, Dallas cleared his throat. "Nothing worse than giving me a hard time on the job."

"So what did you have in mind?" By his body language alone, she recognized he was hiding something from her, but she also knew he'd reveal nothing as the result of nagging. She would let the whole story unfold in due time.

"I heard talk at work of a newly revived practice. Logging horses. A man out of Virginia named Mr. Timmons travels the South, giving demonstrations, trying to get people interested again." The edginess slipped from his voice as he warmed to his subject.

"I thought logging horses had gone the way of the buggy and whip." Julia recognized a spark of enthusiasm in Dallas's eyes that she'd only ever seen when he'd talked of the rodeo. She wanted to fan the flame. "Explain."

"Logging's become big business. The little guy's pretty much been shut out. But with the big operations and the big machines can come big headaches." He'd clearly given this considerable thought. "Clear-cutting doesn't sit well with the public."

"Where does all this fit in with the revival of logging horses?"

"This old practice opens up opportunity for the little guy at the same time it revives an environmental conscience in the industry." Dallas grinned. "It seems a team of men and a team of draft horses can get in places that would bog down a machine. Can slip into old growth forest, can pick individual trees to fell and can be out without doing damage to the surroundings. I hear tell the noisiest part of such an operation is the sound of the wind in the tree tops."

"Heard tell from whom?"

"Walter Marshall, who works in the yard, seems to know a bit about it. Attended a demonstration up in South Carolina.

Got Timmons's card. Said it would be great if someone could get the guy to give a demonstration in Cannons Crossing.''

"And you think Big Daddy would be interested in contacting this man?''

"No.'' Dallas shook his head. "Big Daddy doesn't cotton to anything that he didn't first think up himself.''

"Where is this idea going, then?''

"I thought I—we—could engineer a demonstration. Make it a town event. Walter said he'd gladly help. Aaron Sutter, too. We'll let Big Daddy see the possibilities along with everyone else. If a light bulb goes on in his head, the idea becomes his.''

Julia narrowed her eyes. "This seems like a pretty elaborate plan just to give Big Daddy a new hobby. To get him off your back at work.''

"Believe me. The man has too much time on his hands.''

"You sound grim.''

In two quick strides, Dallas moved to her side. He squatted beside her chair. Took her hand in his. "Julia, if we're going to live and work in this town, if we're going to eke out any kind of independent existence, we need your father out of our hair. Now, I'd rather accomplish that in some kind of positive manner—like getting him involved in a new hobby—than by going head-to-head with him.''

She reached out and trailed her fingertips down the side of his face. "How did you get to be so smart, Dallas Lee?''

"Not smart.'' He grinned. "I've just made a living out of tangling with ornery critters.''

"So tell me about these logging horses. Are they ornery critters?''

"Oh, no.'' Dallas rose, the expression on his face eager. "They're real beauties, from what Walter said. Big old draft horses. Capable of working in close quarters so that the lumber can be harvested in a real choosy manner.'' He began to pace, his body sheer coiled energy.

"But Mr. Timmons runs demonstrations for a business, not

forest management. How do we know the concept's practical?''

"Because he does both. He has a huge logging operation that his son now runs, leaving the father free to travel the country and proselytize, so to speak.''

"You don't think Big Daddy would consider this as a business option?''

"No, although I would if I had the capital outlay.'' Dallas got a dreamy look in his eyes. "I was thinking more of the hobby aspect for your father. The spin-off is the breeding and showing of these draft horses. They're massive creatures.'' He winked. "Something to match Big Daddy's ego.''

Dallas's enthusiasm proved contagious even though this was not the morning-after-the-wedding conversation Julia had expected. Nonetheless, it felt good to be talking plans and dreams again with him. The old oak tree might be no more, but the fact that Dallas now included her in his strategy making showed that something vital remained of their old relationship.

"So,'' she said, prepared to help in any way that she could just to be near her new husband, "what were you going to do about this project today?''

Leaning against the kitchen counter, Dallas glanced at the floor. Some of the unease reentered the room. "I thought we could meet Walter out at the Sutters'. Aaron has agreed we can hold the demo at his farm if Walter thinks it's suitable.''

Julia began to relish the prospects. "Maybe Helen and I could organize a potluck lunch to go along with it. Create a real fair atmosphere. Draw a crowd.''

"I bet Helen would like nothing better.'' Dallas beamed his approval of her idea. "You know, she invited us out for today's Sunday dinner. I haven't given her an answer yet.''

"Why not?''

His expression became pinched. "Today's the only honeymoon we're likely to get.''

She glanced into the bottom of her empty coffee cup, searching for courage to say the right thing. The honest thing.

"I'd like nothing better than to spend the day with you, plotting and planning, making a wisp of an idea reality. Like old times."

He looked relieved.

Her body might have preferred that he protest. That he sweep her off to bed and a day of passionate lovemaking. But her heart needed time and space to create a buffer of safety. She might look at him differently after speaking the wedding vows, but she felt certain he still saw this arrangement as practical. Friendly. What more cautious way to protect her vulnerable emotions than to spend the day with a Richardson-Parker project? Something unemotional, with clear-cut goals. And a virtual guarantee of success.

Just like old times. Familiar territory.

Leaning on the Sutters' corral waiting for Walter Marshall to join them, Dallas avoided looking directly at Aaron. "How much do you know about women?" he asked against his better judgment.

"Now, that's a loaded question if I ever heard one." Aaron took his hat off and scratched his head. "You and Julia aren't having problems already, are you?"

Dallas wished he hadn't started this conversation.

"Are you having problems, son?"

The word *son* sluiced open a dam of pent-up feelings. It sounded so heartfelt.

He'd never had a father to confide in. Later he hadn't even had a mother. He'd only ever confided in Julia. And now he needed to find a way to confide in her again—within the confines of their new relationship. The relationship undefined, he felt locked out. Maybe talking to Aaron would help relocate the key.

"We aren't so much having problems as…a period of adjustment."

Aaron snorted. "Welcome to marriage. By definition, one period of adjustment following close on the heels of another."

"You serious?"

"Never more so." His foster father chuckled. "The movies with their happily-ever-after make it look far too easy."

"Here I thought Julia and I were the only ones feeling strange." Dallas shook his head. "You see, we've always been the best of friends. Suddenly, we've become...more. We were both so darned independent before. Now we're sharing the rent and a bed and a last name. One minute we're smooth as silk together. The next minute we're edgy and tongue-tied."

"Marriage between two strong people is always a little bit of a guessing game."

"What do women want? I used to think I knew what Julia wanted. Now I'm not so sure."

Aaron grew very still. Very serious. "I don't have all the answers, but I do know you can't go wrong with communication and honesty."

Just looking at the older man, Dallas suspected that he'd somehow picked up that knowledge by erring in exactly those two departments.

He flinched. Since promising to marry Julia, he himself had strayed from the same two qualities, which had been a staple of their early friendship. He thought of the search for his father's identity and how he should have shared that important project with Julia by now. He thought of the letter from Boston Big Daddy had tucked in his jacket pocket. Why hadn't Julia told him she'd written to her ex? Was the letter even from her ex or from the friend who'd agreed to sublet the apartment and forward the furniture? How much, really, did Dallas know of Julia's current associations? How much did she want him to know?

"We used to be able to finish each other's thoughts," Dallas said. "Now I wonder if our minds even function in the same universe."

As Walter Marshall approached, Aaron wordlessly reached out and patted Dallas on the shoulder. Although the gesture made him none the wiser, he found it surprisingly comforting.

* * *

"What do men want?" Julia asked Helen Sutter as she set the table for Sunday dinner.

Harrumphing loudly, Helen gave the mashed potatoes a thwack with a big wooden spoon. "Do you want the knee-jerk short answer or the thought-out long answer?"

"First the knee-jerk short answer." A gentle laugh bubbled up inside Julia. "Although I suspect it won't be politically correct."

"Sex and the easy way out." Helen stirred the potatoes with exceptional vigor.

"Now that that's out of your system," Julia said with a chuckle, "what's the thought-out answer?"

Helen stopped her preparations and gave Julia a long, hard stare. "I would guess that most men—most men worth their salt—really want to be better than they are."

Now, that little observation gave Julia pause.

"Why do you ask me such a question the day after your wedding?"

"I've discovered I know Dallas less since we decided to marry than I did all those years growing up. He shares fewer of his thoughts with me. Keeps more of his emotions hidden."

"He has more to lose now by opening up." Helen covered the bowl of mashed potatoes, then put it in the warming oven. "Besides, I don't know a soul who really knows Dallas Parker."

"What was he like when he lived with you?"

Helen crossed her thin arms tightly over her chest. "He was angry. And rebellious. And difficult to love." A sad look in her eyes, she hugged herself.

"Difficult to love?" Julia started at the faint self-accusatory tone in Helen's last statement. Although she'd always felt compassion for Dallas's situation, she also felt sympathy for the Sutters'. "You sound as if you're being hard on yourself. You were a foster parent, obliged to give shelter, understanding and support to a stranger. Love is difficult to come by under the best of circumstances."

"Maybe." Helen scowled. "But maybe Aaron and I had something that boy needed. Something we withheld."

"He needed a mother and a father. Lacking them, he needed to know who his father was. So that he could add that knowledge to the memory of his mother. For closure. Could you have given him that?"

"Yes." Helen's answer came from far away. She started, then looked at Julia with a faintly guilty expression. "I mean, yes, I agree he needed that."

It seemed that Julia had struck a tender spot, but for the life of her, she didn't understand what it could be. She moved across the kitchen to wrap her arm around Helen's shoulder. "You opened your home to a troubled young man. You couldn't have done any more."

"Perhaps I could have forgiven enough to—" Tears misted Helen's eyes.

"Forgiven whom?" The scorched smell of secrets hung in the air.

"Oh—" Helen swiped at her eyes "—God. Circumstances. Life. For making me childless and others…" Her words trailed off. She brusquely kissed Julia on the cheek, then turned to the sink. "I'm a silly old woman. Sometimes I let my weaknesses get me down."

Julia could identify with feelings of vulnerability. And because of her own fears, she hadn't been completely emotionally honest with anyone—herself included—since she'd returned to Cannons Crossing. Perhaps that was why she felt compelled to confide in Helen Sutter now.

"Helen," she began. Tentatively. "Don't blame yourself for being human. We all feel unprotected at times. Like me. Marrying Dallas."

"What are you talking about, girl?"

"Dallas and I didn't marry for love."

"Oh?"

"We married because I'd gotten myself into a sticky situation—"

"You're pregnant!"

Julia swallowed hard. As she'd needed to tell Dallas all a week ago, she needed to tell Helen all now. Holding everything in had been a tremendous burden. "I'm pregnant, but Dallas isn't the father. Dallas is my friend. And my knight in shining armor. But now I'm afraid I've involved him in too much. To the point where I've sacrificed his future for the sake of mine and the baby's."

Her eyes wide, Helen let out a low, soft whistle.

"Mind you, he was the one who suggested marriage. But why would he do all this for me?" Julia needed to know. "I thought maybe you could shed some light on his past. The part I didn't share. Maybe there would be the key."

"The only key I can see is that the boy must love you a whole lot."

"He's never once said so."

"Not in words, maybe."

Helen's assertion was pure speculation. To avoid the hurt of getting her hopes up, Julia steered the conversation in a different direction. "The other reason I wanted to talk to you is that you've had experience with foster care. Because Dallas isn't the baby's father, I worry…I mean, it takes a special person to love another's child."

"I know," Helen said with finality. "Will the baby's father be in the picture?"

"I doubt it." Julia screwed her courage to the sticking place. "He's married."

A look of raw pain passed over Helen's face.

"I've written to him, asking him to give up any legal claim. I'm waiting for an answer, hoping that if the child was free, Dallas could begin to love him or her as his own."

"Does Dallas know you've done this? Written."

"No. I didn't want to tell him until it had been settled."

"Tell him. Now. You're married. Your lives run together, not parallel. Don't keep things from each other. It only weakens a relationship." Helen spoke with such conviction that Julia suspected she spoke from hard experience.

"I want to tell him…but finding an opening is so difficult."

Julia shook her head. "The irony is that communication and honesty were our strengths all through childhood. Now we seem to have misplaced them in the complexities of this new relationship."

"Complex or simple, relationships always have room for honesty and communication." Helen patted Julia's arm. "Trust your feelings for one another."

"Helen, this is a marriage of convenience. Practical. The result of a bad situation and a good friendship."

Helen snorted. "Don't give me that. I didn't see any shotguns at the wedding yesterday. You two young folks *chose* to marry. The reasons, I admit, might be a little different from those of the ordinary bride and groom. But you're both of age and of sound mind. Recognize that you each made the decision freely."

Julia admitted to herself that she'd made her decision freely. A part of her would have married Dallas—had he asked from the heart—even had she not been pregnant and out of work.

"Besides," Helen added, "you're married. The deciding on that score and the ceremony are history. You need to concentrate now on staying married. That's the real challenge."

Even knowing Helen for a plainspoken woman, Julia found her pronouncement particularly harsh and daunting.

Because the weather had turned seasonally cold, Dallas had raised the Caddy convertible top for the ride home from the Sutters'. The subsequent confinement nearly gave Julia claustrophobia after the open afternoon spent in Aaron and Helen's company. An openness fueled by laughter and the exchange of ideas. An easiness between Dallas and herself brought on by the familiar energy of a joint project.

In the enclosed Caddy interior, warmed by an eager heater, mellowed with a soft country radio station, Julia found it difficult to shift emotional gears. This afternoon Dallas and she had been friends again. Now...

Now, husband and wife, they headed home. To what? Another night of intimacy? The thought both excited and frightened Julia. A sprinkle of guilt, as well, flavored those two diverse feelings. Wanting Dallas, craving *all* the rights that came with marriage, somehow felt like stealing. Considering the circumstances.

He didn't love her.

"You're shivering." His voice jolted her. He reached out his right arm. "Come here. I'll warm you up."

A thief and shameless, she slid across the bench seat to enjoy what wasn't wholly hers.

"I didn't think Aaron and Helen could get so enthused about hosting a demo day." He gave her a peck on the top of her head and a gentle hug. *Friendly* gestures.

At his touch, she tried to suppress the longing that rose within her. "Why would you be surprised? They love you. They love good horseflesh. They love a community event."

"Why do you say they love me?"

"It's obvious."

"That's a fundamental difference between you and me, Julia. In my life, love has never been obvious."

"Well, get used to it where the Sutters are concerned. Talking to Helen today, I got the impression she—or maybe even she and Aaron as a couple—had gone through some tough times. Understood adversity and how it can close a person off from others. She's reaching out, Dallas."

"Why? And why to me? To us."

"Maybe because you're the closest she ever came to having a child. Maybe because she knows family doesn't always have to mean blood relations."

Dallas stiffened next to her, and Julia wondered if he was thinking of her unborn child. Turning into the driveway in front of their cottage, he removed his arm from around her, placed both hands on the wheel. Was the withdrawal merely expedient or a deliberate attempt to distance himself both physically and emotionally? Despite last night's passion, the fact remained that they'd entered into this marriage to give an innocent baby two parents. Not to declare those parents soul mates.

Now was the time to ask Dallas his true feelings. They were alone. Nothing stood between them and honesty. But dusk had fallen. After the day's activities, weariness seeped into Julia's bones, sapping her strength for discussion and emotional daring. She wanted to curl up in front of the fireplace. With Dallas. Maybe their bodies would say the things their hearts would not.

"I'd like a fire in the fireplace," she said as they got out of the car.

Dallas strode to the front door. "I'll make you one."

"Me?" She wanted to hear *us*. "Are you turning in?"

Unlocking the door, he glanced at her. "I have a couple of calls to make about the logging demo. I don't think Big Daddy would take kindly to me planning it on company time." He pushed the door open for her. "I have some paperwork for the yard, too."

"Anything I can help with?" She wanted their cooperation of this afternoon to continue.

He scowled. "No. It'll go faster if I just take care of it."

"You'll join me when you're done?"

"Of course."

His words gave promise, but his actions—a quick concentration on fire starting—made her wonder if this sudden interest in work masked his desire to avoid her. To avoid further intimacy.

She sat on the sofa and watched him. With a masculine grace and an efficiency of movement, he built her a fire. In contrast to the flames, however, he appeared cool in every sense of the word. She certainly wished her insides would chill out, but fiery doubts continued to dog her every thought. Why were matters so difficult between them? Easy one minute, fraught with tension and unspoken longing the next.

"Dallas…" Tired as she was, she had to reestablish communications. "Are you having second thoughts?"

"About what?" He kept his back to her.

"About the wedding."

Crouching near the growing flames, he turned to face her. "It's a little late to have second thoughts about the wedding."

Wanting him to think her a thoroughly nineties woman, rarely helpless, seldom at a loss, she replied, "It's never too late." She tried to make her words breezy.

His expression softened as he stood. "Julia, we agreed to make a home for this baby. Are you having second thoughts about that?"

"No!" The baby needed them. She only wished she hadn't proved as needy.

"That's all that matters." He dusted his hands on his jeans.

Wouldn't it be absolutely lovely, she thought ruefully, if the baby's well-being were all that mattered?

"Can I get you some of that herbal tea Mary Louise sent over?" he called from the foyer.

"No, thank you." Tea had no power to cure what ailed her.

Gazing into the leaping flames, she admitted to herself that, against all reason, she'd slipped into an incurably lovesick state. Even with the baby to think of, how did she propose to carry on in a relationship of unrequited love?

Dallas rubbed his eyes. The lines on the spreadsheet before him on the kitchen table had begun to wiggle and wander. He glanced at the clock. Ten past midnight. He hadn't heard a peep from Julia in the parlor. How had he let the time slip by?

Stuffing the paperwork into the leather rodeo satchel he'd been using as a briefcase, he headed toward the front of the house.

He knew exactly why he'd let work consume him tonight: fear of failure. Big Daddy had given him thirty days to prove himself at work—work that he had neither aptitude nor inclination for. Work he would never have given a second thought to if it weren't for Julia and her baby.

As matters stood, he needed to succeed at the lumberyard to prove himself to Julia.

Failure had never been an option in his life. As a boy, the

need to hold his head high had kept him from failing. As an adult, his pure, God-given talent had provided the safety net. Now, however, failure loomed a distinct possibility on the horizon although the stakes and his motivation had never been higher.

He stepped through the archway into the parlor to find the fire in the grate no more than glowing embers and his wife sound asleep on the sofa.

As he drank in her beauty, a sudden jumble of feelings erupted deep within him. Physical yearning clawed its way to the top of the heap. Followed closely by a vivid possessiveness and a pride in that unearned possession. She was his. For better and for worse. He was hers.

He'd done nothing to deserve her except be in the right place at the right time.

She slept with her hands under her cheek, as a child might sleep. Tenderness filled him. Soon they would have a child. The only reason for this marriage. A fierce tightness grabbed his heart. He would protect Julia and the child with his last ounce of strength. With every bit of ingenuity he could muster, even if it meant selling his soul to the devil himself. To Big Daddy Richardson.

Stretching in her sleep, Julia whimpered. If he had the power, he would protect her to the extent that she never had bad dreams.

Moving to her side, he bent, then gently scooped her into his arms. Instead of waking, she nestled against him as if his arms were home. His emotions danced a jig again, and among them one—love—begged for attention. Dallas pushed it emphatically to the back of the others.

Talk about failure. If he let himself love Julia—truly love her—he would let himself in for heartbreak. In hastily designing this marriage, neither she nor he had ever uttered the word *love*.

Their mutual concern for the baby would have to be enough.

That didn't mean he couldn't secretly relish the feel of her in his arms. Her womanly softness. Her warmth. Her sleepy fragrance. Carefully, he carried her up the stairs and into their bedroom. Gently, he placed her under the covers of their big bed. He removed her shoes but couldn't bring himself to remove her clothes. Last night, with all its passion, had etched itself on his senses. He couldn't afford to awaken that side of their relationship again. Not until he could offer her a truly worthy man.

After one last, long look at her peaceful features, he returned downstairs to douse the lights and lock up.

The sound of a car pulling into the gravel driveway set his reflexes on alert. Who could be out this way at this hour? He moved cautiously to look out the curtained sidelight.

Big Daddy hauled himself out of his monstrous Lincoln.

To avoid waking Julia with what always turned out to be a loud discussion between the two men, Dallas stepped outside to meet his father-in-law coming up the walk.

"Julia's in bed. Asleep," Dallas said without preamble.

"That's fine." Big Daddy planted his feet on the walkway. "I came to chew the fat with you."

"Came to welcome me into the family?" Planting his feet, as well, Dallas grinned.

"Came to tell you that I know *my* grandbaby is no kin of yours." The old man fairly spit the words.

"So?" Dallas shrugged. "I happen to know that you've been fooling around with your secretary."

Point. Counterpoint. Stalemate. Dallas's grin grew broader. Big Daddy couldn't possibly think an old rodeo bum would scare easily.

"You knew about the baby's real father?" Big Daddy growled.

"Yes."

Big Daddy's mustache drooped disappointment. "Then what's your game with *my* daughter? You figure to cash in on the Richardson fortune?" The fight hadn't quite left the old boy.

"I figure to settle down with Julia and raise a family."

"Working—or pretending to work—in *my* lumberyard," Big Daddy muttered.

"Me. My. Mine." Dallas chuckled. He suddenly realized his father-in-law had no power to hurt him. Or Julia. Or the baby. Not if Dallas didn't let him. "You sure do have a self-centered view of affairs, Norton. You suppose that would still be so if Julia and the baby and I moved, say, clear across the States to the West Coast?"

"You wouldn't dare!"

"In a heartbeat, if you try to make trouble between Julia and me." Dallas stroked his chin, enjoying the power. "Which, I assume, is the very reason you dropped by to-night."

"Are you threatening me, boy?"

"I'm not saying anything Julia hasn't said to your face already. In front of witnesses."

"You'll soon learn how mighty the pull of home is for Julia."

"I know." Dallas cocked one eyebrow and skewered Big Daddy with a righteous stare. "We're making a home right here in this cottage."

Big Daddy let out a blustery snort, but Dallas could see that the turn in conversation had taken the old man off guard.

"Care for a beer or a cup of coffee before you head on home to Miriam?" Dallas couldn't help it. The devil made him do it. He'd stew the old man in a hospitable gesture.

Without a word, Big Daddy turned, then marched back to his car. He looked as if he might throw down one more gauntlet before leaving, but must have realized he'd already spent his ammunition. Fruitlessly. With one last, silent glower, he threw himself into the driver's seat.

Dallas waved heartily before heading into the house.

Who said you couldn't teach an old dog new tricks?

Two old dogs had just now learned a thing or more out in the front yard. Under the stars. Big Daddy Richardson had learned that he couldn't mess with Dallas Lee Parker. And

Dallas had learned that he, even washed-up in rodeo, had clout. Right here in Cannons Crossing.

Imagine.

It was all a matter of backbone and perception.

Chapter Twelve

In the waning afternoon sun, Julia looked out over the Sutters' paddock, appreciated the enormous draft horses going through their paces and the observers packed in at the fences. She gave a satisfied glance at the picnic tables laden with now empty potluck dishes, the families enjoying a country holiday. She sidestepped a group of happy children playing a noisy game of tag. No doubt about it, the hastily put together logging demonstration had turned out a rousing success.

She wished she could say the same of her week with Dallas.

As it was, she felt like an abandoned wife.

Leaning up against a fence post, she kicked herself mentally for being petulant. In addition to putting in long hours at the lumberyard, Dallas had worked hard to pull this demonstration together in a week. She knew he felt pressured to prove himself to Big Daddy in a limited space of time.

But deep down inside, she wished he'd reserved a little time for her. A little more private time.

Oh, he hadn't abandoned her. Not really. He'd consulted

her daily about work in the yard and about plans for this demonstration. Had listened to her ideas and had treated her as an old friend and partner. Still, she wished against all logic that he'd treated her more as a lover. A new bride. This last week was just one more reminder that sex didn't change anything.

The fact that they'd shared a night of passion only proved that there was nothing wrong with their physical magnetism.

But why was it she craved the one thing she couldn't have—a deep and lasting emotional attachment? Love.

"Where's that cowboy husband of yours?" her father muttered as he approached her from the side and put an arm around her shoulders.

"Last I saw, he was signing autographs."

"A real big shot."

"Why, you're jealous!" Julia turned to face her father. Funny, but he didn't intimidate her anymore. Edgy from a week of unresolved issues, she set her hands on her hips, itching for a confrontation. "It really bothers you that Dallas commands respect, doesn't it?"

"Respect!" Big Daddy huffed and puffed out his cheeks. "Why would I be jealous of starry-eyed kids asking for an autograph? From a washed-up rodeo bum."

Suddenly grinning, Julia shook her head. She really didn't want a fight. She just didn't want her father to get away with his usual bluster. "That's not the whole of it, and you know it. Three-quarters of the people who showed up today are Richardson Lumber employees. They showed up out of respect for their new boss. Dallas. Out of enthusiasm for his ideas."

"They showed up out of curiosity," Big Daddy mumbled. "They knew, if nothing else, they'd get a view of good horseflesh and some fine home cooking."

Unaccountably, Julia felt magnanimous. She stood on tiptoe and planted a kiss on her father's beet red cheek. "I still love you," she declared, satisfied to surprise and defuse rather than ignite.

Big Daddy pulled away, suitably flustered. "Why ever wouldn't you?"

"Because you're trying to make trouble between me and my husband."

"I wouldn't if you'd chosen a proper husband," he muttered.

Julia raised one eyebrow in warning.

"I know. I know. Not another word." Big Daddy raised both hands in mock surrender. "But I don't want to see any crocodile tears when that rovin' cowboy gets itchy feet and finds the opportunity to move on."

It took every ounce of self-control Julia possessed not to start a verbal brawl with her father. Protecting Dallas's honor had always been instinct with her. Instead of arguing, however, she took a deep breath. When she'd let it out, she cautiously changed the subject. "Speaking of opportunities, what do you think of these logging horses?"

"They're beauties, I'll say that much." Despite his obvious attempt to appear disinterested, Big Daddy couldn't suppress the covetous glint in his eye. "What made Parker set up this demo?"

Julia and Dallas had been very savvy in setting up the event. They'd treated Big Daddy with no extra attention, letting him find out about the affair by word of mouth and the flyers they'd stuck up all over town.

"Because there seems to be a lot of interest in renewing the practice," Julia replied cagily.

"Who all's interested?" Big Daddy's competitive nature flashed clear and true. Interest meant rivals, in his book.

Julia smiled and let out the line a little at a time. "Oh, Aaron Sutter, Walter Marshall…others. Now, I'm not sure if they're interested in the business or the competitive aspect. You know…breeding, showing."

Big Daddy scowled, and Julia knew she'd hooked him. If a new breeding movement began in the area, he'd want to be at the forefront. He'd want his name associated with pioneering the effort.

"Maybe I'll go over and have a few words with that fella from Virginia."

Julia beamed. "You do that." With a feeling of pride, she watched her father lumber away to conquer new territories.

The pride came from standing up to him. Not letting him rattle her. Avoiding a needless conflict. Manipulating him, instead of vice versa.

"P. T. Barnum would be proud of you!" Dallas's voice rumbled close to her ear. "Shall I get you a carny cane and straw hat?"

She turned to find him grinning down at her, his Stetson low over his eyes so that most of what she saw was a heart-stopping flash of white teeth. White teeth and attitude. "How long have you been standing there?"

"Long enough to see you stand up to Big Daddy." He tipped his hat back, revealing his startling blue eyes with their devilish twinkle.

"It wasn't much in the way of standing up to him." She blushed, knowing that wasn't true. Colored at the thought of how much effort it had actually required. At the thought of how long overdue the effort was.

"It doesn't have to take some history-making battle to declare your independence." His eyes flashed in a reflection of the brilliant blue and cloud-free fall sky. "Although I've never mastered the technique, I always admired subtlety."

She basked in his praise. In the absolute sunshine of his regard.

"Come on. I want to show you something." Unexpectedly, he placed his hands at her waist, then lifted her to a sitting position on the top rail of the high fence. His touch left a heated circle on her flesh. "Timmons says he'll let me handle a team."

A protective anxiety ran through her. "But your injuries!"

"I'll be okay." Gazing up at her, he ran his hand over her thigh, sending a shiver clear to her toes. "This isn't rough stock. These babies have been trained to respond to a flick of the fingers. But just in case..."

He reached out and loosed the yellow ribbon she'd worn to tie back her hair. Tucking it into the watch pocket of his jeans so that just the end peeped out, he winked. ''A favor from m'lady.''

Julia could not control her heart rate. Neither could she control her tongue to speak. Mutely, she watched this man, her best friend, her husband, leap the fence, then stride purposefully across the paddock toward the draft horses and their owner. With Dallas's entrance into the ring, the whispers among the spectators started in earnest. The cowboy certainly commanded attention.

Dallas was a large man, but the big gray Percheron geldings dwarfed him. Hooked up to a fourteen-foot-long, three-thousand-pound tulip poplar log, the equine team waited patiently for the master's command. Dallas conferred briefly with Timmons before taking the reins off to one side.

Julia held her breath. Even in relatively flat pastureland, the combined tonnage of horse and log alone presented a control problem. She prayed silently that no injury come to Dallas.

She'd underestimated her husband's horse sense, however.

Under Timmons's watchful eye, Dallas appeared to be completely at ease. Responding to his ''gee'' and ''haw'' commands, the brawny Percherons neatly picked their way around the obstacle course set up in the paddock. The dust kicked up by their massive plumed hooves rose and eddied around Dallas until he became a silhouette of lean muscle and spare movement. Regardless of the size difference between man and beast, it was obvious the man retained full control.

The crowd murmured its appreciation.

The course complete, Dallas seemed not to notice the spectators. His smile came from a pleasure private and faraway. He ran an admiring hand down the near horse's flank before Timmons and he sank deep into conversation.

Julia felt a twinge of guilt. This was Dallas's milieu. Horses and hard work. Not an office. Not paperwork. Not feint and parry with a father-in-law who didn't appreciate his best qualities.

If he couldn't have rodeo, he needed an occupation like this logging operation. But there was no way on earth that, saddled with the responsibilities of a wife and baby, Dallas could put together the money necessary to set himself up in such a business. Even if he had the money, the itinerant life-style wouldn't be conducive to family.

A euphoric grin on his face, he waved to Julia to join him.

Dallas couldn't have suppressed the grin if he tried. How good it felt to be back in boots and jeans. Back in a ring with the sound and smell and feel of magnificent horses. After the shadows of the lumberyard warehouse, the open air and sunshine felt like a tonic.

Julia walked across the paddock toward him. His Julia. An uncertain look on her face. He worried over that look as much as he worried over how he'd neglected her this past week. He'd worked himself ragged all week for them. For their future as a family. But to Julia—without their old deep and full disclosure—it must have seemed that he'd been avoiding her.

And the idea of avoiding her couldn't be further from his intentions. If she could see into his heart, she would see that every time she came near, he wanted her more and more. Wanted her friendship, wanted her body...wanted her love. But before he could enter love's arena, he had to demonstrate that he deserved her.

Proving himself worthy was emerging as neither an easy nor a black-and-white issue.

Timmons's assistants began to unharness the Percherons.

"Julia." Dallas reached out his hand to take hers. "Timmons here has made me an offer."

"Oh?" Her regard grew veiled. Cautious. Perhaps justifiably so.

"Your husband's a quick study," Timmons said. "He only wants experience. And right now, I need able hands for a hurricane-cleanup project on the coast."

Julia scowled at the logger. "Dallas already has a job."

"I'm not offering a full-time job. At least not yet. It's more an opportunity to apprentice. This project will take a few weeks tops. But I'll take him any time he can get away from his regular job. It would give Dallas some highly marketable skills to start a career outside rodeo, and you two newlyweds a nice cash bonus to start your marriage."

Julia turned to Dallas. "You'd walk out on your commitment to my father?"

He thought she might see it this way. He turned to Timmons. "Would you excuse us?"

"Of course. Talk it over. But, Julia, I've never seen a man so naturally suited to this line of work as your husband."

Julia's mouth had become a tight line, and Dallas didn't quite understand her hard expression. If he could just explain the situation clearly, he had no doubt she'd see this as an opportunity for *them*. Wordlessly, he guided her outside the paddock, around the back of the barn to a spot that hadn't been discovered by the demo crowd.

Facing her, he placed both hands on her shoulders. "Julia, talk to me."

She seemed to distance herself emotionally. "No. *You* talk. You seem to be the one with the news."

"It's not a done deal." He lifted her chin so that he looked directly into her eyes. Tried to pull her back to him. "I'm not going to make a decision that would affect the two of us without consulting you."

A flicker of interest showed in her tawny gaze. "What do we have to decide and how would it affect us?" He'd counted on her natural-born curiosity.

"This is it. Shall I use my days off from the lumberyard— a half dozen at the most—to help with this hurricane cleanup? I'd get paid good money, but, more importantly, I'd get valuable experience."

"You're interested in this logging business?"

"More than interested." In the long run, it could provide satisfaction in a career he was suited for and independence amid the overpowering Richardsons.

"I thought you set this demo up to hook my father on the

idea." Her gaze grew clouded. "Are you planning to compete?"

"No. If Big Daddy shows an interest, it's going to be in the hobby end of it. I'm looking to make a living, eventually. For us. For the child."

He wanted to say *our child,* but, not having discovered how much Julia was willing to share in the realm of parenthood, he didn't want to get off on a possible side discussion that might derail their present attempt at communication.

"That's a half-dozen days we could—" She stopped in midsentence.

"We could what?" He scrutinized her features for a clue to her thoughts. If she would just say to him, *That's a half-dozen days we could spend working on a real marriage,* he would kick this logging idea clear to the Atlantic. If she'd just say, *That's a half-dozen days I'll spend missing you,* he would suck it up and spend his life toiling in Big Daddy's employ. Hell, he'd rather spend those half-dozen days making love to her. But if his love proved unreturned, his time would be better spent building respect.

"Oh, I suppose repairs on the cottage can wait."

Cottage repairs? She'd been thinking cottage repairs? His heart sank.

Sighing, she worked at a small smile. "And I'll soon be busy with my new job at the radio station anyway." Her smile disappeared along with Dallas's hopes of a declaration of love. "Do you really hate working at the lumberyard?"

"I've never shied away from hard work in my life. You know that. It's just that working for your father is a lose-lose situation."

"How so?"

"Even in a best-case scenario, folks look at my position as a result of nepotism. Worst case, I'm a gold digger."

She reached out and touched his chest, sending a jolt of pure pleasure sizzle through him. "One of our strengths was always standing up to popular opinion. Together."

He wanted to draw her into his arms. Wanted to breathe her

scent. Wanted to tell her that the word *together* held new meaning for him. New meaning and a dangerous vulnerability. Instead, he said, "We're going to need to hang tough because talk's already flying, I'm sure."

"Dallas, this isn't the Cannons Crossing of your boyhood."

"Maybe not. Maybe it's just my pride that wants a job that's not a handout."

"I can understand that." Slipping her arm around his waist, she began to move back toward the demo. Back toward the crowds. Where had the old ease in solitude gone? Or was he simply reading things into the stiffness of her touch? Her readiness to return to a less secluded spot. "When would you start with Timmons?"

"My next day off is Thursday."

"You'll do well." Her voice caught, but she gave him a quick squeeze. "You always have. You always will."

She spoke the words as if his life were somehow separate from hers. He appreciated her support, but his intent had been to convince her that a decision to explore the logging possibilities would be good for them. For the two of them as a couple. The three of them as a family. He wanted the possibility of gaining independence from her family to draw them closer together. Instead, she walked stiffly at his side as if they'd drawn an invisible dividing line of sorts. Creating separate but equal futures. The thought caused him considerable pain.

They swung around the corner of the barn and almost collided with a knot of people in animated discussion.

One woman turned angrily to Dallas. "Well, here's the cock of the walk now. I suppose you sleep well at night, knowing the suffering you've caused an innocent girl."

For the life of him, Dallas didn't recognize the woman. "Ma'am, you tell me the suffering I've caused, and I'll try to rectify it."

Narrowing her eyes and flicking her gaze toward Julia, the woman snorted derisively. "I'm Mandy Quaid's mama. Mandy. Big Daddy's secretary. That ring any bells?"

"No, ma'am."

The connection still didn't call up any visions of gross injustice on his part. Any undue emotional distress caused by Mandy's job or his supervision. In fact, from their first introduction, Dallas had tried to steer clear of the disgruntled secretary. True, her private relationship with Big Daddy might be cause for an uncomfortable twinge of conscience or two, but Mandy could blame no one but herself for that discomfort. That fact didn't stop the creeping unease in the pit of Dallas's stomach. The mother's venom-filled regard set his survival instincts on alert.

"Mandy and I've had our differences at work, but I don't think that constitutes suffering on her part," he said evenly.

The woman seemed to have trouble meeting his gaze. She turned on Julia. "Your new husband seems to have trouble keeping his hands to himself. That's why my daughter decided she had to quit Richardson Lumber."

Now, that false accusation made the hair on the back of Dallas's neck rise.

He could barely control the twitch in his tensed jaw muscle. "You care to explain what you think you know?"

"I don't think. I know." She looked back at the knot of observers, some open-mouthed. "Dallas Parker went after my Mandy from the first day he came to work in the yard. When she rebuffed him, he harassed her. When she couldn't take the strain anymore, she quit."

"That's a lie."

Mandy's mother still wouldn't meet his gaze. "You calling my daughter a liar in the bargain?"

"I'm saying I never pursued or harassed your daughter. In any way. Never."

"We all know your reputation, Parker. And we all know Mandy's."

Dallas found himself on the horns of the damnedest dilemma. He'd been unaware that Mandy had quit her job. But he could guess the real reason—her relationship with Big Daddy—either ongoing and risky or broken off and soured.

Dallas could attempt to expose her for what she was. Unfortunately, in the process of trying to save his own reputation, he'd have to sully hers and his father-in-law's.

Frankly, saving his neck at the expense of others never had fit in with his personal code of ethics.

He'd stated his innocence publicly. He would ride out the storm of controversy should it arise.

"I think if you ask the other employees at the yard," he replied, sharply controlling his temper, "they'll tell you how I've conducted myself since coming to work."

Mandy's mother remained unmoved. "No matter how many people are around, there's always the opportunity for hanky-panky behind closed doors."

Dallas thought of Big Daddy and Mandy. The mother had spoken a bitter but twisted truth. "If Mandy has a beef with me, I'd like to hear it from her face-to-face."

"Understandably, she's not about to put herself in that position." Squint-eyed, the woman turned to Julia. "Heaven help you," she snapped before turning, then stalking across the barnyard.

The small crowd of observers dispersed uneasily.

"Julia…" He turned to her, realizing that, for the first time in his life, his reputation had the power to affect another. And not just any other. Someone he'd vowed to protect. Someone whose respect meant the world to him. Someone he loved and whose love he secretly coveted.

The look on her face was one of horror.

"Julia, please, believe me."

"What ugliness!" she whispered. "But why?"

"It's not true."

She turned to him, her regard clear and steadfast. "I know."

"You do?" Her assertion astonished him.

"Yes. I believe you because I know you, Dallas Parker." She scowled. "And I know Mandy Quaid for a manipulator."

Julia's unqualified belief in him nearly bowled him over.

Julia could have kicked herself for her naïveté. Just a few minutes earlier, she'd been miffed at Dallas for seemingly making a mountain out of a workplace molehill. She hadn't really believed him when he'd said that spiteful speculation swirled around his appointment at the yard. She should have remembered Mandy's jealousy.

"Your first day of work, Mandy approached me," she said, "unhappy that Big Daddy had made you personal assistant. She said the job should have been hers. But I never thought she'd resort to *this*."

"People will surprise you with the things they'll do to survive." His look held a barely suppressed anguish that tugged at her heartstrings.

"We could bring her up on slander charges."

"Don't go corporate on me, pigtail girl." He actually grinned. "With you by my side, we'll ride out any rough stuff that comes our way. Without benefit of lawyers."

"But she shouldn't be allowed to get away with spreading vicious rumors."

"And I'm not about to get down and wrestle in the mud with her." He put his arm around her shoulders and pulled her close. "Forget it, Julia."

"Forget what?"

"That wicked gleam in your eye tells me you're getting set to do battle."

"If we don't, there may be trouble."

"If we do, there may be trouble. Life's a gamble."

"She's not worth your little finger."

"Exactly." He bent and planted a kiss on her brow. "That's why I intend to pay Mandy Quaid and her mama no never mind. None whatsoever."

"What about the few people who witnessed the exchange right now?"

Dallas shrugged. "Some will believe the Quaids. Others, me." He glanced around the Sutter property. "I'm not going to worry about it. Not with the future staring me in the face."

She looked for what he'd called the future. She saw the massive horses now tended by a team of handlers. She saw the better part of Cannons Crossing scattered about the grounds. She saw Aaron and Helen Sutter standing arm in arm, beaming at the assembled community. Could Dallas have finally come to see all this as his future?

Or did he see only the logging enterprise? A one-way ticket out of town.

Again.

Catching Julia's eye, Helen broke away from Aaron and came across the barnyard.

"What a success!" she exclaimed, actually reaching out and pinching Dallas's cheek with glee. "Folks'll be talking about this demonstration for weeks on end. You two are just what this dusty old town needs. Hot new blood. Exciting new ideas."

Dallas wrapped his arm around Julia's shoulders. "We always did make quite a team."

A surprise thought entered Julia's head at Dallas's statement. This week and today had really been a tiny reflection of their childhood relationship: shared dreams, hard work in tandem and a unified front against a sometimes hostile environment.

And when all was said and done, here they stood. Together. Unscathed.

Julia rethought the notion that their relationship had regressed. Perhaps, before building a future, they needed to embrace the rock-solid foundation of their past. As they had this past week.

"Julia, honey?" Helen's words cut into her thoughts. "Have you seen your daddy working the crowd? He's about to bust with the competition possibilities. I wouldn't doubt his stables will see an addition or two before the week's over."

Dallas grinned. "That was the idea."

Helen shot Dallas a quizzical little look. "Will you two stay for supper?"

"No!" Although quick to decline, Dallas didn't seem uneasy or standoffish. On the contrary, a lazy twinkle danced in the depths of his eyes. "I've made reservations for Julia and me."

"Reservations!" the two women responded simultaneously with surprise. Dallas Parker was not a dinner-reservations kind of guy.

"Y'all wound me." He affected an adorable mask of dejection. "I thought Julia deserved something special for putting up with the chaos all week."

"In that case, go." Helen gently pushed the two of them toward the field of parked cars. "Aaron and I will take over here."

"But the logging crew's still here and almost half the crowd." Suddenly, Julia felt shy at the prospect of being alone with her husband. "Then there's the cleanup."

"Oh, pooh!" Helen waved them off. "Aaron's dying to help ready those logging horses for the return trip. As for the folks still here, well, I have years of experience with church-fair crowds and community picnics. Besides, the Boy Scout troop has offered to take care of cleanup detail." She winked. "Looks like there's nothing left for you two but to enjoy those reservations."

Julia guessed not.

With a grin that grew warmer by the second, Dallas took her hand, then led her to his Caddy.

"You didn't have to make reservations," she said, finally seated in the car.

"Oh, yes, I did. You didn't get much of a honeymoon week."

Julia blushed. Although she'd been thinking the very same thing, she replied, "I'm perfectly aware this isn't your normal marriage situation."

"Even so, I wanted to let you know I appreciate your support and patience."

She glanced out the window so that he couldn't see her gathering tears. She didn't want appreciation for her support and patience. Rather impatiently, she wanted him to say that this dinner was so that they could spend some time alone together. Because he loved her as she loved him.

They rode in silence. Having paid little attention to the direction Dallas had taken, Julia was surprised to discover him pulling into the driveway in front of their cottage. Candlelight flickered from the front parlor windows.

"What—?" She swung her gaze to Dallas.

"When I asked, Mary Louise said she'd be glad to help."

As if on cue, the Richardson cook opened the front door, then came down the walkway toward Hiram Ledbetter, who'd just pulled up in the Mercedes behind the Caddy. Mary Louise knocked on the Caddy windshield in passing. "Hustle on inside before the food gets cold or a candle tips over and burns the place down."

Dallas placed his hand over Julia's on the seat. "I'm taking that as an order." His voice floated to her, husky and inviting. "Ready?"

No, quite frankly, she wasn't.

Inside the house, Mary Louise's best romantic efforts beckoned. A fire crackling in the parlor fireplace. Softly glowing candles on the mantel. Flowers in abundance on the hearth. A white linen cloth spread on the hardwood with a picnic for two. This was no wicker-basket picnic, however. Mary Louise had made use of the family silver and crystal, creating a scene of sensuous opulence. She'd even strewed rose petals amid the covered dishes and place settings.

"Well?" Dallas stroked Julia's back. "We missed that first picnic you planned—the housewarming picnic. I thought we'd try again."

As quickly as tears rose in Julia's eyes, she attempted to dash them away.

He reached out and stayed her hand, then turned her chin so that she looked at him. "Let 'em fall." He chuckled softly. "I've grown used to the hormones."

She attempted a smile. Oh, but this time the tears weren't the result of hormones. This time they were for something she couldn't have. This evening had all the markings of a romantic interlude, but Dallas had planned it as a thank-you for her patience and support. Her tears were tears of frustration at the contrast between longing and reality.

Dallas took careful note of Julia's reaction. He didn't want to frighten her off with his intentions. He'd planned this evening with Mary Louise, all the while telling himself that Julia deserved a special thanks. Period. He'd repressed the thought that he'd really prefer to plan an emotional seduction.

The room before them all too clearly spelled seduction rather than thanks.

But Julia's tears just now warned him of her vulnerable state. He made a mental promise to take it easy. To let their relationship develop over time. She had enough pressures in her life without the added disclosure of his true feelings for her.

With a forced nonchalance, he moved to the sofa, which had been pushed off to the side of the room. Gathering the seat cushions, he then spread them around the picnic cloth on the floor.

"Never let it be said I forced my lady to rough it." He kept his words light, teasing. Kept his gaze on her to determine her response.

Her tawny eyes widened. A smile flirted with the corners of her sensuous mouth. Blushing—a familiar reaction since childhood, one that she hated but one that he loved—she entered the parlor, then, with a sexy elegance, took a seat on a cushion. She gazed up at him expectantly.

Suddenly, his appetite for food left him, replaced by a hunger for Julia.

He had to remind himself that she'd entered into this relationship out of expediency. He thought of the letter from Boston and the negative possibilities it held. If he was to win Julia's love, he needed to woo her cautiously. Needed to demonstrate to her that her future lay here, with him, in Georgia.

He took a seat on a cushion opposite her.

"So...you and Mary Louise cooked this up." Her voice was silky soft, an audible caress. "What's under all these silver covers?"

"Comfort food." Grinning, he raised a lid. "Fried chicken. Biscuits. Coleslaw. Creamed corn."

"Are you trying to fatten me up?"

"You *are* eating for two." He winked. "And Mary Louise assured me comfort food has fewer calories when eaten by candlelight."

"How can I resist?"

"Don't." He reached to uncover another silver serving dish, but in so doing, his little finger snagged on a loop of the yellow ribbon sticking out of his jeans watch pocket. The talisman slithered to the picnic cloth, where it lay on the snow white linen, a golden reminder of the bond that lay between Julia and himself. A bond of shared experiences and mutual respect. A bond he wanted to deepen with passion and love.

She looked deep into his eyes. "Do you remember wearing my yellow hair ribbon that one time back when you were riding junior rodeo?"

"Remember? Hey, I carried that thing with me on the circuit until it disintegrated a few years ago." He fingered the ribbon in front of him. "I needed a replacement."

Her eyes widened. "Why did you wear the original in the first place? You were just a kid. It was a silly, romantic request on my part. I'd just read King Arthur—"

"You'd just read King Arthur to me up in the old oak tree. I knew full well the significance of a lady's favor." He furrowed his brows. "I guess I felt it was payback time. Seems you'd been carrying my favor into battle on my behalf for years."

"Did you really see it that way?"

"You believed in me when no one else did. If that's not doing battle on my behalf, I don't know what is."

She cocked her head. "And here I thought I owed you."

"For what?" Surprise filled him.

"For believing in me. Unconditionally. For seeing me as a whole person. Not some pretty, trouble-free ornament my father expected."

Moving around the picnic cloth to be closer to her, he reached out and touched the creamy softness of her cheek. How could anyone not believe in Julia Richardson?

Julia Richardson Parker.

Her married name excited him.

Her smile provided the invitation.

Against his better judgment, he leaned close to kiss her.

"Thank you," she whispered against his lips. "For believing in me."

"My pleasure," he whispered in return, savoring the satiny feel of her skin, the heady fresh-air-and-sunshine scent of her hair and clothing.

She moved first, sliding her hand behind his neck, applying a gentle pressure to bring his lips full upon hers. In a fraction of a second, the kiss slipped beyond thank-you.

And in that lost second, he misplaced his silent vow to proceed slowly. Cautiously.

Gathering her into his arms, he could only think how right she felt in his embrace. Julia. His Julia. And their child.

He ran his tongue over her lips, savoring the taste of her. Comfort food of the highest order. She opened for him, sought his tongue with her own. The deepened kiss sent ripples of pleasure through him. He felt himself harden. Felt longing and need increase. He wanted to touch her. Claim her.

Cradling her in his arms, running kisses over her mouth and cheek and neck, he unbuttoned the soft flannel shirt she'd worn for the demo. Heard her sharp intake of breath. Looked to her to see if he should stop.

No warning met his gaze. Instead, in her half-lidded, golden eyes, he saw a physical desire to match his own. Her slightly parted lips beckoned. As she arched into his embrace and ran her fingers through his hair, the last vestige of his reserve snapped.

Sliding his hands along her bare flesh under the flannel shirt, he pulled her to him in a rough kiss of passion and possession. She responded with a fiery abandon that scorched his synapses, claiming him with her touch, urging him on with soft little moans. The mutual hunger grew—palpable—in the flickering candlelight.

He couldn't rein in his desire. Couldn't make this a slow

and languorous joining. Propelled by the mounting week-long tension of proximity and denial, he stretched out on the floor, pulling her with him.

"I want you," she murmured from atop him, her words a husky siren's song.

"I want you, too," he groaned, reaching to rid them both of boots and jeans.

"Now," she whispered, longing sizzling the edges of that one tiny word. "Now," she repeated as she tugged at his jeans, nipped at his earlobe.

Now, his body screamed as she lay back on the hardwood floor, drawing him above her.

For a moment, he held her gaze in his. Tried to read her heart's mysteries. She might rationalize this joining as a purely physical act. A release of tension. A rebound from hurt. But for him it was lovemaking, plain and simple. He loved her and their baby.

Truly loved her.

"Come," she urged. "Now."

Unable to hold back, he entered her with a silent and a secret declaration of his love. Entered her warmth and felt himself home at long last.

Chapter Thirteen

A changed woman and alone, Julia entered the Richardson kitchen.

Last night she'd given herself up to Dallas, body and soul. He might not know it, but she loved him. Loved him with a whole-heart, forever kind of love.

And that love made her feel lost.

Because Dallas didn't return it.

Not once in the passion of last night had he uttered the word *love*. For all she knew, he may have regarded their joining as the perk of being consenting—married—adults. She, on the other hand, had given her heart to him, as well as her body. Last night she, at least, had made love.

Even though she hadn't the courage to speak the word. To test his feelings.

When she'd awakened this morning, he was gone. Gone without even making coffee. To work, most probably. This past week, they'd fallen into the habit of coming and going independently. More like roommates than husband and wife.

But today—after their second night of passion, in which Julia had found herself in love and most vulnerable—she couldn't abide the emptiness of the cottage.

She didn't fault him for going, but she felt his absence as an ache.

That was why she sought the company of her family.

Big Daddy sat at the kitchen table, reading the financial section of the newspaper. He looked up when Julia entered the room. "You all right, baby girl?"

"I'm fine." Normally, she'd have bridled at the diminutive, but today she took some comfort in it. "I thought I'd catch breakfast with Mama and you. I only have a week left as a lady of leisure before I go to work."

"Your mama's sleeping in." Big Daddy scowled. "If you'd married a man who could support you properly, you wouldn't have to go to work at all."

"Daddy…" Julia shot him a warning glance. She ignored his dig at Dallas, and tried a different approach. "Did it ever occur to you that I derive satisfaction from my work?"

"It occurred to me, but I never understood it."

"If I'd been a son, would you have understood it then?"

"Of course. But you're my daughter, and I raised you to relax and appreciate the finer things in life, work not being included in the list."

Julia sighed. It appeared her father would never view her as more than a passive female ornament in his active male life. How fortunate she no longer needed his approval to feel strong. She had her own solid résumé of independently achieved accomplishments.

"Mornin', Miss Julia." Mary Louise bustled across the kitchen with a tray loaded with fruit and muffins and eggs and ham. "You and that handsome husband of yours didn't let that supper get cold, now, did you?"

"No, ma'am." To hide her blush at the half truth, Julia lowered her head, plopped down in a chair across from Big Daddy, then reached for a section of the paper, which she made a show of studying assiduously. "It was delicious.

Thank you,'' she added. It had also been microwaved back to life at a sinfully wee hour in the morning.

"Any time, honey bunch," Mary Louise replied, mischief creeping into her voice. "I do like to see a couple get off to a lovin' start."

Julia kept her head down, her eyes on the print before her. "Why aren't you at work this morning, Daddy?" she asked in an evasive maneuver.

"Thinkin' about logging horses."

"Oh?"

"Well, it shouldn't come as a surprise. A new movement like this cropping up. Everyone in town expects me to be at the forefront. A pioneer. A leader."

Julia let his glowing self-testimonial slide. "Are you planning to work them?"

"No, no. Breed them. Train them maybe, if I could find a good man. Compete."

Julia's blood began a slow boil. "If you could find a good man?"

"Sure. Maybe that fella from Virginia would be willing to give me some recommendations."

"What about Dallas?" Julia asked between clenched teeth.

"What about Dallas?"

His dismissal infuriated her. "Dallas knows horses," she replied, straining to control her temper.

"You mean consider Dallas as a trainer?" Big Daddy's face grew red. "Have you gone daft? The boy rode rough stock on the circuit. He knows nothing of purebreds and finesse."

"Mr. Timmons said he'd never seen anyone so naturally suited to this line of work."

"Pshaw!"

"Why do you belittle Dallas's abilities?" Angry, Julia rose from her seat. "Who do you think had the idea for the demo in the first place?"

"Marshall. Sutter."

"No. Dallas." She jammed her fists on her hips. "Dallas was the one who contacted Mr. Timmons to set up the demonstration. Dallas was the one to bring it all together in less than a week.''

"Well, that accounts for it. Timmons knew Parker was my hired hand. It was *my* name that greased the wheels surely.''

"Of all the pompous, self-centered ideas!''

"You watch your mouth, girl. The Richardson name is known far and wide. Has been for generations. Long before that fatherless trespasser came on the scene.''

In exasperation, Julia turned to leave. Then stopped. Leaving had always been her response to her father's excesses. But Dallas had become too important to her not to stand and take his side against her own blood.

She leveled a glare at Big Daddy. "For your information, Dallas, with his reputation and his experience with stock, could go anywhere in the country as a trainer. Mr. Timmons has already offered him an apprenticeship in the logging business.'' Pleased to see a startled expression appear on her father's face, she went on before he could answer. "He doesn't have to stay here in Cannons Crossing and take your lumberyard job or your grief.'' Tapping her foot in accompaniment to her rapid pulse, she shook a finger at him. "And the truly sad thing is that if you'd just open your myopic eyes, you'd discover that Dallas Lee Parker is everything you've always wanted in a son.''

Big Daddy gasped. His eyes looked about ready to pop out of his head, and his mustache quivered.

"Yes, he is,'' Julia declared. "He's strong and proud and stubborn just like you. He's loyal to a fault. And talented. And hardworking. And...and...and if you'd only swallow your pride, you could have a daughter *and* a grandbaby *and* a son-in-law to brag on.''

When she finally stopped talking, she discovered that she was trembling, stunned by the audacity of her tirade and stunned by the intensity of her attachment to Dallas.

"Are you finished?'' Big Daddy asked coldly, rising.

"Yes. I am.''

"Then if you'll excuse me, I need to get to work.'' He

paused, then reached into his suit-jacket pocket. "Oh, yes...this came for you the other day. With all the hullabaloo, I forgot to give it to you." He thrust a rumpled letter toward her.

The letter appeared to have been steamed opened, then carelessly resealed. Because she knew for a fact Big Daddy would have no qualms about opening another family member's mail, she felt renewed anger begin to rise at the lack of adult privacy in her own home. Glowering at her father, she hastily noted the letter's postmark. Boston.

All anger ceased, replaced by a dull dread.

Dallas had left the cottage early to seek out Helen Sutter for a before-work cup of coffee and counsel. Now, standing on her front porch, he wanted to turn back. He didn't know which of his decisions surprised him more—the one after last night's lovemaking, wherein he'd admitted to himself his love for Julia and vowed to earn her love even at the cost of causing himself pain, or the other, this viewing the Sutters as family, people he could count on in time of need.

The log cabin's front door swung open. "Dallas Lee, you gonna stand there, scaring off the birds, or are you comin' in?" Helen asked, her expression softer than her words.

Removing his Stetson, he stepped over the threshold.

"Well, what's eating you?" Helen always was a woman to cut to the chase.

"I'll need a cup of coffee. Or two or three."

"I have fresh brewed." The little woman turned toward the kitchen.

Dallas followed, wondering how he could ever begin to ask for the things he needed.

"The demo went real well," Helen remarked, bustling about the kitchen. "You and Julia should be proud. It reestablished your roots here in Cannons Crossing."

Dallas saw an opening in the conversation as he sat at the long trestle table. "Speaking of those roots, I need to find my father. Or at least his identity. And I need help."

Setting a cup of coffee before Dallas, Helen stiffened. "You're back to that, are you?"

"Helen, it's not just for me. It's for Julia."

"What could it matter to Julia? She didn't marry your past. She married you. As is." Helen slid into the seat opposite Dallas.

"She married me because she's pregnant, and I convinced her no baby should face the fatherless childhood I experienced."

"She told me the baby's not yours."

Helen's declaration stunned him because it meant Julia had trusted her enough to tell the truth. As far as Dallas knew, she hadn't been as honest with her own mother.

"I'm not being judgmental, mind you," Helen continued. "I'm just trying to figure out why you did marry Julia."

Dallas hesitated. Baring his soul was not an easy, everyday occurrence. "Because I love her," he finally admitted. "Maybe even I didn't know it when I offered to be the baby's father. But it was there. Always has been."

"Then love should be enough."

"I'm realistic enough to know that it often isn't." Dallas scowled. "What do I have to offer her in terms of real assets? I'm a broken-down rodeo rider with no sense of family. Julia's nesting. She wants to stay in Georgia. If not always in Cannons Crossing, then close enough that the Richardsons play a part in their grandbaby's upbringing." He shook his head. "And Big Daddy Richardson can't seem to forget that I'm the local bastard."

Helen winced. "Seems to me that bringing love and fatherhood to a relationship should be more than sufficient. No matter what Big Daddy thinks." She crossed her arms and hugged herself, the set of her shoulders rigid, the expression on her face anxious. "But considering all you have facing you, it doesn't seem fair to drag an unknown grandfather into the mix. Maybe drag in some long buried pain."

"You talk about pain." Dallas shifted uneasily in his chair. "I've lived with the pain of not knowing. As a kid, I never knew what it was about me that would make my father not want me. As an adult, I wonder what bad or good qualities I've inherited from that man. What I have to guard against. He was irresponsible. Does my wandering rodeo life mean I have those tendencies?''

Quickly, Helen reached across the table and covered his large hand with her small weathered one. ''You're not irresponsible, Dallas Lee. And neither was your pa.''

The conviction of her statement made him start. ''How do you know?''

She pulled her hand back. Averted her eyes. Didn't answer.

''How do you know?'' Dallas repeated, urgency rising. It was his turn to reach out. He took both her hands in his. Hers were icy cold. ''Look at me. Please.''

She did as she withdrew her hands to her lap. Her eyes seemed to harbor an inner conflict.

''There's a big empty space, right here,'' Dallas continued, placing one hand over his heart. ''Where my pa should be. Even on my best days, it makes me feel less than whole. Now, I've found a woman who deserves a whole man, a baby who deserves a whole daddy. For God's sake, if you know anything—good, bad or indifferent—about my father, tell me.''

Helen stood, then silently left the room. Believing the strange, tension-filled discussion at an end, Dallas rose, too. But before he could leave, Helen returned with a very old book, which she laid on the table before him. It was the Sutter family Bible.

''I'm breaking an oath for you, boy.'' There were tears in her eyes. ''But I've come to love you like a son.'' Opening the Bible's cover, she ran a clean butter knife under the endpaper, loosening it. A yellowed envelope fell out. ''You're a good man. And as a good man, I want you to handle this new knowledge with some sensitivity.''

''I don't understand.'' He accepted the envelope she handed him.

Opening the fragile letter, he noted that the date was his birthday, twenty-eight years ago.

"Read it," Helen urged.

It read:

Aaron,

I'm writing to tell you of the birth of our son today. I'm naming him Dallas Lee Parker. I know you've reconciled with Helen. That's why I didn't tell you of the pregnancy after our break-up. I guess I always knew your rightful place was with Helen, after all. I won't push myself or our son into your marriage. That would prove a disaster all around. But I'm asking that you promise one thing. If anything should happen to me, please look out for Dallas. He needn't know that you're anyone more than a concerned friend.

Rhetta

Dallas felt the bottom drop out of his world.

"Where did you find this?"

"Right where you saw me take it from. Aaron sealed it in the endpapers."

"I don't understand."

"Aaron would have hurt two women if he'd publicly acknowledged you all those years ago. One, he would have gone against your mama's wishes. And two... Well, I don't know if I'd have had the maturity to deal with the full disclosure back then. I hurt enough, knowing he'd been seeing Rhetta."

"But he kept the letter." Awe filled Dallas's words.

"He kept it *in the family Bible*." Helen's eyes misted over. "Sealed away, yes. But not hidden from the Lord. I happened on it several years ago when the glue gave out."

"He must have thought of himself as my father all along. Must have held out hope for a reconciliation." Dallas felt emotion constrict the muscles of his throat. "Otherwise, he wouldn't have kept the letter over the years. Even in secret."

"You needn't worry about your paternity, son," Helen offered softly. "You come from good stock."

Astounded, Dallas felt as if the flimsy pieces of paper were two-ton weights, immobilizing him. "Aaron's my father and...and...you allowed me into your home. I don't understand."

"None of this was your doing." Helen reached out to touch his arm. "And in time I found the strength to forgive Aaron for straying during our separation." Her expression softened. "Can't you see that you don't have to be perfect to be loved?"

"What will Aaron say when he finds out you've betrayed his trust?"

"I think he'll find the strength to forgive me when he comes to understand I did it, hoping to complete the too-long-broken circle of family."

"Can I tell Julia?"

"She's the chief reason you wanted to know all this, isn't she?"

"It was supposed to be a gift for her." He felt himself choke up. "I didn't realize how much of a gift it would be for me."

"I'm glad." Gently, Helen took the envelope and letter from Dallas. "Just don't think that this will solve all your problems."

"How's that?"

"Your bride is vulnerable. Don't push her. She's been betrayed herself and badly hurt. It may take time for her to open up again. Trust. Share. Accept your gifts. She told me she worries that the two of you no longer know each other. The fact that you now have family won't automatically bring back that old communication. That old honesty. You'll have to work at that."

Dallas began to feel a lightness seep through him. "I have all the time in the world."

Helen's features grew still and serious. "Sometimes you must sacrifice—and experience hurt—for the one you love."

"What do you mean?"

"It wasn't easy for me to let go of my anger at either your

mother or Aaron. Nor you in the beginning. But I did in the end because I loved Aaron.''

"I love Julia."

"Have you told her?"

Uneasy under Helen's stare, he glanced out the window. "I haven't found the right opportunity, considering the practical circumstances surrounding our marriage.''

"Remember, I asked you once what you had to lose by letting yourself fall in love."

He shook his head ruefully. "That's a moot issue now that I find myself already in love."

"Then go to her. Start with a little honesty."

He couldn't wait.

The feeling had been growing in Julia since last night. She needed to tell Dallas that the marriage was off. She'd made a horrible mistake.

Clutching the letter from her ex-lover in her hand, she stood looking out over the charred site of the old oak tree. The day after the lightning strike, Big Daddy had mobilized a cleanup crew. Julia wished he hadn't. The leveled stump and the raked environs depressed her more than the blackened skeletal remains of the ancient tree had. The scorched debris had provided a tangible reminder of Dallas and her past solidarity. The emptiness now, however, proved unsettling. As if their future was a void.

She walked to the stump and sat. Running her hand over the newly sawed wood, the myriad rings, she was amazed at how moist and vital the heart of the felled tree still felt to the touch. She bet that, within a year, saplings would spring from its roots.

If only her relationship with Dallas could be so naturally resurrected.

This morning had proved one big reminder of the obstacles facing them. At breakfast Big Daddy certainly reinforced the fact that he wasn't about to let up on his son-in-law. Add his infuriatingly obstinate attitude to that of Mandy Quaid and her mother, and Julia knew that Dallas was right about the hostility that still dogged him in Cannons Crossing. They could move, yes, but because of the baby, they would always be bound inextricably to their hometown.

As if on cue, the baby moved. Placing her hand protectively over her abdomen, Julia took notice of the letter she still held. She'd written to her ex-lover, asking him to relinquish all legal rights to this child. He'd done so with an alacrity and eagerness that felt like a slap in the face. But as much as his rejection of this new life saddened her, she was relieved that the cad wouldn't become a future threat. One more reason Dallas didn't need to protect another man's child. One more reason Julia didn't need the services of a knight in shining armor.

And about this knight. He'd talked about the tarnish on his armor. The end of rodeo. The need to reinvent himself. This morning, as she'd argued Dallas's merits with Big Daddy, the fact that the logging-horse business provided a perfect career for an ex–rodeo champ became apparent. It was a career that would satisfy Dallas's need for space and movement. A career that surely would be hampered by a wife he didn't love and another man's child.

No getting around it, this marriage of convenience was unfair to her new husband, especially with all the negatives she brought to the bargain.

Julia stroked the wood of the old oak's stump as she cataloged the reasons to set Dallas free. This morning had certainly reinforced her determination, but the seeds had been planted last night with their lovemaking.

What really stood in the way of making this marriage work was the fact that Julia loved Dallas, heart and soul. That he didn't return the same kind of love discouraged her. Made her want to exit early to retain some shred of dignity.

It became clear as the days wore on that she couldn't exist on the half loaf Dallas offered—protection spiced with a raw physicality. Perhaps others might be content with that, but she never would be. She'd caught a glimpse of what life with Dallas could be, and it had spoiled her for anything less than the whole. If she couldn't have it all—his love included—she would make it on her own and let him go. For his sake.

"Julia!" His voice, filled with an urgency, came to her over the field. "I've been looking all over for you." He ran toward her through the tall grasses, his movement laced with a sinewy masculine grace, his face set in determination. "We have to talk. About last night."

"I know," she whispered, rising to meet him, determined to speak first before she lost her nerve.

As he came to a stop in front of her, she noted the set of his jaw, the resolute look in his eye, the sense of barely contained energy in his stance. All traits she recognized from childhood. All precursors to facing a challenge. She knew, without a doubt, that the prospects of logging had put the fire back in Dallas. He'd discovered the route to his freedom. Because she loved him, she would give him the key and a guiltless farewell.

He started to speak, but she laid her fingers on his lips.

"Listen to me, Dallas." She tried not to let the longing engendered by touching him distract her. "This marriage isn't working. I want us to go our separate ways."

His regard increasingly wary, he grasped her wrist to remove her fingers from his lips. "I don't understand."

"We married in haste for a lot of practical reasons, all of which have been resolved this week." As much as it pained her, she drank in the sight of him, pressed it in her memory for the time when he'd no longer stand beside her.

"Nothing's changed." He scrutinized her face.

No, nothing important had changed. Unfortunately.

"I have a job," she declared, trying to shore up her courage. "You have prospects for a job. A real job that suits your talents." She held up the letter from her ex. "*He* has agreed to remain out of my child's life. Legally. Permanently." She hurried on so that he couldn't interrupt. "After the initial shock, it's clear my family will support the baby and me emotionally. Neither my baby nor I need your protection." She inhaled deeply. "And both you and I need our independence."

"But last night—"

"Was simple physical attraction. An inevitable release from all the tension." That most certainly hadn't been the case for her, but she didn't want to seem as if she was fishing for reassurances. She needed to make a clean break, appear strong, so that he'd feel free to pursue his future.

"A separation." His eyes had gone cold. "This is what you want?"

No, it wasn't what she wanted. She evaded a direct answer, nonetheless. "This marriage idea was crazy from the beginning. A wild Richardson-Parker plan." She attempted a smile. "Not one of our more well thought out plans."

He tensed. "What can I say to convince you otherwise?"

"Nothing." The lie dug deep in her heart. *Say you love me, and I'll stay. Forever.*

Knowing that response would never come, she turned and ran. Through the field. Toward Ten Oaks. The tears blinding her vision.

Feeling dead inside, Dallas let her go because he had an ominous sense that this time she meant it. And from long experience, he'd learned that you cannot force relationships. Perhaps she'd simply discovered that she couldn't grow to love him.

In love with her, he'd let her go. For her sake.

And then it hit him. Like the lightning that had hit their sheltering tree. There had been no word of love in this awful conversation. For his part, he'd failed to tell her that he loved her. And she'd never mentioned that she *didn't* love him.

There was hope yet.

Praying he wasn't too late, he made a mad dash for the house. As he raced through Hiram Ledbetter's gardens, the normally retiring gardener shouted testily, "Now, what have you done to our girl?"

In the kitchen, Mary Louise nearly cornered him. "What's going on? Miss Julia came through here, tears streaming down her cheeks, her eyes all puffy."

"Julia!" he shouted.

Martha shook a duster at him from atop a stool in the hallway. "Go see if you can calm her. Our baby's locked herself in her room."

All this did not describe a woman happy with her decision. Dallas's margin of hope increased as he sprinted across the foyer to the large winding staircase.

"Now, just one minute, Parker!" Big Daddy's voice from behind threw a wet blanket on Dallas's rising optimism.

Slowly, Dallas turned to face his father-in-law. "Don't mess with me, Norton. I have to talk to Julia."

"Well, I want to talk to you about Julia."

"Not now." Dallas turned to climb the stairs.

"Now!" Big Daddy clamped a heavy hand on Dallas's shoulder. "Before I change my mind."

This didn't bode well. The second Richardson today who needed to unload. Dallas glowered at the old man. "Make it short."

"We had a row this morning. Julia and I."

"What's new?"

"Julia's attitude, for one thing." Big Daddy scowled.

The two men obviously had something in common. Dallas hadn't liked Julia's change in attitude earlier, either.

"The girl showed some spunk," Big Daddy grumbled. "Some gumption. Although I'd rather she hadn't aimed it at me."

"I don't understand." Dallas didn't understand his father-in-law's discomfort. It was apparent he had something unsettling to share. Not anxious for more bad news, however, Dallas turned to go.

"Wait!" Big Daddy hemmed and hawed before finally muttering, "She made it clear she loves you, good-for-nothing rodeo bum that you are."

"What?" Dallas froze in his tracks. "That's impossible."

"That's what I thought. But obviously, Julia doesn't see it that way."

"Now *you* don't understand." Dallas narrowed his gaze. "She just told me she wants to end the marriage."

''Pride!'' Big Daddy sputtered.

''Come again.'' Dallas thought he hadn't heard right.

The old man looked distinctly uncomfortable. ''My daughter and I are two of a kind when it comes to pride.'' He winced as if the admission hurt him physically. ''We'd rather wrap ourselves in it than be hurt.'' He skewered Dallas with a beady-eyed stare. ''Have you done anything to make her think you might not love her anymore?''

Hell, he hadn't even told her he loved her in the first place.

''You hurt my daughter, and you'll be looking down the business end of a shotgun.''

Amazing how encouragement could come from the most unexpected sources.

Dallas grinned. ''You don't have to worry about that...sir.'' He turned, then took the stairs two at a time.

It wasn't the image of a well-maintained shotgun that spurred him on. It was the thought that Julia loved him. *Loved him.*

''Julia!'' He shouted her name as he raced down the upstairs corridor. The sound of it on his lips gladdened his heart. ''Julia!''

Her bedroom door was closed. He tried the knob. Locked. ''Julia, honey, let me in! You can't leave me till you've heard me out.'' He knocked on the door with enough vigor to wake the dead.

Instead, he woke Auntie Ouidie. ''For goodness' sake, son, break down the door!'' she urged from behind her own closed door. ''That's what they do in my bodice rippers!''

Dallas shook his head. These Richardsons found the most peculiar ways to cheer a body on.

''Julia, please!'' He knocked on the door again. ''Don't make me say what I have to say in front of the entire household.''

The door opened a crack. Julia, her face pale, peered out at him. ''I told you there was nothing you could say to change my mind.'' She glanced over his shoulder as a second door creaked open behind him. ''Oh, come in,'' she urged, tugging at his arm, "before an account of this whole scene gets pressed in the family Bible."

He didn't need a second invitation.

Inside her room, he quickly closed the door behind him and drank in the sight of her. Beautiful Julia. How could he have been so blind?

"Dallas...I'm listening."

He wasn't about to waste breath on preamble. "I love you."

Disbelief registering on her face, she took a step backward. "You don't have to say that. I'm a big girl. I understood what I was getting into from the beginning."

"Well, hell." He grinned. "I didn't."

Sweet confusion reigned in those golden eyes. It wasn't often he could lay a genuine surprise on his Julia. "You love me...as a friend, right?" she asked tentatively.

Laughing, he took a step toward her and swept her into his arms so that her feet came clear of the floor. "Honey, I love you every which way!"

Her eyes widened as he swung her around in a circle. He'd answered Helen Sutter's question and discovered that the only thing he had to lose by letting himself fall in love was fear. With Julia in his arms and his true feelings out in the open, he was fearless. "I was crazy not to tell you."

"I love you, too."

Her soft declaration made him come to a halt. Gently, he released her so that she stood before him, her tawny gaze clear and steady and penetrating. A joyous smile wreathed her face. "I love you," she repeated. "I always have. That's why I set you free."

"What a pair." He shook his head. "That's why I set you free."

"I don't want to be free if it's without you."

"Me, either."

Something in his brain said, Stop talking and kiss her, fool. So he did.

Long and hard and with an urgency that no longer scared him. Wrapping her arms around his neck, she kissed him back so honestly, so passionately, that he realized he'd come close to making the biggest mistake of his life.

She loved him. And all it took for him to discover it was honesty and communication.

Feeling her lips curve into a smile, he drew back. "What's so funny?"

She ran her fingers through his hair, making the skin all down his back tingle. "What brought this confession on?"

"Not what. Who. Helen Sutter. Big Daddy—"

"My father!" She kissed his chin. "Now I know you're hallucinating."

"No." Dallas chuckled. "Believe it or not, your father and I are going to be okay."

"Dallas Lee, what has come over you this morning? Tell me everything."

She began to pull him toward a settee in the corner of her room, but he pulled her back into the shelter of his arms. "I'll tell you everything, but you're not going anywhere." The feel of her warm, lithe body pressed against his energized him. He wasn't about to let her go. He kissed the hollow of her neck just because he had the freedom to do so.

"Whatever it is, I like it," she purred.

"Oh, Julia." He held her close. "Helen told me the most incredible story of love and forgiveness." He took a deep breath. "Do you know that my father's right here in Cannons Crossing? He's Aaron."

With a gasp, Julia pulled away. "Aaron! And Helen told you this?" Awe washed over her features. "But she welcomed you into her home. Came to treat you like a son. How could she do it, knowing…? Was it all for show?"

"No. It was all a part of her philosophy—hard come by— that you don't have to be perfect to be loved." He gave Julia a hearty squeeze. "That's what made me bold enough to lay my imperfect self before you, Julia Anabeth Richardson Parker."

"*Your* imperfect self!" Julia drew back to look him right in the eye. "What about *my* imperfect self?"

"As I said before, we're quite a pair." He chucked her playfully under the chin. "For two people with our list of accomplishments, we've both been a little dense in recognizing self-worth."

"I never doubted your worth."

"And I never doubted yours. I just got stuck, trying to prove myself worthy of you."

"I didn't want proof of anything." She outlined his lips with her finger. The tease gave him shivers. "I just wanted you to love me."

"Oh, I love you." He hardened in response to that declaration. "I love you so much that, knowing how much family and roots meant to you, I wanted to find my father. Wanted to either bring some closure or some possibilities to that arena."

"Aaron is your father," she said breathlessly. "I can't believe it. Our baby is going to have two sets of grandparents."

Suddenly, her expression clouded. She pulled away before Dallas could stop her. Pulled away and turned her back. When Dallas set his hands on her shoulders, he could feel the stiffness in her entire body.

"Julia, what's wrong?"

"The baby. I was always afraid to ask you how you really felt about the baby."

Gently, he turned her to face him. "You mean *our* baby?"

Tears pooled in the corners of her eyes. "It's another man's baby."

"Sorry." With his thumb, he wiped away a fallen tear. "You can shoot me for a chauvinist, but when we made love I claimed the baby for my own. Our own."

"Oh, Dallas!" She threw her arms around his neck and showered him with kisses. "Is that a lesson from Helen, as well?"

"No." He ran his hands over her sides, felt the warmth of her skin through her top. Hunger grew with the feel of her. "That little lesson I picked up from loving you."

She wriggled closer to him, then stiffened again. "Oh, no."

"What now?"

"Your job." She thumped him on the chest with her fist. "You can't work for Big Daddy forever, and you can't stay home with a family if you're on the road logging."

"Julia, honey, you can make problems where there are none." He drew her close and murmured in her ear. "After the apprenticeship, I have no intention of traveling. I want to train logging horses. Period. I can do that from wherever we decide to call home."

"*We.* I like the sound of that," she assured him.

"Is that it for questions?"

"I think so. Why?"

With one powerful motion, he swung her into his arms. As he carried her to her high tester bed, he said, "We've taken care of the logging. We've taken care of the baby. Now I have a need to take care of the loving."

Laying her gently on the bed, he paused to take in the look of unconditional love she bathed him in. He'd come back to Cannons Crossing with the need to reinvent himself. Almost too late he'd recognized that his future hinged on his past.

Almost.

He smiled down at Julia as she deftly undid his shirt buttons. My, but they had a lot of catching up to do. He lowered his mouth to capture hers.

"Norton!" Auntie Ouidie's plaintive voice came from the hallway. "They've been in there an awfully long time."

"Honestly, Ouidie!" Big Daddy replied. "They're newlyweds and in love. Leave them alone."

Epilogue

Julia was more nervous today than she had been the day a month ago when she'd married Dallas for very practical reasons.

Today was different. Today was for real.

A blustery November day, the sun had broken out just as she and Dallas had set out over the field toward the site of the old oak tree with Big Daddy and Miriam and Auntie Ouidie and Helen and Aaron in tow. Most of the autumn foliage had dulled. Some of it had started to fall. But Ten Oaks's signature leaves still hung on, a hearty bronze.

She carried a spade while Dallas, whistling a merry tune, wheeled a barrow carrying a sturdy oak sapling. They were about to plant a replacement to their old meeting place and respeak their wedding vows.

Five months' pregnant, Julia couldn't be happier. The doctor assured her that her increasingly active unborn child couldn't be healthier.

"Darling," Miriam said, coming alongside her daughter, "I wish you'd let me plan a little reception."

"You did. Last month. And it was beautiful." Julia put her arm around her mother's shoulder. "This time it's Dallas and my show."

Miriam waggled a foot in front of her and commented wryly, "The mother of the bride wore Wellingtons. I can see it in the society pages now."

Big Daddy pulled up beside them in a golf cart he used for surveying his property. Auntie Ouidie rode on the seat next to him. A huge wrapped and beribboned present sat where clubs would normally go. "Hell, Miriam. You'd look good with plastic garbage bags on your feet," Big Daddy declared.

Miriam blushed. A female Richardson trait, Julia thought. In the past month, she'd seen a difference in her parents' relationship. A new closeness. A new bantering lightness. A more loving quality.

"Norton, you silver-tongued devil!" Auntie Ouidie gave him an elbow in the ribs. She looked at Julia. "Pay the naysayers no never mind, sweetie. You and Dallas, with your rather unorthodox ceremonies, have brought a breath of fresh air to this town."

Up ahead, Dallas stopped. "Did I hear my name spoken in vain?"

"They're singing your praises, son," Aaron called out, bringing up the rear, hand in hand, with Helen.

Rubbing her abdomen and her fidgety unborn baby, Julia smiled broadly. Everyone in the world she loved was gathered around her. If she and Dallas ever decided to move from Cannons Crossing, it would pain her deeply. Dallas had finished his logging internship. He still worked at the lumberyard. They hadn't talked about moving. They'd been too busy making day-to-day plans, making a nursery for the baby, making love.

Her grin expanded at the thought of their uninhibited lovemaking.

"Come on, folks!" Dallas waved them on enthusiastically. "It's not much farther. I can see the old stump."

They reached a spot not far from the original oak. Julia took her place next to Dallas as the others circled them. Dallas's smile warmed her as her big woolly jacket never could.

"Ready?" he asked, a smile on that generous mouth, a twinkle in those ever changeable sky blue eyes.

"Ready." She plunged the point of the spade into the red Georgia earth. "Dallas Lee Parker, I love you. You've been my rock through the years. You've been my passion lately. Now you'll be the father of my child. Before God and our families, I take you for my husband."

With rising emotion, she turned over a clump of sod, then handed the spade to Dallas.

"Julia Anabeth Richardson Parker, I love you." He filled the spade with dirt. "This is where it all started. At the old oak tree. You believed in me and never let me forget it. You brought me back here where I discovered the truth. I thank my lucky stars that you are my wife."

Everyone applauded. Then everyone—Miriam in her farm boots included—took a turn at digging the hole for the sapling. When Dallas finished it off, he and Julia lowered the new tree into the ground as Helen took pictures.

Aaron cleared his throat. "I have a gift."

"Not another antique Caddy," Julia joked.

"No, but something I've been saving for Dallas for a long time, nonetheless." He pulled a business envelope from his coat pocket, then handed it to Dallas. "Shortly before her death, Rhetta signed this over to me to hold for you until you either needed the money from it or you needed it for roots. It looks to me as if you'd prefer the roots."

With Julia curious and close at his side, Dallas opened the envelope. It contained the deed to the old Parker property that ran alongside the railroad tracks not far from where they stood. Prime bottomland.

"It's my mama's land."

Dallas scowled. "The lawyer told me it went to settle debts."

"In a way it did." Aaron's voice grew raspy. "I think your mama regretted withholding my true identity."

Dallas beamed at Julia. "Our land."

Julia's heart swelled with powerful emotion. Land for a home. And not just any land. Land that came from Dallas's roots. Land that lay alongside her roots. Steeped in a rich personal history. A history that acknowledged the pain as it embraced the joy. How fortunate could they be?

"I always wondered why I couldn't, even lately, get hold of it," Big Daddy grumbled.

"Well, it's in the family now, Norton!" Dallas crowed.

Everyone laughed, and Big Daddy, contrary to expectation, grinned. "Not to be outdone," he said, reaching for the present in the golf cart, "I brought a little present from the Richardsons." He placed it on the ground before Julia and Dallas.

"A toaster!" Julia teased, tugging at the ribbons and wrapper.

"Pshaw!" Big Daddy puffed himself up. "It's for my grandbaby."

Opening the lid to the box, Julia revealed a beautiful cradle. Dallas lifted it high for everyone to see. "It looks handmade," he said, admiration clear in his voice.

"It is." Big Daddy went kind of shy and mumbly. "You two seem to have such a big deal going for that old lightning-struck oak." Uncharacteristically, he scuffed his shoe in the dirt. "When my men cleared it, I had them plane the trunk down to see if there was any usable, uncharred lumber." He looked at his hands. "There was just enough for this."

"Oh, Daddy!" Julia threw her arms around his neck and planted a loud kiss on his cheek.

"Well, you deserve it. You're going to make good parents." Her father looked right at Dallas. "Both of you."

They were. Oh, they were. She slipped her hand into Dallas's. They were going to be good parents because they understood fully the ups and downs of relationships. And because the love that bound them together came from being friends, partners and lovers.

*   *   *   *   *

▼™ SILHOUETTE
SPECIAL EDITION®

AVAILABLE FROM 17TH SEPTEMBER 1999

MAKE ROOM FOR BABY Cathy Gillen Thacker

Marrying after a whirlwind weekend was the most exciting thing Tad
McFarlane and Abby Kildaire had ever done. It had been crazy,
impulsive and romantic. But now that Abby was pregnant, it was time
to get serious…

THE RANCHER AND THE AMNESIAC BRIDE
Joan Elliott Pickart

Follow That Baby

When Max Carter first met Josie Wentworth he ordered her off his
land. But as she was leaving, she had an accident. The fall made her
lose her memory and Max found himself this stranger's keeper—and
her lover.

A FAMILY KIND OF WEDDING Lisa Jackson

Katie Kinkaid's new neighbour was as handsome as he was mysterious.
And the more she bumped into the six foot hunk, the more she was
smitten. But why did he insist he wasn't husband—or father—material?

DR DEVASTATING Christine Rimmer

Prescription: Marriage

Nurse Lee Murphy was perfectly happy just to day-dream about gorgeous
Dr Derek Taylor—after all her heart was safer that way. But Derek was
determined to let Lee know the real man behind the white coat!

MARRYING AN OLDER MAN Arlene James

Widower Jesse Wagner had no intention of marrying again. But despite
being sixteen years his junior, Caroline Moncton had other ideas. She
just had to convince Jesse that she needed his passion, not his protection.

TERRIFIC TOM Martha Hix

Blythe Redd was not going to let Tom Tillman retreat into solitude. She
knew his latest act of courage had left him scarred inside and out. But
she was determined to show him how terrific he was—and how terrific
they could be together!

AVAILABLE FROM 17TH SEPTEMBER 1999

Intrigue
Danger, deception and desire

SHATTERED LULLABY Rebecca York
A FATHER'S LOVE Carla Cassidy
ONLY A WHISPER Gayle Wilson
TWILIGHT MEMORIES Maggie Shayne

Desire
Provocative, sensual love stories

CALLAGHAN'S BRIDE Diana Palmer
THE BEST HUSBAND IN TEXAS Lass Small
THE COWBOY'S SEDUCTIVE PROPOSAL Sara Orwig
THE OLDEST LIVING MARRIED VIRGIN Maureen Child
THE OUTLAW'S WIFE Cindy Gerard
THE FORBIDDEN BRIDE-TO-BE Kathryn Taylor

Sensation
A thrilling mix of passion, adventure and drama

ENGAGING SAM Ingrid Weaver
HARVARD'S EDUCATION Suzanne Brockmann
MIDNIGHT CINDERELLA Eileen Wilks
THIS HEART FOR HIRE Marie Ferrarella

Sometimes bringing up baby can bring surprises —and showers of love! For the cutest and cuddliest heroes and heroines, choose the Special Edition™ book marked

That's my baby!

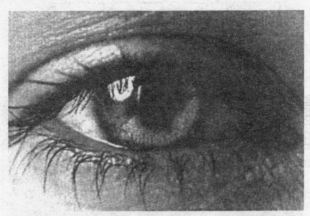

SWEET REVENGE

NORA ROBERTS

Adrianne led a remarkable double life.
Daughter of a Hollywood beauty and an
Arab playboy, the paparazzi knew her as a
frivolous socialite darting from exclusive
party to glittering charity ball. But no one
knew her as The Shadow, a jewel thief with
a secret ambition to carry out the ultimate
robbery—a plan to even the score.

The Shadow was intent on justice.

MIRA®   **Published 22nd October**

FREE

4 BOOKS
AND A SURPRISE GIFT!

We would like to take this opportunity to thank you for reading this Silhouette® book by offering you the chance to take TWO more specially selected titles from the Special Edition™ series absolutely FREE! We're also making this offer to introduce you to the benefits of the Reader Service™—

- ★ FREE home delivery
- ★ FREE monthly Newsletter
- ★ FREE gifts and competitions
- ★ Exclusive Reader Service discounts
- ★ Books available before they're in the shops

Accepting these FREE books and gift places you under no obligation to buy; you may cancel at any time, even after receiving your free shipment. Simply complete your details below and return the entire page to the address below. *You don't even need a stamp!*

YES! Please send me 4 free Special Edition books and a surprise gift. I understand that unless you hear from me, I will receive 6 superb new titles every month for just £2.70 each, postage and packing free. I am under no obligation to purchase any books and may cancel my subscription at any time. The free books and gift will be mine to keep in any case.

E9EC

Ms/Mrs/Miss/Mr ....Initials............................
BLOCK CAPITALS PLEASE

Surname...

Address..

....

....Postcode ....

Send this whole page to:
UK: FREEPOST CN81, Croydon, CR9 3WZ
EIRE: PO Box 4546, Kilcock, County Kildare (stamp required)

CATHERINE LANIGAN
in love's SHADOW

On a cold December evening, a shot rang out in a wealthy Chicago suburb and the lives of three women were changed forever. Bud Pulaski, successful businessman, committed suicide, leaving behind a shattered wife, an estranged sister, a bitter mistress and many unanswered questions.

They are three women—searching for answers that will affect the rest of their lives. Searching for a ray of hope in love's shadow.

Published 17th September 1999